DOCTOR
GRAY

SHARON WOODS

To the single dads who turned the page on heartbreak and found a new chapter of love...

CHAPTER 1

DAMIEN

"SAMUEL, IT'S TIME TO get up," I whisper as I enter my son's room. It's 7 a.m. He needs to get up for school, and I need to get to the hospital because I have a full day of patients. My mom will be here to drive him to school, but I need to get him moving or he'll be late.

He snuggled his little body under his red Lightning McQueen blankets that match his red racing car bed, so all I can see is the top of his messy brown hair and forehead.

The morning light seeps through his curtains. I walk toward them and push the fabric wide open, trying to let the natural sunlight wake him up, but it doesn't work. He's still fast asleep.

A deep sigh leaves me, as I know I'm waking him from his favorite hobby: sleeping. The total opposite of me who thrives off very little sleep. I've been lucky he's always been a great sleeper. Even as a baby.

I walk closer to him. "Come on. Get up, bud," I plead, adjusting my navy work tie. I'm already dressed in my navy dress suit and black work shoes. After my early morning home-gym workout and shower.

Samuel grumbles and rolls onto his other side. "I don't want to go to school," he mumbles sleepily into his pillow.

I smile, finding his grumpy side amusing. I know he gets that gruffness from me. And I don't think it's a good thing as an adult, but as a child, it's adorable.

If I didn't have to be at work already, I'd let him stay home. But it's a workday and I have a long list of patients and doctors who are depending on me.

"You've gotta. I need to go to work, and you need to go to school." I rub his soft, short hair. His hand comes out from under the blanket, and he tries to swat my hand away.

"Fine." He huffs and pushes his blankets off him.

He sits up lazily, his blue eyes hitting mine. Everyone says he's my mini-me, which I can see. Not only is he a spitting image of me, but the scowl between his brows and the way his lips thin are a dead giveaway.

I can't help but chuckle as I stand. "Let me fix you some Lucky Charms," I say, walking away. I'm pulling out the bribery today. That's how desperate I am. I ignore my thoughts on how bad the cereal is for him and remember it's not like this every day. Some days are just harder than others. Heck, parenting is hard. I'm surviving here.

"Nana said they're not good for me," he says, causing me to stop moving and spin around at his doorway. He swings his legs off the bed, getting ready to stand, and rubs his eyes.

I walk back over to him and squat down in front of him, so my eyes are at his level. "Well, she's not here yet, so you have to hurry and eat them, so she won't know." I wink and poke his nose.

His nose wrinkles in response, and that one look reminds me of my ex. The one who walked out on us one year ago. Having my mom help me raise a kid was never in my plans. But shit happens, and now I'm going to be the best mom and dad I can be to Samuel. He deserves to know he's enough. The smartest, most handsome, and kindest little boy I've ever met. I know I'm biased, but fuck, what do you expect? He's mine.

He runs past me in his car-themed PJs, and all I can do is shake my head, stand up, and follow him into the kitchen, where I make him breakfast.

"Are you picking me up from school?" he asks, watching me from his seat at the counter. I grab the milk and pour it into his cereal bowl.

The guilt of disappointing him is always so hard to swallow, but sometimes I've gotta do it. I'd love not to work as a plastic surgeon and be the only one to pick him up and drop him off, but that's not an option. I've got to work and parent. I can't do both without some extra help.

"No, buddy. I've gotta work late today. Nana is," I explain, pushing the bowl in front of him.

"Yay! Nana!" he replies, grabbing his spoon and eating.

Fifteen minutes later, the doorbell rings and I check my watch to see she's right on time.

When my ex-wife Lucy left, she gave me full custody of Samuel. Which is hard when I work and my schedule isn't great, but I make it work. With the help of my parents, I can manage both. It leaves minimal free time for me, but when time permits, I see my friends. Like my best friend Elijah, who is hosting a BBQ this weekend as a housewarming party.

"Where's my favorite people?" Mom calls out as she enters the house, her words echoing throughout it.

Samuel giggles as if he's never heard her say that before.

The sound of her shoes lets me know she is getting closer to us. "There they are!" she exclaims, and Samuel beams at her.

She moves to him first and smothers him with kisses and hugs. His arms and hands hug her back in a warm embrace.

"Eaten your breakfast, I see. Now you're ready to brush your teeth and wash your face." She pulls away from Samuel and moves over to me. She kisses my cheek and greets me, "Son."

"Mom," I reply, before grabbing my briefcase, phone, and wallet.

I'm about to leave when I remember I need to ask her for a favor. "Before I go, I need to ask if you're free on Saturday. I've got a barbecue at Elijah's new house."

She winces. "I'm sorry this Saturday I'm meeting my friends. But maybe—"

I shake my head. "Mom, it's fine. I'll take him with me."

"Eli has games for me. I want to go too, Dad," Samuel interrupts.

"Are you sure?" she asks.

"Yes. I'd miss it if it wasn't for Elijah," I admit.

Elijah's been my friend since high school. I don't want to let him down. He's been there for me in the difficulties of the last few years. And between work and Samuel, there's little time for me. It would be nice to have a little downtime with my friends.

"No. Go. You need to have some fun. Maybe even find—"

"Not happening," I say, cutting her off. I know exactly what she was going to say. And there's no chance. I'm a single dad. My needs are not important. Love isn't worth the pain. I loved a woman once and look how well that turned out.

It didn't...

"I hate how bitter and angry she's made you. You need more fun in your life. It's time."

I'm bitter and angry because I didn't see the red flags. I should've known she didn't want to be a mother. She didn't want that life. She wanted to be free. I can't understand why she could easily leave us or, more specifically, leave him. Hurt me as much as you want, but to hurt your child, how could you do that?

I'll never understand.

"I'm happy and also late for work," I reply. My eyes shift to those big blues still sitting at the counter. I walk over and kiss and hug Samuel before I leave. I know he won't ask me anything about his mom today. Samuel stopped asking me about Lucy when every time he did, I didn't have answers. I know one day I'm going to have to explain the truth to him. But how do I explain something I don't even know myself?

No clue, but I'll at least have to try.

He deserves that whenever the day comes.

I just hope it's not anytime soon.

Half an hour later, I'm supposed to be pulling up to the hospital building. But I detoured in need of a strong caffeine hit, because ever since I left my house, my mind has been in overdrive.

It happens every time I think about my past.

My mistakes.

I avoid the cafeteria at work, knowing colleagues will stop me, and I'm not ready to chat.

I'm never really chatty, but today is even worse. This is why I'm not going there now. I stride into the coffeehouse, where I'm hit with heat and the smell of coffee beans. It's busy with the morning rush of people on their way to work. A mix of takeaway and eat-in patrons.

I get in line to order takeout and grab my phone to respond to a few emails while waiting for my turn. As I'm reading, the sound of a familiar laugh pulls my gaze to the front counter. I spot Marigold, my best friend Elijah's little sister, and she laughs again.

It's a light, wholesome laugh. No fake or forced hints in the tone.

The green sweater and tight blue Levi's sit nicely over Marigold's curves. She's pulled her hair up in a tight ponytail and she's holding textbooks in one hand and paying with the other.

A book slips down and drops to the floor. I'm moving to pick it up before I've thought about it and holding it out for her to take.

"Hey!" she says brightly. "Give me a sec." She spins to finish paying and then we stand to the side.

"How are you?" she asks with a smile.

I try to not get lost in her brown eyes and answer her. "All right. And you?" Even without the black makeup on her eyes, they stand out.

"I'm well. Are you about to start work?" Her eyes drop over my suit, and I don't miss the slight widening.

I run my hand down the front of my suit, smoothing it, wondering for a second if I look okay. I clear my throat. "Yeah. I just needed coffee first," I say dumbly. *Like, why else would I be in a coffeehouse?*

Her brow lifts. "Don't you have a cafeteria?"

"I didn't want to be annoyed," I mutter honestly.

"And here you find me," she says, biting her lip and trying to hold back a smile.

"You're not annoying," I reply easily. Because honestly, she never has been. If anything, she's always been quiet. She never really hung around Elijah and me over the years. Less so since I became a dad. I haven't had as much time with Elijah at his place as I used to.

Her cheeks flush a shade of pink. "Thanks."

Her name is called out. Relief floods her face, and she turns, grabbing the cup and taking a sip. She moans before meeting my gaze. "I needed this today. It was a late night."

I remember being twenty-five, living off caffeine and no sleep just to work and study. Now my college and residency days are long gone.

"You're in your second year of law school, right?"

"Yes. Thank God. Almost at the end now."

She takes another sip and then licks her lips. I follow the movement with my eyes. For a split second, I wonder what her lips would taste like.

What is wrong with me?

"I need to order," I rush out.

"Yes. Sorry. Go, go." She waves.

I get in line, and she stands to the side. My eyes keep drifting her way. She's wearing a tiny smile, but there's this glow about her. Like even tired, she looks radiant.

I order my Americano with a dash of cream and move to stand next to her.

"Did you get my invite for my birthday dinner?" she asks.

"I did."

"And you never responded..." She looks around before meeting my eyes.

Shit.

"I didn't?"

She shakes her head. "No, but you got the text?"

"Yeah. Sorry." I rub the back of my neck. "I'll be there."

Her birthday is so close to Elijah's; it's hard to forget. I must've been at work when she texted and thought I'd reply later. But I didn't.

My name is called out.

She waits as I go to the counter and grab it before we walk side by side to the door. I open it and hold it out for her. The corner of her lip lifts, and she dips her head as she passes me. I step outside after her. She crosses her arm over her due to the cool morning breeze.

We stand in front of each other, holding our hot drinks, when my phone rings.

"You can get it," she says, sipping her drink.

I check my phone. It's Doctor Natasha Blackwood. We've known each other since college. She's working for the NFL team, the Chicago Eels. I don't know what she could be calling for. Unless it's about a player from her team.

"It's not urgent. I'll call *her* back," I say, tucking the phone back into my pocket.

Her heavy lashes that shadow her cheek fly up, and complete surprise sits on her face. "It's okay. You should call *her* back."

I take a sip of my drink and glance at the time. "Yeah, I probably should get going. I have a big day."

"I bet. Well, have a good day. Don't work too hard," she says with a sparkle of humor in her eyes.

"You try to get some sleep," I say.

"I'll try."

A gush of wind picks up, and she covers her eye with the few fingers she can with her cup and books filling her hands.

"Ah," she mutters.

"You okay?"

She's blinking rapidly. Her dark lashes flutter as she tries to remove something that's blown in there.

I step forward and give her my cup to hold. "Let me look."

"Okay," she breathes.

I lay my hands on the side of her face and tilt her head back. The touch sends a buzz of electricity through my hand that I don't understand, so I ignore it and focus on the task at hand.

But as I stare down at her this close-up, I really take her in. Fuck. She's beautiful. Which is making it hard for me to concentrate. The bow of her full pink lips, the slope of her button nose, and those long black lashes blinking are causing my desire to re-spark. Even more so when her eyes hit mine. But it helps me spot the problem.

"Hold still," I grit out, picking out the particle sitting in her eye.

Once it's out, I drop my hands and step back.

"Better?" I ask.

She bites her lip. "Much. Thanks, I better go. I'll see you Saturday?"

My brows pinch together.

"Elijah's," she replies.

I nod a thanks. I almost forgot. "Right. Yes. See you then."

She gives me a small smile and wanders off. I follow her until she's completely out of my sight. Unable to help the way my eyes drop over her curves one last time.

I unlock my phone to call Natasha back. I'm in urgent need of a healthy distraction. And work is the best one I have.

My head is down, reading an email before I see my first patient of the day, when a knock on my office door sounds. Without lifting my head away from the email I've almost finished, I call out, "Come in."

The door swings open and Doctor Alex Taylor strolls in and plops himself down in the patient's chair.

My eyes dart to him before I return my focus back to the email. The guy is so laid back about work and life, I don't know how he does it.

"Do you actually get any work done?" I ask.

"All the time."

I snort and hit send on the email before facing him. "I doubt that." I lean my elbows on the desk.

His brow lifts curiously. "Why do you say that?"

Other than the fact he's not wearing a tie at work...

"You're always talking to people and avoiding being in your office. Doing actual work."

He waves his hand in front of him. "Paperwork isn't my strong suit, but I actually get shit done, you know."

I stare blankly at him, doubting that.

"I dictate," he answers my silent question.

I push my glasses up.

He pulls out a little black rectangular box and waves it toward me. "I talk into this, and I pay someone to type up my notes."

I nod.

My desk phone rings. "Damien," I answer gruffly.

"Your first patient is here, Doctor Gray," my receptionist informs me.

"Give me five minutes. Doctor Alex Taylor is here," I say, intrigued by the dictation that could save time and allow me to spend more of it with my son instead of being buried in paperwork.

"Okay, she's filling in her paperwork anyway," she replies.

I hang up.

My eyes are back on Alex's. "Send me the details. I'll look into buying one. Might give me more time at home."

His brows reach his hairline. "Oh, some new girl, huh?"

"I'm thirty-eight. I wouldn't date a girl. I date women..."

Well, I did. Past tense.

"Sooo, it is a woman," he drawls, sitting up eagerly in his chair.

I cross my arms. "No. My son. I want to be home with him more."

"And you've never thought about dating again since Lucy?"

Her name makes my stomach harden. I hate hearing it. It's always an unwelcome reminder.

"I don't need someone. I'm happy," I argue, through clenched teeth.

He chuckles loudly, shaking his head. "Fuck, if you're happy, I'd hate to see you actually in love."

"Never going to happen," I growl. I don't intend to repeat my mistake.

"Well, don't you miss pussy?"

I pinch the bridge of my nose. I'm not even sure how to respond to him. I've not been with a woman since...well, fuck. Since Lucy.

"No. When you're busy with a kid, you don't have time—"

"Bullshit," he cuts me off, sitting up in his chair so he's closer to my desk.

I look down at my watch. Five minutes have passed already, and I don't want to keep my patient waiting any longer. "I don't have time for this. My first patient's out there. I'll catch up with you later."

"I can't," he states matter-of-factly.

I sit back in my chair, ready to spin around, but I pause midway. "Why?" I ask.

He wiggles his brows at me excitedly. "I'm heading home to Tahlia."

"Right." I grunt back and swivel to face my computer. Bringing up the new patient's notes. Alex looks like he has no intention of leaving.

A soft tap on my door sounds.

Alex finally gets up. Thank fuck.

"Come in," I call out, taking my glasses off and putting them on my desk. I don't have any idea who this could be now. But I really need to get a start on work and not already be thirty minutes behind.

A door opens and a throat clears. "Sorry." I hear Marigold's voice.

I twist in my chair to see Alex standing in the doorway. His eyebrow arched, his finger pointing at Marigold, and he's miming. *Who's this?* Alex has a look of amusement written across his face.

I flick my gaze to hers, ignoring Alex.

"You left your coffee," she says sheepishly, and she's still juggling her coffee and books. I push my chair away from my desk and stand. I stride around the desk to take my cup from her. My fingers brush hers, causing her to suck in a sharp breath and jerk. A splash of her coffee spills from the lid onto my suit sleeve.

She winces. Embarrassed.

I touch her arm gently, ignoring the way she feels beneath my palm and the stain that the coffee leaves. "Are you alright?" I ask.

"Yes. I'm sorry. I didn't mean to ruin your suit," she replies in an apologetic tone.

"It's fine. I'll be in scrubs soon."

Her shoulders drop away from her ears, and I know Alex is still watching us. But I don't care right now. My focus is on Marigold.

"I always wondered what your office looked like," she mumbles, looking around at my basic modern office.

"You did?" I ask, unsure why she'd want to see it. It's nothing exciting; it's bland just like me.

"Yeah, and it's what I imagined."

I am intrigued now. "It is? How?"

I never cared about what anyone thought of me or my office, but suddenly, her opinion matters.

"Modern brown timber and white." She laughs and says, "You have organized everything perfectly. Seriously, not a paper or pen out of line."

I look around, noticing for the first time that I have an impeccably clean office. But I prefer no mess, no clutter, and simple furniture pieces because it all makes me feel less stressed.

She peers down before meeting my gaze again.

"I better get to college. I just wanted to drop off your coffee."

"Thanks."

"You're welcome." She dips her chin and turns around, offering Alex a goodbye on her way out.

I stare at the door she just left through for another moment before I walk back to my desk. I take my seat in my office chair and put my glasses back on.

Alex steps toward me, and I immediately shake my head. "Don't get any ideas. She's off-limits."

"What? I was just going to say that you two look cozy."

I roll my eyes. "You're imagining things."

He shakes his head. "No chance. You're not grumpy or snappy with her. You're different. Happier."

Now I'm sure he's making things up.

I groan. "Go away and work," I say, the need to bring my first patient in and get to work taking over.

Alex steps away, laughing. He walks to the door, opening it but not before calling out, "Ignoring it won't make it go away. Trust me."

When he closes the door behind him, I sit back and take a sip of my now cold coffee, but I welcome the way it cools down my overheated body. Marigold brings out a reaction that I haven't felt for a very long time. And I'm unsure what to think about that.

CHAPTER 2

MARIGOLD

I GET HOME FROM college and grab the mail from my mailbox. A letter from the University of Chicago is one of them. I drop my bag on top of the counter and begin opening it.

"Oh. Hi. I didn't hear you get in," my mom says.

As soon as I see the word *urgent*, I quickly put the letter back in the envelope and throw it in my bag. I'll read it later. I know what it is, and I can't pay for it right now, so it's not a big deal if I don't read it right this second.

My eyes flick up to meet hers. "Yeah, I just got home."

My stomach growls, reminding me I haven't eaten since lunch. I walk to the cupboard to grab a snack and find mom has baked today. My mouth waters at my mom's famous fresh banana bread.

"What do you feel like for dinner?" Mom asks, opening the fridge and handing me the butter.

"Anything," I answer, grabbing a slice of banana bread and putting it on a plate to add a decent layer of butter. It melts when I take a bite.

Mom sighs. "That's not much help."

I swallow the bread before replying, "Sorry, Mom. I love anything you cook."

She turns to find me moaning and eating the bread way too quickly.

"I can see that."

"I need to study, so maybe something quick and easy?"

"What about a stir fry? Your dad will be on his way home from work now."

I pop the last bite of banana bread in my mouth and swallow it before answering.

"Sounds good. I'm going to chill out in my room and call Clara. Unless you need a hand?"

She grabs some beef strips out of the fridge, then closes it and turns to me. "No. You go relax and I'll call you when dinner is ready."

"Thanks." I take my plate to the dishwasher, then I grab my bag off the counter and take the path to the guest house.

It's just me and my parents living here now. My brother moved out in his early twenties.

I plan to move out as soon as I've got a full-time job at a law firm.

It's not bad living here, though. They live in the main house, and I live in the guest house.

Thankfully, they don't come over to the guest house too often and not when I work, which is at night, as a cam girl, which means I always keep my door locked. Just in case.

When I get inside my house, I head to my room, grab the letter out of my bag, and collapse on my unmade bed to read it.

It's a reminder notice for tuition.

I grab my phone out of my bag and check my bank account. There's currently not enough money to cover it. However, after this week's work, there should be enough to pay for it. I just need a couple of new subscribers to join my page or one subscriber to join my premium where we live chat.

Obviously, I'm risking my law career if I were to get caught, which is why I always wear a mask and hide my face. No one can find out it's me. I know that means I'm walking a fine line, but I'm so close to finishing school and right now, that's my goal. Pay my tuition without owing my family.

My parents barely check on me. I'm twenty-five, so they give me the space I want—to do things like online apps. Of course, they don't know about it, but it means I've never had to worry about them barging in. They're happy that I'm doing law. They see me as their innocent daughter. I am, but I desperately need money for school that I can't ask them for.

I only just started the online work this month. After I used all my savings on my last semester's tuition, I knew I had to find a job. That night, I stumbled across an online article. I thought it was too good to be true. The figures the girls were getting on the app Mysterious Fan would cover my college tuition and more. Plus, it doesn't require eight hours on my feet. My studies have to come first and getting a degree in law, there's a lot of studying involved. I figured I could try it out. If I didn't like it, I could quit. It's not as bad as I thought. I'm still nervous when I first get on with someone new. But luckily, I haven't met too many weirdos that I've had to block. A few subscribers just want to talk or ask for a picture. It's been easy money so far.

Putting the letter away in a drawer, knowing I'll take care of it later this week, I take a seat on my bed with my books ready to read.

I start, but I'm too restless, and I can't stop thinking about bumping into Damien today. He has always had this effect on me. I'm always hoping to see him. Anytime he and my brother are together, I'm there watching him. It's been like that for years and I'm aware I'll never be able to have him...unless it's in my dreams. And I have many dreams about him. Now seeing him today, I know for sure that I'll have a new one tonight.

The memory of him keeps replaying in my mind. His hot breath on my face. His close proximity. The darkened eyes. His soft touch. And finally, his strong spicy pear scent. It's all making me hot and bothered. I rub my head, trying to clear it, but it's no help.

I get up and grab my phone to call Clara. Maybe talking about today will get me to concentrate again.

She answers on the first ring. "Hey!"

"Hey, can you talk?"

"Yeah, why?"

"Guess who I bumped into this morning?"

"I dunno. Who?"

"Damien," I whisper.

"You've always had a crush on him."

I laugh as I imagine her rolling her eyes. I sit down to remove my old nail polish.

"I do. He's hot." I sigh, remembering how he looked in his suit today.

She makes a disapproving noise before replying, "He seems like a grumpy old dude to me."

I get why she says that. And I've explained to her how his wife left him and his son. For reasons we don't know. Which has made him different. But she also doesn't see the soft side of him like I do. I hope it's just for me, but I'm not stupid. He doesn't look at me the way I look at him.

I'm his best friend's little sister. He'll never look at me as anything more than that.

"You haven't known him for as long as I have. He's so sweet under the hard exterior," I argue.

"He's all hard."

I know she's being dirty and heck, I wish I knew if he was hard or not.

"I wouldn't know, but he was sweet today."

"What happened today?"

I finish removing the nail polish and throw the rubbish in the bin. Then I retake my seat.

"I bumped into him at the coffeehouse close to his work and he chatted with me."

"Sounds romantic," she teases.

"Hey! He is. Something blew into my eye, and he held my face and removed it."

She snorts. "Look out. Next, he'll kiss you."

I grab my favorite purple polish and paint my nails.

"God, I wish. The number of dirty dreams I've had about him is so unfair. He was so close to my face today. Those hands on my face felt amazing."

"Your brother will lose his shit if you go there," she reminds me.

I breathe out heavily. "I know. But it's not about that. I'm hesitant because I don't want to put myself out there to be humiliated. It's only been a year since Lucy."

I finish painting my nails and let them dry.

"Didn't you say they had issues before she walked out on him?"

"And Samuel. But yeah, that's what my brother said. Oh, and I'm seeing him Saturday at my brother's new house for a barbecue."

The image of him out of his suit and in casual clothes enters my mind.

"You need to look hot!"

I grin, totally agreeing with her. "I was just thinking about what I'll wear. Can't be too dressy though..." Looking over my closet, I try to remember what I have.

"That yellow sundress."

I know the one she's talking about. "Yes, it brings out my eyes."

"I'd say your tits, and isn't that what you want?"

I laugh and when I recover, I say, "Yes, but I'm not as blunt as you."

"What? You need to up the seduction, woman. He doesn't even know you exist."

"He does," I argue.

"Yeah. As Eli's little sister, not as a woman."

I look out my window into the cloudy sky. "Hmm."

She's right.

"Lucky I'm working all week. I can work on my confidence and pay my overdue college tuition."

I'm honest about my money issues with Clara. But with everyone else, I hide it. I don't want people feeling bad for me.

"Why don't you ask your parents or your brother for money? He's loaded."

It's the exact reason I don't want to ask them. I want to earn it.

"No. I want to do this. I enjoy being online. It's helping me grow confident."

"You're insanely beautiful. I don't know why you aren't confident."

I don't feel beautiful. Guys have never treated me right. So over time, I've never felt good enough. "Not with guys."

"That's because your ex was a dick."

A loud giggle leaves my mouth at her honesty. "That he was..."

"Well, if it can bring the kitten out in you, I'm all for it. And do your homework because I expect a good story about Saturday."

My intercom buzzes. I check my nails and they're dry, so I stand.

"I'll try, but I better go now. My mom's calling me to come eat dinner and then I need to shower."

"Better get yourself prepared for work," she replies.

"Exactly. Call you tomorrow," I say and hang up after she says bye.

There's a fresh spring in my step now that I've got a plan for the weekend. I just have to get through this week first.

CHAPTER 3

DAMIEN

"HOW WAS SCHOOL?" I ask, tugging at my tie to remove it as I enter the living room.

"Alright," Samuel answers.

I walk up to him and rub his damp hair.

"Just alright?" I ask with a frown.

He shrugs his little shoulders. "Yeah."

"Did you need help with your homework?" I ask. I'm wiped from the long day at work, but always find the energy to help him.

"No, I've just done it, darling," my mom calls from behind me. She'll be tidying the bathroom just how I like it.

I exhale a deep breath, grateful for her help. "Thanks. Do you want to stay for dinner?"

"No, we ate already. Samuel was hungry earlier today, so I cooked and ate with him. There're heaps in the fridge."

I'm just not up to cooking right now, so to hear that she's cooked is like music to my ears.

Elijah enters the kitchen. "Hey!" he says, coming to kiss my mom on the cheek.

She says hi back with a smile. She adores Elijah.

"I really need to take back my key," I mumble.

He smirks. "Don't be like that. You love me coming over to hang with you. I bet you were sad I couldn't do it last night."

He usually comes every Sunday, but he had a conference this weekend.

"You're not my girlfriend. But you have one that probably wants you to spend time with her."

Jackie is nice and I hate the guilt I feel from him being here instead of being with her. Yes, our weekly hangouts started when Lucy left. We never had a conversation; it just happened. He kept coming over every week, usually on Sundays, and one day, he was here before me, so I gave him a spare key to let himself in if he did again.

"Nah, she understands I like hanging out with my asshole of a best friend."

I roll my eyes. "Smartass," I murmur and move to the fridge. There's a big plate of lasagna. I take it out, cut it in half, and set it on two plates before heating them up. Elijah wanders off in the direction of Samuel.

"How was work?" Mom asks, joining me in the kitchen.

"Fine. How did it go with Samuel?"

I don't like to talk about my work. It's a mix of pure exhaustion from the long day, and I don't want to bore people with my work talk.

"I picked him up from school. We went to the park to play and then came home."

"Thanks," I say, taking the plates from the microwave.

Samuel is setting up Mario Kart with Elijah, ready for us to play. It's becoming our thing. Before bed, we play together. Usually, I cook, shower, and put him in his PJs, but tonight, I was on call after my shift, so Mom's already done it all.

Elijah comes and eats his food.

"I'll let you go. I better get home to your father and cook him his dinner," Mom announces.

Elijah says goodbye and puts his plate in the dishwasher.

I swallow the last bite of food, along with the guilt of taking my mom away from him.

"He's fine. Don't worry about him," she says, reaching over to rub her hand over mine.

I nod, not knowing what else to say. They've been married for over forty-five years and have two kids, me and my sister Kylie. And they still like each other.

I used to want that.

Now I don't believe in marriage.

I follow her to the living room, where she hugs Samuel goodbye. I walk her out and head back to watch Elijah play with Samuel for twenty minutes before Samuel yawns.

"Time for bed," I say.

"One more race?" he pleads.

"Yeah, I want to beat him," Elijah argues, as if he's actually been trying to beat him. I know he purposefully has been losing. I never win either, because I love to watch the pure joy on Samuel's face when he beats me. And Elijah is the same.

My resolve falls. I can't seem to say no to Samuel. Because if playing one more round means I'm making him happy, then I'll take it. He deserves a little happiness.

So, we all play one more race before I'm reading a book and tucking Samuel into bed. I sit on the end of his bed until he's sound asleep. He knows I'm there. This is more about me than him. I need him to know I'll always be there for him. Need him to know I'll never leave him. He's never alone.

Being alone sucks.

I return to the living room where Elijah and I watch a basketball game, grateful that Elijah doesn't want to talk too much tonight because I'm wrecked. He leaves after the game, and after checking on Samuel, I head to my room to shower. I remove my suit and step in, welcoming how the water washes the stress from the day. Back-to-back patients and being on call meant a lot of talking and I wouldn't say I'm good at that. It's forced, but I do my best. I don't need to have the best bedside manner to have a long waitlist. I just need to do my job well. And I do. My schedule is jam-packed, and I'm booked out for the next five months.

Going to sleep should be easy tonight. I succeeded in another day of being the best dad I can be and being the best plastic surgeon. So then why is it that when I curl into bed, I can't sleep?

I toss and turn for an hour. My mind drifts to Marigold and then to Alex and our conversation. Back to Marigold and her ass in her jeans, her big, kind smile, genuine laugh, and the sexy flush on her cheeks after I touched her face.

I pinch the bridge of my nose and stifle a groan. I shouldn't be thinking about her. And definitely not imagining what she would sound like under me, which reminds me that I haven't been with a woman...Fuck! I haven't seen a woman naked in over twelve months. I wouldn't even know where to start. That thought alone makes me want to see Marigold.

How would I feel seeing a woman naked again? Would I still be angry and hurt? Or could I actually enjoy myself?

Today, when I touched Marigold, I enjoyed it. However, I can't help but wonder if I would be less myself if it had been someone else. I need to ignore these silly feelings because fuck, I can't go there. It's so fucked up. Like, why am

I suddenly thinking about her? I'm having these wayward thoughts, and I don't want to date a woman. I'm simply horny.

Then why am I thinking of her?

Then it clicks...Marigold is familiar, a friend, so it makes sense I would think of her.

I just didn't expect her to stir feelings I haven't felt in a long time.

I glance around my dimly lit bedroom, wondering if Samuel can somehow hear my thoughts. I get out of bed and see that he's still sleeping soundly. Relieved, I walk back to my bedroom and shut the door. There's no way I'm going to sleep without relieving some of the tension. I lie on my mattress and scroll through the web for something to stimulate me. Some sites I stumble upon are cringy and gross and they definitely don't turn me on. The noises and faces of the women look fake. Just like their tits. I want to see a real woman.

I'm embarrassed at myself for doing this, but before I hook up with someone, I want to see if I still work. Near the end of my relationship with Lucy, we stopped bothering. Sex was a chore, not only for her but for me, too. I swear she faked most of her orgasms, but pretended she didn't. So, this is definitely a better way to ease into getting back out there.

I type different words into the search bar. I find a website that looks okay. But I need to sign up.

I groan in defeat. Entering my details, I officially sign up and click around until I find a username that doesn't make me feel creepy.

Finding one called Wild West 25, I click on it and flick through all her pictures and videos that she's already posted on the site.

I can't help but admire her long brown hair with soft highlights and the way it contrasts against her pale skin. One particular image captures my attention. It makes me hard instantly. She's wearing a black glitter mask and a black bodysuit that hugs her in all the right places. I can see she's curvy, yet she has a more athletic build. She has me utterly transfixed and I accidentally hit the like button.

A message pops up, interrupting my runaway thoughts. My eyes widen and I quickly open it.

> **Wildwest25:** *Hi, how are you doing tonight?*

Nervous. Like I wanna fucking vomit. I shake my head. I can't write that. Her message is simple yet polite.

I haven't answered, still feeling guilty about doing this. Here I am, acting like she's asking me on a date. I'm a fucking teenager all over again. I'm considering bailing, but then what? I'll remain in the same space I was in. What if this helps me figure out if I'm ready to be with a woman again?

I'm already here...way past my comfort zone. What's the harm in talking to her? Nothing!

Nothing bad can come from simply messaging her.

Before I can type a message, another one pops up on my screen.

> **Wildwest25:** *Do you want to do a live?*

I stare at the message for a second.

Do I?

> **Wildwest25:** *Would it make you feel more comfortable?*

I think nothing right now could calm the tsunami of nerves in my stomach right now. The last time I felt like this was when Samuel was being born. The whole un-known and lack of control messes with me. I wipe my hand over my perspiring forehead.

She doesn't give me any more time to think because there's a pop up alerting me to the fact she wants me to join her in a live video chat.

I stare at the tempting button, wondering if the woman will be just as sinful. Based on the photos, I'm going to say yes.

My mind flicks between yes and no. Before I decide, fuck it.

She's hot. And if I can get hard from looking at her photo, imagine a video. I will definitely make a mess. But at least I'll walk away with answers.

With nothing else to lose, I hold my breath and I hit...accept.

CHAPTER 4

MARIGOLD

I LET OUT THE breath I was holding the moment his body comes onto my screen.

Finally, a guy is willing to do a live. I thought he was going to decline, and I'd have to accept a dreadful night's pay.

I take him in. He's lying in bed. I assume it's his. A pile of plush white pillows propped behind him. I can't help but notice all the bedding surrounding him is white. The way he's tilting the phone screen, I can only make out from his lips down. He has dark day-old scruff on his jaw. He's wearing a gray t-shirt that he must sleep in, and I can't see lower because his torso is long and takes up the whole camera.

The outline of his stomach and chest make me run hot. There's ab definition on his solid body. The dark hair on his toned free arm makes me think he works out.

"Hi," I say, using a slight accent.

When I turn the camera on, I play a different person. One who doesn't have to do this to pay for college. Instead, I play an older, sexy and desirable woman. Free from money worries. I know my bedroom lights complement the shape of my body. Enhances my features and focuses more on my body and less on my face. Knowing they don't know me makes it easier, and it adds to my self-confidence.

His lips stay thin, and he says nothing back.

"You've never done this before, have you, sir?" I say with a purr of seduction. I don't know if he's a guy who likes names, so I start with the simple "sir" instead of "Daddy" or something that can have him turning off his camera.

"No," he grunts.

And the sound of his voice is deep and sexy, scattering goosebumps all over my skin.

"It's okay. I'll take care of you," I breathe. "Is what I'm wearing pleasing to you?"

I watch his Adam's apple bob as he swallows hard.

"Yes," he replies, his voice thick with desire.

And that causes a flame of heat to take over my body. I love the idea of pleasing a man. And after the way my ex and I broke up, I'm ready to feel needed again.

"Good. What do you want to see?" I say, staring at his image in front of me. Wondering where his head is at.

I expect him to think about it, but he doesn't.

"Your body," he grunts, and it's barely above a whisper.

The heat now hits between my thighs, something that hasn't happened with a client before. This is just for him. I smile into the camera, loving how direct he is, but I can't help but wonder if he's shy. He doesn't speak much, but there's something about him that has me intrigued.

And it makes me playful. "You mean naked?" I ask curiously.

He clears his throat and shuffles on the bed, trying to get comfortable.

"Yes."

He adds nothing else, but taking in his body makes my lip catch between my teeth. Before I can stop myself, the words, "Will you take your shirt off for me?" leave the tip of my tongue.

As soon as they leave my mouth, I don't regret them, even though it could make him log off. Because, technically, he's paying to see me naked. But I desperately want to see what's under that gray top of his. It's already lifted in the corner of his hip since he shuffled around in bed. He's teasing me with his firm, tanned skin.

He doesn't speak. And my heart beats frantically as I curse myself for asking. For sure, I've scared him away, but just as I'm about to apologize, he lowers the phone and lays it on the bed so it's staring up at his white ceiling. I automatically step closer to the camera and soon see his torso on display. I have to swallow a moan because he's just as I suspected...hot.

He has a tanned and toned body with just the right amount of muscle and soft edges. The dark hair on his chest makes my hand curl, wondering what it would feel like under my palms. I've never come on here and met a guy like him. Not that I've been on here long, but I've seen a few to know they're at least double my age. Hairier, rounder, and lonelier, too. So, I wonder why a guy like him would need me. Surely, he wouldn't have trouble finding a woman to please him. I know I haven't seen his full face, but the jawline, lips and nose are causing my stomach to flip.

My gut tells me he's handsome. And it's never wrong.

His chest is rapidly rising and falling. I can't help but pause and take it all in, holding on to this moment.

"You're beautiful," I say with a husky voice. My whole body is overheating now.

He chuckles deeply. The sound is so soothing and real. It's as if he's never heard those words before. And it makes me want him to know it.

I step closer to the camera. "It's true. I haven't seen anyone on here like you before," I explain.

He licks his lips and my sex clenches at the sight. His wet tongue has me dreaming about how good it would feel between my thighs with that scruff adding a roughness to my pussy that I've never felt before. The thought alone causes my pussy to ache. I shuffle on my feet, trying to rub the ache. It won't take me long to orgasm with him tonight.

"That's sad," he mumbles, pulling my thoughts back to the conversation.

"Is it? I'm on here as a cam girl so I can't exactly choose a specific type of look. Can I? It's not a dating app," I say, glancing down at my freshly polished purple toes.

"Yet I'm here." His voice pulls my gaze back up.

"And I'm glad." I stand straighter and pop my chest out. A new rush of arousal hits my core when my hands skim softly over my thighs, all the way up to my shoulders. "Enough about me. Let me give you what you came here for."

I'm watching him intently, and I don't miss the way his lips part as my hand moves to the strap on my left shoulder.

I slip it off, then do the other side before slowly pushing it down to my waist. Exposing my full round breasts. His breathing is now faster and louder.

My nipples pebble into stiff peaks under his gaze.

I reach up and touch both of my breasts and moan. With one in each hand, I alternate in squeezing them. Then roll my nipples between my fingers. I imagine it's his firm hands on me instead of my own.

"I wish these were your hands," I breathe.

"So do I." He grunts.

My head rolls back as I succumb to the euphoria pulsing through me.

"Would you be rough or gentle?" I ask.

"Rough," he rasps straight back.

Knowing he's aroused too makes me wild. I straighten my head, desperate for more. I push the lingerie off my body slowly as I sway my hips sensually. It drops to the floor with a faint thump, and I push it away with my foot. I'm standing completely naked for him. My breathing hitches and I suddenly feel nervous. But instead of showing him nerves, I own my desire.

"Beautiful," he murmurs, but I catch it.

He asked to see a woman, and I'm going to open myself wide for him.

"I'm going to lie down for you and touch myself. You're making me horny." I give the camera a flirty expression.

He exhales heavily.

I move the camera to tilt it toward the bed. I lie myself down on the mattress before checking if the way I'm lying is giving him the best view of me.

I part my legs and he audibly sucks in a sharp breath. "Incredible," he says in a gravelly tone. Heat pools in my already-soaked sex and I suddenly find it hard to swallow.

One word and I'm getting more turned on than ever before.

I slide my hand over my stomach and straight to my pussy, but as I touch the top of my mound, he says, "Look at me," his control snapping.

I bite the corner of my lip and bend up on one elbow. I've propped myself up enough to stare into the camera. He adjusts the camera angle. My view of him suddenly increases, allowing me to see more of him. His sloped, crooked nose is now on display, and I can see him wearing navy shorts; I also don't miss the massive bulge he's sporting. But movement catches my eye. His hand slips down and I'm breathless with anticipation, watching his hand slip beneath the waistband of his shorts.

He's going to get off with me and with that knowledge, I skim my fingers over my body until they touch my clit. I rub circles around the swollen, achy nub. The pressure has me gasping loudly and arching my back for more. His hand moves rapidly as he gets himself off. I assume it's all for me and that is incredibly hot. I lower my fingers through my wet pussy and when they hit my hole, I hum in pleasure. My knees cave in.

"Open wider," he gruffs out.

Spreading my feet wider earns me a deep sensual growl, and my pussy tingles from the sound.

My fingers move faster.

"Show me how hard you are," I beg.

His hand ceases moving, and I'm worried this is the end.

"I just want to see what seeing my body did to you," I explain. I'm hoping with a little honesty it might get his walls to come down.

Unexpectedly, he tilts the camera. I can see his hand inside his shorts but not his dick. He shuffles the shorts down so I can see his fingers wrapped around his thick cock.

"Yes," I breathe out as my fingers move faster in my pussy. The sight of his slick precum leaking on the tip of his erection causes my tongue to slide over my bottom lip. I keep fingering as I stare at him, transfixed. He's slowly stroking himself. The muscles in his arms flex as he squeezes hard, and imagine it's me doing it for him. As if he can hear my thoughts he begins pumping his cock.

Heat spreads over my lower back. I'm trying to keep my legs open as I chase my orgasm.

"Tell me you're close," I whisper. "I want to come with you."

He pumps his dick faster, and the grunts out of his mouth are too much to bear. But thankfully, after a few more strokes, he rasps out, "Fuck. I'm coming."

My head tilts back and my legs quiver intensely as my orgasm takes over.

I ride the wave until I'm utterly spent. That was the best orgasm I've ever had. What a shame it was through a camera. I shiver at the thought of his cock pumping hard into me until I shatter around it. Imagine...

As my mind and body calm, I suck deep breaths, trying to settle my beating heart. Then I peel my eyes open and sit up on the edge of the bed. He covered his tanned abdomen in his mess. His cum gleams all over himself, and hell, if I thought he was hot before, he's sweltering now.

He's going to want to clean up, so I have little time to talk to him...

"Did you enjoy yourself tonight?" I ask with a cheeky grin.

"Yes. Thank you. You were perfect," he says in a deep voice.

I get full-blown butterflies from hearing those words.

My cheeks flush and I plead, "Please show me your face. I want to see the only man that has made me come that hard."

I bite down on my full bottom lip as anticipation turns to surprise when he tilts the camera to show me his face. Before he quickly turns his camera off.

I blink rapidly, thinking I'm dreaming.

But I'm not.

My dream is real. Because the guy on the other side of the camera was Damien Gray, my brother's best friend.

CHAPTER 5

MARIGOLD

AFTER A COUPLE OF minutes, I get a notification on my phone from the app. My heart rate picks up as I quickly open it. I see it's from *Grays_online* which is Damien's username, and I nibble on my lip as I read his message.

> **Grays_online:** You're beautiful. Thank you.

I stare stupidly at my phone with a giddy smile. I knew he was sweet, but those words turn me to mush.

It should disgust me. I just orgasmed in front of my brother's best friend...who's thirty-eight.

Thirteen years older, to be exact.

But I'm not.

The quiet, intriguing guy ended up being him. Surprised is an understatement of how I'm feeling inside right now. As I sit on my bed in shock, I drop my phone on my bed and put my face in my hands, shaking my head.

The memory of his body flashes in front of my eyes. He's broad, athletic, and masculine.

I need to write something back. After taking a moment to collect myself, I sit back up and grab my phone to type out a response.

> **Wildwest25:** Thanks! And you're very hot. :)

I shouldn't be encouraging this, but I can't help myself. There's something about him that has me being completely honest. If he was in front of me right now, I couldn't say it. I like the fact I can hide behind the mask and my phone. It allows me to speak freely.

I've been fantasizing about him for a long time, so finally seeing him naked in all his glory was a dream come true.

A message alert tone breaks my trance.

> **Grays_online:** Can we do this again tomorrow night?

All rational thought escapes. I grin stupidly as I type back.

Wildwest25: *Bit keen, are we?*

He responds instantly.

Grays_online: *You have no idea.*

Wildwest25: *For me, only, I hope?*

Grays_online: *Only you.*

I stare at those two words. Simple yet powerful. Should I confess it's me?

If I do, will this arrangement end? Because I don't want it to.

I decide to keep it to myself for a little longer.

Wildwest25: *Am I corrupting you?*

Grays_online: *Yes. If I'm being honest, I never thought I'd want to talk or see a woman again. I was burnt in the past. Yet. Somehow, you make me* change my mind. There's something about you.

Wildwest25: I'm glad I can be the one to show you not all women are bad.

Grays_online: Oh, you're definitely bad. But in the best way.

Wildwest25: I'm an angel.

Grays_online: You definitely are. Although I don't want to go, I need to take a shower. I know what I want for tomorrow's video. I'll send it to you now.

I scrunch up my nose, wondering what it could be. Luckily, I don't have to wait very long because I get a new message explaining exactly what he wants.

I open the message and my mouth drops at the elegant and sexy see-through, expensive lingerie and fuck. A toy…

I message back quickly.

Wildwest25: *I love them.*

Grays_online: *I'll send you the money for them now so you can buy them. I can't wait to see them on you. Night.*

I can't argue about him buying them because the 199-dollar set is way out of my budget.

I stare at the messages. I wonder what to do. My mind is reeling.

I text Clara and beg her to come over and debrief. While I wait, I distract myself by showering. An hour later, I usher her inside my guest house.

"You're sure it's him?" Clara, my best friend of ten years, says.

She sits down beside me on my sofa. I lie back with my hands covering my face.

"I saw his cock, for fuck's sake."

She laughs so hard it turns into a snort. "Hopefully it was worth it. Tell me it was. Please."

I stay silent a moment too long, thinking just how perfect he was.

"It was. You fucking liked it." She slaps my upper arm.

I drop my hands beside me and tilt to face her, frowning. "Ouch. What'd you do that for?"

"Sorry. I'm excited," she exclaims.

"Why?" I ask, sitting up.

"This is so interesting. Did he know it was you?"

I shake my head. "No. I'm lucky that I wear a mask as part of the outfit," I say, as I walk over to the mask I was wearing.

She follows and takes it from me and touches it.

"You say it's good money?" she says while deliberating it.

"Mmm," I hum, wondering where she's going with this.

"I think I might join. I'm struggling with cash right now. Bills are getting higher and God, the gas is shocking." She drops the mask back in my drawer and stands back.

"Yeah, you're telling me." I wander over to my sofa, sitting down again. "If you sign up, make sure you tell me how it goes."

"I'm sure my story wouldn't be as juicy as yours." She raises her brows at me.

It sure is something else...just like him.

I keep that to myself.

"I reckon."

"What're you going to do about it?" she asks.

The million-dollar question.

"No idea. And of course, he wants to chat again tomorrow night."

I rub my eyes.

"Yeah?" She looks at me brightly.

"He requested a turquoise set and a toy." A hint of a smile lifts on the side of my lip as I remember how stunning it was. I'm excited to try it on but nervous to show him. I hope I live up to what he expects it to look like.

I show her my phone with the picture of the items. "You have to buy that?" she asks, grabbing my phone to inspect.

"It's the good stuff from Honey Birdette, but he's buying it. He transferred the money before you came," I explain.

She hands over my phone. "Why didn't he buy them and ship them to you?"

"I didn't want to give him my address."

"Oh yeah, duh!"

I smile at her. I'm glad I can guide her if she wants to do this. At least I can keep her safe and talk stuff out with her. It would be more than what I had. Mine was researching online and a lot of trial and error.

"So, how do you plan to stay anonymous?" she asks.

"I'll wear the mask and if he hasn't recognized my voice by now, I'm safe. Luckily, he's quiet, so we don't speak too much."

She looks at me, puzzled. "That's odd."

I shrug. "Not really. I feel strangely at peace with him other than also being extremely turned on." As I openly admit that, I feel a flush hit my cheeks.

"Isn't that part of why you're online?"

"Unfortunately, most guys who come on are not like him. They're definitely not as hot. Don't get your hopes up. It's a job. But tonight, well, that was a surprise."

"This is so interesting. How long will you play this out?"

A deep breath escapes me. "I don't know. I just want to get to know him."

Her eyes narrow. "I know that look." She waves her finger around my face with a humorous expression.

"What?" I ask, not understanding what she's seeing on my face other than a flush from talking about him.

"Don't go falling in love with him."

I grimace. "Not happening. He has a kid and an ex-wife, remember? Oh, and add to the fact my brother will kill me when he finds out."

She narrows her eyes at me. "I know, but I also know you."

I tilt my head, not understanding. I wait for her to finish.

"You fall in love too easily."

"Pfft," I say, waving her off, "I do not."

"Yes. You. Do."

As I think about my past boyfriends, I can't help but bite the side of my cheek and dissect how every single one of them left me hurt. I loved them more than they loved me. Take my ex, for instance. Our relationship lasted for two years. I fell head over heels in love with him. Looking back, I realize I loved him more than he loved me. I would constantly message and call him. Try to make plans with him. All he wanted was his friends and to party. He cheated on me with a co-worker because he said I was too vanilla.

I'm not so vanilla now.

I sigh, defeatedly. I can't argue. All I can say is, "I won't fall in love with him. I promise."

She dips her chin. "Good because you have too much to lose, and I don't want my best friend in pieces again."

I smile at her kind words.

I lean forward to wrap my arms around her and hug her. Her arms reach around my back and hug me back harder.

At this moment, I wish I could find someone dependable, like my best friend.

The next day, when I return home from school, I see a package on the counter in my parents' house. I look and it's addressed to me. I grab it and carry it to the guest house with a spring in my step, knowing it's the stuff I ordered.

Inside my room, I rip open the package and examine my purchases. I also see they added some free chocolate sauce.

My face drops in surprise.

Seems Damien is going to be in for some fun tonight. I'm giddier seeing this stuff in person and I can't wait to try on the lingerie.

I snap a picture and send it to him through the app. Along with a message.

Wildwest25: Look what arrived.

He doesn't respond straight away. So, I go about getting ready for later and then study.

I'm reading a case at my desk as my phone sounds.

I pick it up and see a notification from the app. I open it and read the message.

Grays_online: Chocolate sauce?

Wildwest25: Damn it. I forgot about leaving that as a surprise. Bad luck now.

Grays_online: I'll tell you a secret about myself. I don't like mess. Like at all.

Wildwest25: *I'll get really messy then.*

Grays_online: *Wish I could lick you clean.*

I shiver from reading those words. What would it be like to have him licking my body?

I force myself not to think too long about it and type back.

Wildwest25: *I wish too…*

Grays_online: *Same time tonight?*

Wildwest25: *Yes. I've got studying to do.*

Grays_online: *Good girl. Study hard, and I'll see your pretty face later.*

I nibble on my lip as I think about being his good girl. And how that would sound coming from his lips.

I refocus on my case.

The next few hours pass and when it's finally time to dress and get ready, I become a little nervous. But I ignore the nerves and finish dressing.

Butterflies fill my stomach as I wait for him to come online.

When the green light flicks on, letting me know he is, in fact, on, I shift on my bed, getting the angle just right.

Grays_online: *Are you ready?*

I adjust my mask and take a big steadying breath. I send him an invitation to join my live as an answer.

"Hi," I breathe. My playful voice is in full force.

"Hi," he darkly replies.

My body tingles in response to him. He's topless tonight. Again, only from the nose down to the top of a black waistband. His five-o'clock shadow comes through and how I'd love to feel it against my face.

His toned abdomen contracts from the way he's sitting tonight.

I imagine his gaze running over me. Admiring what he bought me. I stand and turn slowly. My hands touching my thighs and hips to settle on my waist.

"What do you think?" I ask in a sultry voice.

I feel sexy in the satin fabric. The way it pushes my breasts up and compliments my skin. I can imagine him growing hard from just looking at me.

"Beautiful."

My lips part into an open smile.

"It would be a shame to ruin it." I skim my hands over my hips again and then down across my stomach, pausing on my outer thighs. "But then I don't want to take it off."

I bring my finger to my lip and tap. Deliberating it.

"Take it off." The strain in his voice tells me he's affected by me.

"Already?" I ask teasingly.

"Actually, no. Get on the bed and on your hands and knees. Ass in the air and face me," he orders gruffly.

It sends a thrill through me as I take a breath to calm my excitement and strut to the bed, purposefully pushing my hips out. When I'm in front of my made bed, I follow his instructions. I keep my knees closed just to get him to order me around.

I usually take charge in my lives, but with him, I'm living out my fantasy and letting him give out the orders.

"No. Part your knees. Wide."

I do, and he groans with appreciation.

"Perfect. Now reach between those pretty thighs and tell me if you're wet."

I slide my hand over my stomach slowly and then slip my hand under the waistband of my thong. My fingers hit my warm, wet pussy.

I mumble incoherently.

"I want to see. Bring your hands out so I can see how wet you are for me."

I do it, and it earns me another loud groan.

I decide I can't be the only one getting hot right now. I want to make him equally horny, so I take over.

I sit back on my heels, reach around, and remove my bra with one swift motion. Then I scoot off the bed, slip my thong off, and stand in just black stilettos before I grab the chocolate sauce.

"Dirty girl," he rasps.

"So dirty," I whisper as I look into the camera and pour sauce over my tits until it drips down over my body, and I smear it everywhere.

I make the biggest mess I can.

"Fuck." He barks.

I bring my fingers to my mouth and suck hard.

"Look at me as you do that."

My eyes flutter open, and I stare at him through the camera. I move my fingers in and out and I know he's picturing me sucking his cock like this. I grunt and hollow out my cheeks with every stroke and suck. Everything with a purpose to bring him closer to climaxing. Because I bet if I put my fingers back on my pussy, I'd find myself dripping.

"I'm all messy. I wish you were here to help clean it up, sir."

"Me too," he mutters.

I grab the pink vibrating dildo from my bedside table. It's soft to touch and close to lifelike with all the ridges.

I spread my legs. My eyes are closed as I bring the toy to my wet pussy. The vibrations make me moan.

"Show me," he says.

I grab a chair and lower the camera down so that I can lift a leg and let him see what he's so clearly desperate to see.

"Better?" I ask.

"Much. Now fuck that toy as if it was my cock."

Who knew Damien had this dirty mouth?

Not me, that's for sure. But I enjoy knowing this secret side of him. As if it's something special that only I know about.

"I'd much prefer it was you," I say, pouting.

As the words leave my lips, I'm shocked at how much those words ring true. It's not like I haven't had similar words spoken to me, and every time bile rises to my throat and I have to fake every word. But with him, I don't feel repulsed.

I feel turned on.

What's happening to me?

I close my eyes and imagine the toy is him and the hum through my body takes over. I glide the toy in and out slowly. Then I pull the toy out to slide it over my clit before easing it back inside me.

The heat in my lower back quickly becomes unbearable and I know that I'm climbing.

My legs quake. "I'm close."

I peel my eyes open and look straight into the camera and I'm pleasantly surprised to find his eyes boring intensely into the camera. Dark, broody and so much heat.

Yep. I will not last with him looking at me like that. Why him? What's so different about him? Even though I know I shouldn't, I am attracted to him, and it will end in disaster. I can't help it; I'm like a moth to a flame.

I don't close my eyes because I want to keep the image of his face as I come.

I pick up the pace. I fuck the toy with his eyes on me and before I know it, I'm coming.

"Fuck, you're incredible." He grunts.

I lick my lips and remove the toy before standing up.

"Seems you have good taste in lingerie and toys."

"I'll have to buy you more. So much more."

The idea has me smiling.

If that's what I'll feel like if he does, I can't say no.

I know Damien has money, so I don't feel guilty. Well, not for that. The only guilt I feel is about me hiding my identity when I know him. But he'll end this when he finds out, and I don't want him to.

"What are you thinking?" I ask.

"Red and a—"

He's cut off by a knock and a faint voice. "Dad, why's the door locked?"

I know it's Samuel, but before he can speak, the screen goes black and I'm blinking at a blank screen.

I think Samuel just interrupted us.

Shit. That was close. A little too close.

Chapter 6

Damien

I ADJUST MY ERECTION back into my sweats. Another one for the day if you count waking up hard this morning. I rub my face roughly with my hands as I get off my bed, quickly unlocking my bedroom door. Grateful, I added a lock today.

Samuel walking in to see his father masturbating would scar the poor kid.

I'm still worked up by seeing her fucking herself with the dildo, so I take a deep breath before I open the door to find Samuel screwing up his sleepy face.

"Hey, what are you doing up?" I ask.

"I had a bad dream," he mumbles, looking up at me with glossy eyes.

I rub his head and then pick him up.

"Let me sit on your bed until you fall asleep again."

He nods, but his head lowers to my shoulder. I grip him. And it's moments like these that remind me I shouldn't think about myself or a woman. I should remain focused on being there for him.

I carry him down to his room, lower him onto his bed, and tuck him in.

"You'll stay here until I fall asleep?" Samuel asks with a wobble in his voice.

"I promise." I squeeze his hand.

Samuel nudges his head into the pillow, getting back to sleep. I take a seat at the end of his bed and drop my head in my hands.

And for the next ten minutes, all I see is her.

She won't leave my brain. What is it about her that has me wanting more? I know it's more than just seeing her naked. Even if that's why I was on the app. In fact, she has the sweetest pussy I've ever seen. But if that was all it was, I wouldn't be constantly thinking about her. She's consuming every spare moment. Even now at work, I daydream about a woman with rosy lips and a mask. Which is rather odd to me. I haven't dreamt about a woman in many years.

I sit up and look across at Samuel, who's fast asleep again. Getting up, I kiss his forehead and make my way to my room. I spot my phone on my bed and I immediately pick it up. There's a message notification on the app. It's her...

Wildwest25: *Is everything okay?*

Reading that message makes me tense. I hate how she thought she did something when it's all me. I need to make her feel better, so I respond.

> **Grays_online:** Yes, perfect.

I stare at my phone, thinking it wasn't enough. What should I say? I'm a single dad?

I shake my head. No, I can't say that. I don't know her enough to share that piece of information about myself. This is only about satisfying my needs, and I did that. So what am I doing?

> **Wildwest25:** Did you want to see me again?

I should say no...

> **Grays_online:** Yes.

I'm so screwed over this woman I barely know. Why couldn't I type the word no? I can say the word just fine usually, but I can't with her.

> **Wildwest25:** I have a late-night class tomorrow, but I could do it the following?

I check my work schedule and see that I'm on call.

> **Grays_online:** *It should be good. I'm on call, so if I bail, don't think it's because I don't want to see you!*

> **Wildwest25:** *What do you do?*

To make her feel at ease and trust I really am on call, I'll answer. She won't know exactly what type of doctor I am, and there's plenty in the state that I won't get found out.

> **Grays_online:** *I'm a doctor.*

> **Wildwest25:** *Wow, impressive :)*

> **Grays_online:** *Yeah, it's pretty cool.*

My job is one thing I'm proud of. I love it. Other than Samuel, it fulfills something in me. Maybe it's the helper in me. Which I've never admitted out loud.

> **Wildwest25:** *I better shower. I'm a sticky mess.*

The chocolate sauce smeared over her sexy body. She's still covered in it, and yet, it doesn't repulse me or make me overwhelmed. No, I was harder than I've ever been in my life.

Grays_online: *You're making me change my mind about messes.*

Wildwest25: *Am I?*

Grays_online: *Only if it involves you.*

Wildwest25: *I'll hold you to that. :)*

Grays_online: *Night.*

I exit the app and take a shower, where I jerk off until I come. If I don't, there's no way I'd be sleeping tonight.

∞

Thursday night arrives, and I've put Samuel to bed. I'm reclining in my bed with one of my arms folded behind my head.

I don't bother switching the TV on because I know she'll be waiting for me. I've never had a woman wait for me so...eagerly. And God, to have such a beautiful one actually look forward to pleasing me is unfathomable.

However, I get it. I am paying her so that could be a good enough reason for her to be on before me. I've paid for all of her time. So, she doesn't need to have any other clients. I made the payment above the usual requirement. And I tip well for her services. Not just sexual services, which she is fulfilling. But for the ones I never imagined I'd like. The comfortable nature I've found myself in around her is worth every cent. It feels like this is more than money. Dumb, I know. But there's something I can't quite put my finger on that seems so familiar about her.

I close my eyes briefly as she comes onto the screen and my heart races.

"Hi," she says quickly, beating me to talk. "No callout?"

I shake my head, my body agreeing with my head that it's not ready for me to be called in. "Hi. Not yet."

If I do get one, I have to drop Samuel off at Mom's on my way. Or she'll come here. It all depends on the hour and the callout.

"That's good." Her pink lips part into a seductive smile.

"It is," I mutter, trying to keep my mind from picturing those lips wrapped around my cock.

"Have you had a good day so far?" she asks in a way that makes me believe she genuinely wants to know and isn't just asking to be polite.

Not wanting to discuss Samuel still, I stick to everything else.

"Yeah, gym, paperwork and emails. Riveting." A deep chuckle rumbles from my chest. Even to my own ears, that sounds depressing, but I can't explain any further.

I dropped off and picked Samuel up, too. But I obviously don't tell her that.

"Always working."

Isn't that the truth...

"Yep. How about you?" I ask, wanting to know what she's done all day. This is probably unusual, but I don't want to dive into sexual activities straight away. Don't get me wrong, I'm damn excited to see her delicious body again, but I also just want to talk for a minute or two. I want to savor these moments that normally give me the ick in real life.

"I had college all day, and I went to the gym too."

I shuffle in bed, working to get more comfortable. "What do you like to train?"

"Weight training or attend a Pilates class."

"Not only smart, but you work out. You're my weakness."

"I'm sorry." She hums with a mischievous look.

"Are you?"

"No, because you're becoming my weakness. Talking to you has made my week."

"What happened?" I ask. Her tone is suddenly familiar, but I can't put my finger on it.

She hesitates, adjusting the mask on her face.

"Tell me," I encourage her. But it comes out as a command, and I can't help but feel relief when she spills. "I'm drowning in college debt. Hence why I'm on here." Her gaze drops from the camera.

"You wouldn't do this if you didn't have the debt?" I ask.

Her head lifts to stare into the camera to answer. "No, but I have it, and this job pays well. Well, better than any other job I could get. I don't have a lot of free time to work after my classes and studying, so this works well."

I grunt, and we fall silent. But not for long. Her mouth twists and I know we're done discussing heavy life topics for tonight.

There's a new, determined sparkle in her eye as she asks, "Do you like what I'm wearing?" She steps back so I can view her whole body through the camera. She's wearing a mask with lace and a nightdress to match. The dress has see-through pieces on the sides of her body. I love how she wears heels, even with lingerie. She can wear gym shoes by day and heels at night. The woman is becoming my weak spot or my newest addiction. I was already hard at the sight of her. Now it's damn painful.

"Yes. But I can't see much of your body," I say.

Her hands skim her hips and she bunches it to the side. "You want this off?" she asks, but it's not really a question because she's lifting it over her head, exposing her naked body.

"Fuck." I growl. "Get on the bed."

She turns and her full round ass sashays to the bed and she bends so her ass is in the air.

"I'd give anything to fuck you from behind."

Her head lifts over her shoulder, batting her eyelashes at me. She pauses in that position, allowing me to take in every little detail. I know she's teasing me because it's written all over her face.

"You enjoying pleasing me?" I grab my dick tightly in my hand and work it over.

"I want you," she breathes as she wiggles her hips and then rolls onto her back and opens her legs.

The words *I want you too* are stuck in my throat with air. I'm struggling to breathe.

"Are you always this wet?" I ask in a rasp, working my dick harder and faster.

She peers down and then looks bashfully up into the camera. "Never. It seems only for you."

Those words are my undoing; my balls draw up, and when her knees cave in, I can't see her sweet pussy as clear.

"Spread wider. I need to see you wet and swollen for me." She follows my order with a groan. "Good girl." I praise, my dick throbbing. "Now touch those pretty tits."

Her hand reaches up, and she touches her breast. And man, do I wish I could feel how amazing they are. They look gorgeous. The right amount to play with. She moves her fingers to her nipples and tweaks them. She whimpers at the same time her hips move up. It's as if she needs more. Her eyes stay on mine through the camera.

"You need to fuck, don't you?"

"Ye...yesss," she stammers.

"Bring your fingers to that swollen pussy and rub your clit."

She follows my instructions and I'm lost in the way she tips her head back and moans as she pleasures herself. I watch every rub as if it's important to know just how she likes it.

I keep stroking my cock, chasing my climax. "Put your fi—" I'm cut off by my phone ringing. "Fuck." I bark and thrust my hand through my hair. "It's work." I close my eyes and count to ten. I need to answer the call without sounding like I'm coming down from an almost explosive orgasm.

"It's okay, get it." She pants.

I want to say, *It's not okay. I want to watch you come so hard that I come too and make a mess of myself.* But I grumble, "I'll talk to you soon. I'm sorry."

I hang up with a heavy sigh, taking one last look at her lying there with her legs spread wide and her fingers on her clit.

I exit the app and drag my hand over my face as I answer the call.

I've been called into the hospital, so I quickly shower. Afterwards, I find a notification from the app. I open to see she's messaged. But this time, it's not just a typed message. There's a video message attached.

> **Wildwest25:** *I recorded myself coming for you. Watch me later (kiss emoji). Have fun at work.*

Chapter 7

Marigold

While other twenty-five-year-olds are getting ready to party on a Friday night, I'm here drowning in my studies. There's a pile of textbooks and papers scattered in my living room. I'm deep into reading about a case containing gray-area ethical issues when my phone rings.

I smile, reading Clara's name. "Hey—"

She cuts me off with her panicked voice. "Please come. I've somehow flooded the rental."

I stand and look around for my bag and keys.

"Alright, I'll be there in five."

I hang up and before I leave, I grab a bucket and my emergency tool kit and as many towels that I have in my linen closet.

I drive to hers and dash to her door. I don't have a spare hand to knock, but she must've been waiting for me because the door opens as soon as I hit the top stair.

"Thank god you're here." She exhales and grabs some towels from my hands.

"What happened?"

"I decided to do some laundry, and it's leaking water, and I can't get it to stop."

"Did you turn the water off at the main?"

Clara looks at me, confused. "Did I do what?"

"Don't worry. You put the towels down and I'll turn it off," I instruct in a calm, confident voice.

Clara doesn't get frazzled easily, so in times like these, I take over.

"Okay." She walks off in the direction of the laundry room and I head to turn the water off.

Afterwards, I meet her in front of the washing machine and roll up my sleeve, cursing myself I didn't choose a short-sleeve shirt. I have my leggings on at least.

Clara's trying to mop up the water that's pouring out from under the machine still. It should stop soon, though, because the mains are off.

"Can you help me move the washing machine?"

"Yeah, but...do you know what you're doing?"

"You called me, remember? I'll take a look and see if I can find the culprit. If not, I'll call someone to help."

"I can't afford to. Neither can you."

I can use the money I made from Mysterious Fan this week. My student loans can wait. My friend is more important.

"I've got it, don't worry. Let's see if I can work it out first. Let's worry about money if we need to."

She steps over to the other side of the washing machine. And we zigzag, pulling each side until it's away from the wall.

The problem is obvious, and I can't help the bubble of laughter pouring out of my mouth. My elbows lean on the top of the machine as I stare at the hose on the floor.

"What?" Clara asks.

I point to the wall. "Have a look and tell me if you can spot the problem. I bet you do."

She peers down and then softly shakes her head as she straightens. "Are you kidding me?"

I roll my lips together, trying to hold back from laughing hysterically. This was a nice distraction from the hours of studying and assignments I've been doing. Even though I still have hours more.

"At least we can fix that. For free."

"Except my dignity. I don't even know how the stupid thing fell out of the wall."

"I'll put it back and secure it, so it never happens again."

"You're a lifesaver. I'm sorry to pull you away from your studies. I owe you."

"Clara, shut up. We're friends. I'm here anytime you need me. Let me fix this and clean up. How about you give me one of your cookies you make, and we'll call it even?"

"I wouldn't say that's even but deal. And don't clean up. I can order us dinner and I can do it later."

"I'd normally say yes, but I have an assignment to hand in tomorrow."

She heads to the kitchen, and I go about fixing the pipe. Ignoring how wet my socks are from all the water. I really should've changed, but I didn't think about it when she called me. I fix the hose and add tape around it to secure it.

We clean up the floor of the laundry room and she insists on washing my towels and returning them clean and dry. I don't argue, because by the stress on her face, I know she wants to do this as a repayment. And truthfully, I'd be the same if I were her.

I turn the water back on and while we wait and test the towels in a wash cycle, she hands me a bag of her freshly baked chocolate chip cookies.

After a few more minutes, I speak. "It all looks to be working. I'll go now, but if something happens, call me and I'll come back."

"Thanks. I do hope I don't have to call. Hopefully, one of my roommates will be home soon, so they can help."

"I don't mind. Call me if you need me."

I leave her house after a hug on her steps, and with my bag of cookies, I trek to my car in soaked socks and shoes.

As soon as I reach my house, I put my shoes outside to dry and take a shower.

After a warm shower, I feel clean and refreshed. Ready to sit back down in my living room and continue studying. I take a bite of a cookie and read over the last paragraph I was on before I left.

Time passes, and before I know it, I've eaten three.

My phone chimes with a message. I see it's from the app. I shouldn't check it because I need to hand this assignment in tomorrow and I'm already going to be up all night.

But I need to know if it's him...

It'll be quick and I will return to my studies.

He's on a late shift at work. I know because my brother told me.

I open it.

> **Grays_online:** What do you do on a Friday night?

> **Wildwest25:** Not what other people my age do. No partying here.

I take a picture of my living room and send it with the message attached.

Grays_online: *I remember those days. Long nights. Red Bull and sugary foods.*

Wildwest25: *It sucks. I can't wait to work.*

Grays_online: *Your drive is alluring.*

Wildwest25: *You mean boring?*

Grays_online: *No. I find you anything but boring.*

Wildwest25: *:) What's a word you would use to describe me?*

Grays_online: *Addictive.*

Wildwest25: *Don't hold back now…*

I type it out as a joke. Thinking he would give me more. I want to hear him call me beautiful again. This is so dangerous. What is going to happen when he finds out it's me?

When I wait but he doesn't text back, I return to my assignment. I haven't got much more to do when I finally get a new message.

Of course, I have zero restraint and I need to read it. I pick up my phone and open it at lightning speed.

> **Grays_online:** Beautiful. Intelligent. Just to name a few.

> **Wildwest25:** Thanks :) And just so you know, I feel the same about you!

> **Grays_online:** Have you finished your assignment yet?

> **Wildwest25:** Just about. Maybe a paragraph left.

> **Grays_online:** Finish it now and message me when you're going to sleep. You need sleep.

Wildwest25: Bossy, aren't you?

Grays_online: You have no idea…

Wildwest25: I'd have to argue with you and say you have bossed me around once before ;) and I liked it. I liked it a lot.

Grays_online: That's because you're a good girl. Now go to bed.

CHAPTER 8

DAMIEN

I PULL UP TO Elijah's new house for his afternoon barbecue. Walking up the path, I know I'm walking into a house full of adults. Out of all my friends, I'm the only person with a kid, other than my friends from work, Mike and Alex, who have babies. I feel out of place and like the odd man out. But mainly, I feel sorry for Samuel as he has no one to play with. He's a good sport though and I always give him the option not to come, but he says he wants to.

My friend's shower Samuel with love, but it's not the same. It's not like I'll be having another kid, so he's going to be an only child. Which makes me sad for him. Growing up with my sister, Kylie, was definitely a highlight of my childhood. I think of all the laughs, pranks, and fights we shared. The love you share with a sibling is special, and I know Samuel won't get that. Which is why I need to be the best dad I can. Shower him with all the love so he won't feel like he's missing out. Not just on a sibling, but a mother, too.

Samuel presses the doorbell and I open the door, knowing they're all probably out back with music playing. They are probably out enjoying the weather since it's a sunny day.

The door opens and I step back.

"Hi!" Samuel says to Marigold.

Her eyes are wide as she holds the door open. Her eyes flick between me and Samuel. It's as if she didn't expect us.

"Hi, Marigold," I say.

"Ah. Hi," she says and clears her throat. "Come in, everyone's out back." She steps to the side, pulling the wooden door wider, and Samuel enters the house, pulling me along behind him.

I look straight ahead, spotting a backyard full of people standing around clutching beers and talking and laughing. The door closes behind us, but I continue walking farther inside, following Samuel.

"Hey! Glad you could come," Elijah calls out. He walks into his house to meet us.

"Of course. Congratulations. Nice house," I say, looking around at the white walls and spotless furniture; the kind of furniture you have when you don't have kids.

"Let me take you on a tour," Elijah adds.

I nod. Samuel and I follow him as he walks around explaining the house. Outside, I stop and say a quick hello before we finish the tour and return to his kitchen.

"Samuel, did you want your iPad and toys set up in the living room?" I ask.

"I can put a movie on for you," Elijah says.

"Can I play Nintendo?" Samuel pleads, looking up at Elijah with bright, hopeful eyes. Elijah bought one for his old house when he knew it kept Samuel happy and entertained. Allowing me to hang out with him and not miss out on boys' catch-ups.

"Samuel, just settle down for a second. We just walked in," I say, embarrassed at how excited Samuel is.

"Of course, I can set that up for you, little man," Elijah says with a grin.

I love how my son can make so many of the quiet and big men of this place turn to jelly. There's something about kids that brings us to our knees.

"Did you want to eat first?" I ask.

"Mmm. I am a little hungry," he mumbles, as his eyes look over at the food spread out on the table.

"Let's get you something to eat and drink then," I say and move to the table. I grab a plate as Samuel tells me the food he wants to eat. He knows it's a party, so he can eat whatever he wants. So, to my horror, it's all greasy or packet food. But I hold my tongue and let him go. It's a once-off. We don't attend many parties, so I want him to be comfortable, even if that includes a sugar high.

"You eat and I'll set up Nintendo and you can play after you eat. Sound good?" Elijah asks Samuel.

Samuel nods his head vehemently.

We sit down and eat. After we're done, I clean up and take him to Elijah's living room. I settle him in, surrounded with toys and games, before it's my turn to relax. I head to the fridge to grab a drink when I see Marigold already grabbing one.

"Can you grab me a beer?" I ask.

She jumps and spins around to look at me.

"You snuck up on me," she breathes, holding her hand on her chest. She dips her head and leans forward in her yellow sundress, her cleavage practically eyeballing me. I dart my eyes away. Suddenly feeling uncomfortable. I shouldn't be looking at her breasts, despite them being a good handful and spilling out of her dress at this angle.

She stands and I can't help but notice she looks different.

More dressed up?

More makeup maybe?

But I guess it's a party. I shake it off and take the beer. "Thanks." I remove the cap, cheer the air, and walk off.

"You're welcome," she says cheerily behind me.

"Glad you and Samuel could make it," Elijah says as I walk outside to join him and his friend, Jeremy. There's another group swimming in the pool. I lift my beer in a hi. They wave back. I've known them all for years now. Any time Elijah has a boys' night or catches up, it's with the same people.

"Thanks for having us," I say as I take a sip of my drink.

He elbows me, and I fold forward, wincing. "Where've you been?"

"Working." I groan back.

"I don't believe you. You're hiding something," he accuses with a significant lifting of his brows.

I know he can't read anything on my face. I'm stone. He's just trying to poke me.

"There's nothing to tell."

"I have a friend of Jackie's—"

"Not happening," I cut him off. "You and I don't have the same taste."

Jeremy chuckles beside us. "I have to agree with Damien."

I quirk my eyebrow at Elijah. "See."

"You two suck. I'll be back and we'll continue this conversation, but I need to grab more meat to cook up." Elijah strides off into the house.

Jeremy faces the barbeque and I stare out into the backyard, watching the game of volleyball in the pool. My shoulders drop away from my ears the second Elijah walks away. The way Elijah stared at me; it was as if he knows I'm holding something back.

Which is impossible. I won't say anything. My online life is for me and my masked friend. I also know I'd be the laughingstock of the group if I explained my little crush on an online girl. Hell, I'm paying for her time and for her sweet words. Yet...I can't help the stupid way I wish for a beautiful and confident woman to want me and my son.

"Are you getting ready to move?" I ask Jeremy.

He's tall, dark, and successful. I'm sure Elijah doesn't know how to hang out with anyone who isn't a minimum seven-figure salary earner.

"I've had the house in New York the whole time, but my Grams is sick."

I nod, totally understanding. The thought of losing my mom is unbearable. I'm so grateful for her. And it's not just me. Samuel only has her as a woman's role model. I don't want that taken away from him. My mom is teaching him motherly things like washing, cooking, and saving. It's what she taught me growing up.

"I'd do the same. Is she terminal?" I take a sip of the beer.

"No, but I just want to be around my family now with her diagnosis."

"Fair enough," I reply.

We both sip our drinks.

"What did I miss?" Elijah's voice cuts in. He's carrying a tray of meat.

"Do you need to cook all that? Are you expecting more people?"

I was hoping to keep it less like a party with Samuel here. If it gets out of control, I'll leave.

"No. Everyone's here, but the meats are almost gone."

"I'll cook it," Jeremy says, taking the tray from Elijah's hands.

We're standing under the shade near the barbeque.

Jackie slides up beside Elijah, her hand coming around his waist to snuggle in. I swallow a whine because PDA makes me sick. But for some stupid reason, I can't stop watching. He looks down at her. A softness takes over his face as he stares down at her. Jackie stares longingly back, her head tilted up at him.

Jackie's not what you'd expect from Elijah. She's not a Barbie doll, or a self-centered woman, or a seven-figure boss bitch. She's just a nice, kind-hearted woman.

"I don't know what you see in Elijah, Jackie," I say, shaking my head.

"I have to agree. You're too good for him," Jeremy adds.

Jackie and Elijah share this look. Full of—dare I say it—love.

"That I have to agree with." Elijah smirks and leans in to kiss her.

I look away and take a big drink of my beer. This is the first time in a while I've had fun with my friends. I've missed it. There's something about being surrounded by my friends that relaxes me. Maybe it's the fact I can trust them. I've had a hard time trusting anyone this past year.

The sunshine surrounding us and the stereo playing good tunes add to my enjoyment.

After a while, I get up to check on Samuel. As I enter the doorway to the living room, I pause mid-step with my half-drunk beer midway to my mouth.

Not wanting to interrupt, I lean my shoulder against the door frame. I can't help but soak in the happiness in front of me. My son's face is lit up as he kneels on the cream-colored carpet. Marigold is cross-legged next to him in her pretty yellow sundress. They're playing Mario Kart.

His face is hard as he concentrates on the game. He's winning, but Marigold is gunning for him. She's not letting him win. And I love that.

"I'm catching you," she yells excitedly.

His face suggests he is comfortable with it. No, he's loving every second. The competitive nature in him is coming out.

There's a strange jealous pang in my gut that I can't quite understand. Is it because she's playing with him and not me?

But why?

It's Marigold.

The sweet, intelligent, pretty, and much younger woman.

Yet, I want to join them.

I don't know what's pulling this emotion from me.

But also, if I do, will I interrupt their happiness?

The push and pull of emotions is fucking with me.

Instead, I decide to stay quiet and watch, sipping my beer. Samuel wins and he throws his hands in the air like a champion before jumping into her arms and wrapping his arms around her neck.

I suck in a sharp breath.

I'm taken aback.

I haven't seen him with another woman before...well, not since his mother. But it's been a while since he's had a hug from anyone other than my mother.

There's a warmth that pierces through my heart. It clogs my throat for air at how big of a moment this is.

But also that Samuel instigated it. He's clearly comfortable with her to dive into her arms and hug her.

Does he miss having a woman around?

I don't miss the way Marigold's eyes shimmer with softness. Someone else caring for him and giving him this attention means the world to me. Her arms cover his back, and she hugs him. It causes my breath to catch. I want to thank her, but I don't want Samuel to hear. I don't want him to know how rattled I am by his actions.

When he pulls away, I push off the door frame, ready to turn around and rejoin my friends when Samuel calls out. "Dad. Did you see me win?" he says proudly.

I turn back around and clear my throat to keep my voice even as I say, "I did. Well done."

My gaze drops to Marigold. Whose nose is flushed a cute shade of pink and she's nibbling on her bottom lip. "Seems I suck at Mario Kart."

My lips twitch at her words. "I'm sure you're good at other things."

"Is that a challenge?" she asks, and I know she wants me to play.

"I'll win," I reply.

She wiggles over, making room between her and Samuel. With her eyes locked on mine, she pats the empty spot on the carpet. "Show me what you've got," she says, giving me a challenging look.

I stare back, sipping my drink, debating what to do. I don't want to interrupt them playing so well together because he clearly needs one-on-one time with a woman. But the jealous part of me is pulling me in, so when Samuel says, "Dad, come play with us please," with those damn eyes, I can't say no to him.

I push off the door frame, crossing the line. "Fine. One game. But I'm going to beat you both." I walk into the room, put my beer bottle on the tv cabinet, and sit down between them.

"Come on Mari, we have to beat him," Samuel says, gripping the controller in his hands.

"Don't worry, I've got this," she says as her eyes stare at the screen.

Her side profile is so pretty. Even in her competitive streak, the woman is graceful. Her eyes are wide with the black makeup on her lashes, making her brown eyes stand out. Her skin is glowing and soft, with the flush of her cheeks making her look youthful yet so damn beautiful.

"Are you going to stare at me the whole time or actually play?" She tilts her head and lifts her brow.

I swallow hard and rather than admit I was staring at her, I say, "I'm ready. I was just checking if you are."

I'm lying through my teeth, and I can see the corner of her lips lift. I know she doesn't buy it, but she says nothing else, which I'm grateful for.

The game begins, and so much adrenaline pulses through my veins from playing Mario Kart. It's a high I've not felt in a very long time. Both Marigold and I are actually trying to beat each other as Samuel watches on, ready to play whoever wins.

Usually I'm easy on Samuel, but Marigold is elbowing my arm and I lean her way. We both shuffle on the spot until the last lap. I drop the control as she crosses the finish line.

Her lips part with a wide smile. "I won."

"You did," I reply in awe. I've not seen this fun yet competitive side to Marigold.

"My turn and I'm going to beat you Mari," Samuel says.

"You wish," she replies, and I can't help but notice how wet and plump her lips are.

Why is my mind thinking about her like this?

For fuck's sake, ever since I joined that damn app my mind can't leave sex. I'm now constantly thinking about it. And how much I just want to go back online and talk to Wildwest25.

And maybe Marigold's lips just remind me of the girl online and that's the confusion. Because I keep imagining the online woman's luscious lips wrapped tightly around my cock. Her cheeks hollowing out as she swallows everything as I come down her pretty throat. Yeah, surely, I just associate every woman's lips now with a fucking fantasy. It doesn't stop me from feeling disgusted with myself, though. I get up and grab my drink.

"I'll leave you two," I grumble and head back out of the room.

But her voice stops me. "Wait up."

CHAPTER 9

MARIGOLD

I DON'T KNOW WHAT I'm going to say. All I know is I didn't want him to leave the room. I wanted to have him around longer. Something about knowing him online and now in person has me wanting more. It's risky as hell. He could figure me out. But I'm willing to risk it...just to know more about him.

In real life, we've always had basic conversations. Nothing too deep, but now I want to know more.

"Did you want another beer?" I ask, leaving the living room and ambling to the kitchen.

He shakes his head, following. "I'm driving."

"You've only had one."

His brow rises. "You counting?"

My cheek twitches as I hold back a smile. "No."

He stares at me for a moment, and I expect him to say no, but, of course, he surprises me. "Well, I guess I can have another one."

I dip my chin and grab him one out of the fridge. This time I twist the cap off for him. But the bottle breaks.

"Crap!" I curse.

"What?" he questions with a look of concern.

I open my clenched hand to show him my palm and the blood leaking from the deep cut.

Without hesitation, he grabs my hand in his. His fingers touch the area. Scrutinizing it.

His eyes peer up into mine. They're bright with a deep-set frown between them. "Does this hurt?"

My lungs constrict at him being so close. I can feel the air leave his lips as he asks.

I have to concentrate on what he asked.

"A little," I rasp, unable to speak properly. His spicy pear aftershave is so strong, I'm getting dizzy. I miss what he says the first time he grumbles.

"What did you say?" I ask.

"Let me clean it up," he exclaims.

"I'm fine. I'll wash it under the tap and put a Band-Aid on it."

I try to pull my hand away and out of his grip, so I can take the few steps over to the sink. He winces and keeps a firm grip on me.

"No, it needs pressure." He applies it to stop the bleeding. He clearly doesn't trust me to do it. And I don't want to stop him from touching me. I like this caring and nurturing side of him. It's different to the quieter, grumpier one that I've grown up with or his new, sexier side. But it's also more than that; it's the zap of electricity I feel from his touch. I wonder if he feels it too.

"Are you going all Doctor Gray on me now?" I smile through the nerves. Thankful no one interrupts us in the kitchen. This moment alone is nice, and I don't want anyone to put a stop to it.

He growls. "Yeah. So let me clean it up."

The thrill of his voice sends a shiver through me. It reminds me of the commands he gives me online. It's so freaking hot.

"You're cold," he grinds out.

I want to say no, but before I know it, I'm being taken to a chair where he drapes a blanket over my shoulders.

"I won't hurt you," he says as he stands over me, leaning over to check the wound again.

Those words are like a promise, and I want to say, *But I'll hurt you when you find out the truth.*

I blink away the dread of fear that's filling me.

"You need stitches," he mutters.

Again, I try to tug my hand back, but he holds me firmly in place. His gaze flicks to mine and under the intense stare, I drop my gaze to his hands. Those same hands that have stroked his thick cock on camera.

What would it be like to see him do that in real life? Incredibly hot. The thought is making me flustered. I force my eyes back to his.

"No, I'm sure it will be fine soon. I just need to hold pressure on it longer."

"Are you the doctor now?" his cool voice asks.

"No," I drop my gaze away from his hard one. Not before enjoying how good his jaw looks from this angle. The powerful urge to reach up and touch his day-old scruff is fierce, but I shrug it off and pull myself together. No more daydreaming.

My brother is just outside, and Damien's son is in the room nearby.

"You need stitches." He grunts as he shows me how the blood is still trickling out and is that b—

Everything goes black.

I blink my eyes open. Looking around, I see I'm lying in a bed in my brother's spare room. The last thing I remember was being in the kitchen with Damien.

"Hey, you're awake," Damien's deep voice says.

"Seems so. What happened?" I ask, confused. I sit up on the edge of the bed and he comes to stand in front of me.

He's reading my face. The intensity is unnerving. Is this what he's like at the hospital?

"You fainted."

"Oh God, how embarrassing." I cover my open mouth with my good hand. I wish I could remember him catching me and carrying me in here because how else did I get here?

I'm mortified I fainted from a stupid cut on my hand. I drop my hand away from my face.

"That's never happened to me before," I say, as if to justify my behavior. There's something in me that wants to impress him. Even though I have done the complete opposite.

"Is it sore?" he asks.

"A little." I shrug, knowing it doesn't hurt as much as the embarrassment does.

"Let me take you back to my house, where I can stitch and bandage it. I can give you some painkillers, too."

"You sound like a serial killer," I say, trying to joke to take away the thought of him taking care of me.

"You know me," he deadpans, unamused.

I do...*A lot more than you realize.*

"I know. I just don't think I need all that."

I try to focus on anything but the feeling of embarrassment. Him caring for me will only make me feel worse.

"Come on Mari, listen to Damien." My eyes fly up to my brother. I didn't hear him come in.

"Fine," I say, glaring at my brother. I'm agitated and nervous about going to Damien's place alone. We may not be technically alone when Samuel is there; nevertheless, I'll be in his space. I wonder what his place is like. I know what his bedsheets and pillows look like...

"Let's go," he says and follows my brother out.

His gruffness bothers me. I know I've seen snippets of his tender side in moments when we're alone. But right now, he's reverted back to being aloof.

I sit stunned momentarily on the bed, giving myself a mental pep talk before I get up and get this over with. The quicker I go to his house, the faster I'm back here.

I'm holding a pathetic makeshift bandage made of whatever they could find here. Clearly, my brother needs an emergency kit for times like this.

I walk out to grab my bag and pass the living room, where Damien is talking to Samuel.

"Samuel, we need to go. Please pack up your toys."

"Why?" he asks with his little face screwed up, not understanding. Guilt washes over me as I know he's leaving early because of me.

"I cut myself, Sammy, and your dad wants to stitch me up. But maybe I could go to the emergency room."

"No." Damien cuts me off with a hurt look. It completely unnerves me. "You'll come with us, and I'll fix it."

I swallow hard.

"Yeah, let Dad, he's great at fixing stuff," Samuel's soft sweet innocent voice cuts in.

I flick my gaze from Samuel to Damien, who's now wearing a small smirk on the side of his mouth. I haven't seen Damien smile much, and when he does, it makes my chest ache. His eyes stare at me with a challenging look to say something else. Something I can't read.

"Looks like I don't really have a choice," I say, trying to keep my voice as even as possible. I move out and walk on shaky legs to grab my bag and leave with Damien and Samuel. My brother sees us off outside on his front porch. I tell him I'll see him as soon as I'm fixed.

The drive in Damien's black Porsche isn't quiet, and it's not from Damien. No, he's still and quiet. He's completely focused on the road. Samuel is the chatterbox in the car, replaying his fun on the games he played.

"I love Eli's house," Samuel says, sitting beside me in the back seat.

"What's wrong with yours?" I ask curiously because I can imagine his place is just as nice as my brother's. The glimpse of his bedroom looked nice...Real nice.

"It doesn't have as many games," Samuel recalls.

"You can get your dad to buy more." I twist in the leather seat to give Samuel a wink, and he beams excitedly.

"Hey. Dad's right here," he grumbles from the driver's seat.

As if I didn't know he is sitting there. Inside this car is almost combustible with him in it.

He's hard to miss.

My gaze drops over his olive-green shirt and blue jeans. The green makes his blue eyes stand out more, but what has my mouth watering is the way he grips the steering wheel. It makes the fabric tight on his arm, showing off how toned they are.

"He has this arcade game that I really want."

"Show me and I'll get it for you," Damien replies instantly.

I pinch my lips together to prevent myself from laughing.

He doesn't want Elijah to outdo him. Also, he wants to prove how much he loves Samuel by giving him anything he wants.

"Then we can play it, Mari," Samuel says excitedly.

Samuel's lit-up face makes me smile. "Sounds like a plan."

And for the rest of the drive, Samuel talks about the game, and I nod and reply when needed, but otherwise, I stay pretty silent. My mind is reeling about what to expect next.

Damien pulls up to black gates. They open to reveal a two-story cream house. He opens the dark wooden garage door and then drives into the parking spot under the house. My pulse is racing as I try to focus on breathing to calm myself down.

I follow him and Samuel into an elevator and into their house.

"Nice place," I mumble to no one in particular as I enter. It's a large open house with dark wooden floors and white walls. Gray feature walls warm up the place.

I wonder if this is the house he shared with his ex-wife. It's not like I can ask. My brother and I don't talk about things like this. And I don't recall him ever mentioning Damien moving.

I amble through the house, following the direction they both went. I scan the house as I make my way into the kitchen. My jaw drops at the marble granite wall behind the oven.

"Wow," I breathe in awe.

This is a kitchen.

Gosh, how I would love to cook in a kitchen like this. I'm actually not a terrible cook. My mom taught me well. Plus, I loved learning and well...eating too.

Damien is pulling boxes out of a walk-in pantry and putting them on the counter before looking around for more.

"You keep medical supplies in your food cupboards?" I ask baffled.

"Not all of it. Just some basics," he answers nonchalantly.

I stand by the marble island and watch him move around. I run my good hand through my hair and clasp my hands together to prevent further fidgeting.

He wanders off to another room for a minute. For a second, I wonder if I was supposed to follow. But the thought vanishes the moment he steps back in the kitchen. He lowers a box to the countertop. I look on until he unexpectedly stands in front of me, grabs my waist and lifts me onto the counter.

I audibly gasp in surprise.

What's he doing?

That one slight movement means so much more to me than he realizes. He, however, doesn't seem bothered that his large hands were on my waist hoisting me up effortlessly. It's as if I weigh nothing at all.

I'm shaking all over from the nerves, desire, and pain.

"Painkillers?" he asks.

I nod. "Please."

I think about how my cut feels stingy and uncomfortable now. So, I can imagine how badly it will hurt when he stitches it up with a needle if I don't have pain relief in my system.

He strolls over to one of his kitchen cupboards and looks over his shoulder at me. "Do you have any allergies?"

I shake my head. "Not that I know of."

He opens the door and retrieves a box. My gaze drops over his toned wide back down across his tapered waist and ass. He's ridiculously hot and after seeing what his abdomen looks like naked, I can't imagine what the rest of him would be like...

He stands directly between my legs again. My breath hitches as his face lines up with mine at this height. If I moved my head a couple of inches forward, I could capture those lips.

His touch on my hand shakes me. I look down as he places a glass of water into my free hand. My parched throat is grateful for it, but between my thighs, I'm definitely growing wet. There's something about him standing between my legs, with a look of concern on his face, caring for me that leaves me flustered. Imagine my shock when he brings a tablet to my lips. His fingers brush them and suddenly, I wonder how I'm going to pull off not crossing a line tonight.

Chapter 10

Damien

Her pink pouty lips have the cutest defined bow. Like they were made for kissing.

The way her mouth is parted, I can see her wet tongue. It makes me hard. Fuck. I shouldn't be thinking of my best friend's sister in this way.

I feel her lips touch my fingers and my heart thumps. What the fuck is wrong with me.

I pull my hand away after I drop the pill in her eagerly awaiting mouth. And I step back.

I drop my gaze to my kitchen counter. My mind is on overdrive.

Why do I feel like she's different with me tonight?

Is she playing me?

She must be. Because all women play me.

I peer back up at her and watch her swallow the tablet before I prepare to suture her hand. I give myself a moment of silence and space; I need to collect myself.

Once prepped with the equipment on the counter, I'm pleased to see she hasn't moved from her position. She's stayed directly where I put her.

I take her hand and wash it with a cleansing solution. Ignoring the way my body is responding to touching her small delicate hand. How soft they look and the cute purple nail polish she wears. Youthful and out of bounds, I remind myself.

Now and then, I peer up and see her watching me with heavy eyes.

I drop my gaze, not missing the way her chest rises and falls slowly. Unable to stop myself from catching sight of her cleavage I saw earlier. *Nice handful...*

I refocus on the task. I grab my glasses and put them on.

"You wear glasses?" she asks.

I look up at her surprised face "Yeah. Why?"

"Nothing. You look cute," she says matter-of-factly.

I exhale heavily. Cute?

Who calls a thirty-eight-year-old man cute?

A twenty-five-year-old woman.

See...this is why I can't be thinking dumb-ass shit.

I'm a father for fuck's sake.

I have responsibilities.

I give her some local anesthetic and begin suturing with dissolvable stitches. It'll only need a couple to close the gap. She won't have a big scar.

She squeezes her eyes shut.

A sense of dread runs cold through me. "Can you feel that?" I ask, immediately stopping what I'm doing. I am about to grab some more local. The thought of her in pain is unbearable.

"No, it just feels like pressure."

I exhale my relief. The tense feeling in my body withdrawing. "Good. I was worried I was hurting you. Pressure is normal. I'm almost done. Will you be okay for me to finish?"

A flush hit her cheeks. "You're not hurting me. Finish whatever you need to."

I push my glasses up my nose and step closer again. My hand touches her hand again. I try to ignore the way touching her skin startles me. I bite back a groan and get back to work mode. A safe zone for me. Her presence has disrupted my usual ability to hone in and focus on work. Her breathing, her sweet perfume I'm breathing in, and the way her ample cleavage is in my face taunting me. They are a perfect pair of breasts. But still breasts I have no right looking at. Even though they are at my eye level if I tilt my head back a fraction.

She's pushing past my boundaries that I normally can control. Why can't I control the way I'm feeling right now?

When I finish the final suture, I drop the needle into the safety bin. "There, all done."

She lifts her hand to her face. "Neat."

"I'll bandage it," I say, looking around for the correct-sized bandage.

"Sure. But then can I lie down for a second," she mumbles.

Panic fills me. She's going to faint again.

Fuck the bandage.

"I'll lay you down now," I say, whisking her into my arms, ignoring the weird hum my body produces as I hold her.

"Oh," she gasps from the unexpected movement, but she doesn't fight me. Her arms wrap around my neck and her face moves in close to mine in this position. The hum is much stronger now. Her athletic curves in my arms are playing push and pull with my body. I hold my breath, not wanting to inhale any more of her sweet honey scent.

Who smells like honey?

It's so odd.

Yet...so her.

Her breath fans over my cheek. I grit my teeth and take the last step toward the sofa and lay her down gently. She sinks into my cream sofa. It looks so big compared to her.

I stare down at her while leaning over her.

She gives me a small smile. It's genuine, but I stand, needing to put distance between us. I grab her a blanket.

And drape it over her body, tucking her in carefully and pausing my hands beside her hips.

She's watching me with lust-filled eyes.

Why did I pause, and why is she giving me this look? I need to get out of this room before I do something stupid like kiss her. Because kissing her would be stupid, right?

"Let me know if you need anything else," I grunt out. I turn around and make my way to the kitchen to clean up. Then I get her a glass of water in case she needs it. But by the time I return to the living room, holding the glass, I find her fast asleep. Her pretty brown hair with flecks of gold falling over her face. She's tucked up on her side, looking every bit enticing.

My legs move on their own accord. Before I can stop myself, I reach over and tuck the loose strand of hair behind her ear. Admiring her openly while she's asleep because I'm sure if she was awake, she'd think I'm weird.

And fuck, I can't blame her.

This is wrong. Yet, despite that, I stare openly a moment longer before I decide a cold shower is in order.

I check in on Samuel who's in his playroom. He's at his table happily coloring. I join him.

"Is Mari okay?" he asks, his brows furrowed. He's clearly worried about her.

I reach out and touch the top of his head. "She's all better. I stitched the cut in her hand."

"Where is she?" He looks around.

I drop my hand from his head. The image of her sleeping soundly hitting me.

"She's resting bud."

His face relaxes and his eyes drop back to his book, and he starts coloring again.

I color with him. But I find some of his pencils dull, so I sharpen them.

After I color a page, I decide it's time for a shower and some time alone. So when he's settled, I go.

I stand under that shower for longer than needed as punishment.

After putting on sweats, I call Elijah.

"Hey! How's Mari?" he asks when he picks up.

"Yeah, her hand is fine. I gave her some painkillers and stitched it up. She's lying on the sofa fast asleep." I walk from my room to the living room, raking my hand through my damp hair.

"Let her sleep," he says casually. As if it's no big deal.

As soon as I hit my living room, my feet stop moving on the cream plush carpet. She's still out cold. She hasn't moved at all.

Panic fills me. "What if she doesn't wake up? Do you want me to wake her and drop her home?" I ask with hope. Having her under my roof while I have some strange connection with her feels wrong.

"Nah. Let her crash on your sofa. If you don't mind."

It's not like I can say no. He'll ask why and I don't want to admit his sister turns me on.

Fuck. He'll punch my head in.

I know I would if I had a little sister.

"Sure," I mutter in defeat.

"Sweet. I'll let you go. Call me if you need anything."

"Will do," I say and hang up.

I stare at the phone, cursing under my breath.

I can't have her sleeping on my sofa all night. No matter if it's comfortable, she needs a bed. But her hand catches my eye. First, I need to bandage her hand. I grab the bandage from the counter and return to her and gently wrap it up.

I take my time, and she doesn't stir at all.

Once I'm finished, I pick her up again, but this time, she snuggles into my neck. The tip of her nose running along the side of my neck as she murmurs, "Mmm, yummy."

I freeze momentarily. Surely, she's not talking about me?

No, don't be fucking stupid. I shake off the silly thought and walk carefully to the spare bedroom.

With her in my arms, I carefully pull back the blanket and lower her down. Her arms still locked around my neck. My cheek against hers. Reaching behind me, I peel her arms from around my neck and stand up. She snuggles into the pillow. For a minute I stare and wonder if I should dress her? Change her into what? A shirt of mine?

But I scratch that idea straight away. Seeing her naked skin would make the situation worse. There'd be no good from me changing her.

I tuck the blankets in and move to step out, but not before hearing a soft whimper. "Damien."

My name on her lips in a sleepy yet sultry way stills me.

I run my hand over my face with a deep sigh; I take a second and walk out. I need to put Samuel to bed and then have another cold shower. The new tension from being close and touching her is too much. I close my bedroom door when I get back to it.

Lying down on my bed with a deep exhale, I message Wildwest25, thinking she'll help me release tonight and get Marigold out of my head. But after ten minutes, I receive nothing back. I sigh heavily and tuck myself into bed and try to sleep. Despite, my best efforts, I quickly realize there's zero chance I'll be sleeping tonight. Not with the constant images of Marigold in my arms, or my name leaving her lips.

There's a banging noise followed by a fit of giggling.

I groan.

I feel like I've only been asleep for five minutes.

Which is probably exactly what happened.

I never heard from Wildwest25 last night, so I'm grumpy about that too.

Another crash sounds and I wince. This time it was louder. I curse and shove the stupid blankets off me. I rip open my bedroom door and stomp down until I hit the kitchen.

I rub my eyes and try to focus on the vision in front of me. Marigold has found a white mug, but she's opening all my cupboards to find something. I should ask what she needs, but my jaw hits the floor when I find her wearing one of my white shirts. It barely covers her ass. Her toned legs are on display as she reaches up to scour my cupboard.

I wonder if she's wearing panties...

"I'm sorry. I hope you don't mind that I borrowed one of your shirts. The dress has blood on it. So Samuel found the shirt and gave it to me," she rambles before chewing on her lip. Her gaze peers around before her eyes meet mine again.

I don't mind...

But I should because it looks better on her than on me.

And my mind is straight back to how her body looks in it.

"It's fine," I mumble out, but my eyes continue to stare at her legs.

"She's trying to find tea," Samuel explains. Totally interrupting my perv session. Which I'm a mix of grateful and bummed about.

Tea. Right.

I don't even remember owning any.

But my housekeeper might've bought it on one of her weekly shopping trips.

"Let me look," I grumble in my rough morning voice.

I open the cupboards one by one.

"We looked in all of them," she states, pointing to the same ones I'm opening and closing.

"Have you checked the pantry?" I ask.

She turns to face me, and I drop my gaze, which was a terrible idea because I struggle to not stare at her erect nipples.

Is she trying to fuck with me?

I swipe my forehead with my hand and walk into the pantry. Not finding any tea. I wouldn't even have a clue what type to buy.

"I don't get why you wouldn't drink coffee. It's weird," I grunt as my eyes take in those taunting buds.

She raises her brows and crosses her arms over her chest. She caught me. "You're weird," she argues.

Samuel laughs.

"What are you laughing at?" I question him with a smile. No matter what, he can always turn my mood around.

"She called you weird," he answers with a goofy grin.

"And?" I ask, grabbing him and giving him a hug as he wriggles in my arms.

"It's funny," he replies as he tries to get out of my grip.

"She's weird too. She drinks tea and not coffee," I say as I tickle him under his arms.

He stops thrashing and stands. He's screwing up his face. "I'm weird too because I don't drink coffee either."

I smile at his innocence and peer over at her. She's pinching her lips together.

"You're a kid. You don't drink coffee, it's not good for you," I say, roughing up his hair with my hand.

He ducks his head, getting away and laughing. "But you drink it."

Marigold giggles, and a twitch forms in the corner of my mouth as a smile starts to form.

I flick my gaze to her. She covers her mouth with her free hand. It reminds me of why she stayed last night.

"How's your hand this morning?" I ask, stepping forward to inspect the bandage.

She bites the corner of her lip. "Good, but I must've passed out from the tablet."

"Seems so," I mumble.

"I'm sorry," she whispers.

"It's fine. I spoke to Eli and told him you fell asleep here."

Her brows rise. "Yeah, and what did he say?"

"He told me to let you stay," I mumble.

She nods but says nothing else.

The air is strange between us. Samuel is watching in fascination. I take her hand and inspect it.

"Looks fine. But I'll write you a script for some antibiotics. You're not going to pass out from them, are you?" I ask with a slight tease in my voice.

She shoves my shoulder playfully. "Ha. Ha. Smart as—" She looks at Samuel and then me. "Pants."

My body relaxes from all the tension of the last twenty-four hours. Her morning energy is addictive. And normally, other than my son, nothing can make me smile. Especially not a woman.

I drop her hand and step away to make a coffee. She turns to the kettle to make hot water?

"You're going to have hot water over a coffee?"

She shrugs. "Yeah, well, you don't have tea." She grabs the kettle and pours water into the white mug.

I watch on in shock before sipping on my latte and moving toward the fridge. I grab some eggs, sausages, and turkey bacon from the fridge.

"Are you making that for us?" she asks, looking at me over the rim of her cup.

"Are you hungry?"

"Starving," she replies eagerly.

"Well then, I'm cooking."

She lowers her cup to the counter and steps closer to me in the kitchen. "How can I help?"

I stare dumbly as thoughts pop into my brain.

Let me kiss those damn sexy lips or let me feed you breakfast while you sit on my counter with your legs spread.

Fuck! I can't say any of that.

I clear my throat that's tightening with arousal. I need space. "Just hang out with Samuel, and I'll call you two when it's ready."

She beams. "I'd love to."

My stupid heart flips at her reaction to hanging out with my kid.

She spins and reaches for her cup, but she spills it on her hand.

"Crap," she mutters.

I hiss and move instantly, grabbing her hand and bringing my mouth to her skin to suck the water off.

My brain clearly disappeared because why didn't I grab a cloth?

Why my mouth?

Where the hell has Doctor Gray gone?

Because I'd been thinking of my mouth on her. The sweet, unusual taste hits my tongue.

I remove my mouth from her hand. Her hand is slightly pink, but it's not too bad; it won't blister.

"How was the water?" she asks.

I swallow hard as I meet her dark eyes that are now filled with heat.

"Delicious," I gruff out.

I meant her, not the water.

"Play with Samuel and I'll cook," I add.

It'll give me a second to breathe and find my brain.

"You don't have to. I promise I can cook." Her lips twitch with a hint of a smile forming.

"Thanks for the offer. I believe you, but I want to cook for you...two," I say as my eyes hold hers. She dips her chin and walks away, carrying her cup, and I see her and Samuel head to his playroom.

When I'm alone, I rub my face with my hands, knowing right now I'm in over my head.

CHAPTER 11

MARIGOLD

I WALK AWAY IN his shirt, not missing the way his eyes roamed hungrily over my body. He loved me wearing his shirt and no bra.

I wanted to tell him I'm Wildwest25, but I had Samuel right beside me, eagerly awaiting to play. I'll take care of it before I leave today, so his little ears won't hear. I survey the room. The playroom is in order. All the boxes are neatly labeled and completely different from how I remember a toy room being as a kid.

Toys were everywhere, but here, it's neatly organized. Samuel walks to one box in particular.

"What did you want to play?" I ask.

"Legos?"

He glances up at me as he tips the box of Legos out.

"Sure," I say and sip more water.

"What do you like to build, Sammy?" I take a seat at his little table and chairs as he brings a box over.

"Buildings or a police station," he says eagerly.

"Got it. Let's build this together."

"I like this," he states.

"What?" I ask, not understanding.

"Playing with someone."

My heart drops. "No one plays with you?"

But Damien seemed good with him before...I don't get it.

"No, my dad works a lot and Nana doesn't like to."

I blink rapidly as I digest this information and find the best way to respond.

"Have you asked your dad to play?"

He scrunches up his nose and shakes his head. "No."

"Well, maybe ask him next time. Your dad seems pretty cool."

"He is. It's just he's been sad."

I frown. "Why?"

"My mom left," he states matter-of-factly.

Building blocks together seemed easy, but now I'm not so sure. I feel like he's unloading all his feelings on me. Which on one hand I love, but on the other, I'm not sure how to properly handle the questions. I'm only twenty-five and not a parent. But he's opening up to me and I don't want to shut him down.

"That must be hard. Are you sad?"

He lifts his little shoulder. "A little. At school when they talk about moms and dads. I don't have one."

I continue stacking little colored blocks on top of each other. "That would make me sad, too."

"But it's okay."

"It sounds like your dad and nana love you dearly."

"Mmm," he mumbles, but he's too focused on his building to answer.

I blow out a breath in relief. He understands he has no mom, but his dad is doing a great job at being both. The only issue is the playtime. It seems Sammy needs more time with Damien.

I continue stacking.

"Woah. Cool. Look how awesome your building is," Samuel exclaims.

"Yeah, good work, Marigold," Damien says from the doorway.

I side-eye him and enjoy the view of him only wearing sweatpants. "Thanks."

His naked torso is burning me up with memories on the camera. But seeing it in real life is something else.

My fingers twitch, wishing I could touch him.

"Food is ready," Damien announces.

Samuel jumps up and runs out of the room.

I laugh.

"Thanks for playing with him," Damien grits out.

"Anytime. It was actually kind of fun." I hold his eyes as I answer.

His brow lifts. "I doubt that."

"Try it. Legos are actually fun and sorta relaxing."

"You and I have different versions of relaxing."

I swallow the words, *but Sammy wants you to play with him*. Not wanting to overstep. Did Samuel say that to me in secrecy, or should I share it?

I don't know Damien enough as a dad to know how much I can say.

It's not my place. I'm just a visitor....

We're sitting around the table eating breakfast as a family. Both Damien and me sit next to Samuel, who's at the end of the table. Every so often, I look up and into Damien's eyes. I soak in the hard lines around his eyes and his morning scruff over his jaw. I try to remember all the little quirks and this relaxed version of him before this ends. Because it will.

The only other side I'll see of him is online.

However, that side is more for sexual relief. There's no friendship, fun or relaxed Damien.

Samuel finishes breakfast and runs back to his playroom to finish our building.

Damien stands to clean up the plates. I follow to help him clear the table.

"You're good with him," I say quietly, not wanting Samuel to hear.

"Thanks," he replies. But it's gruff and I feel like I've said something I shouldn't have.

I stay quiet and pack up before I ask to take a shower. Even if I have to put on yesterday's dress, it'll still feel better when I'm clean.

In the shower, I grab the body soap and the moment I open the lid, a waft of pear hits me. It's his scent. There's something about using his soap and walking out smelling like him that makes me bathe in it. I make a mental note of the label, planning to order a few bottles once I'm back home. Stepping out of the shower makes me feel and smell better. I wonder if he'll mind if I keep his top. I want to...

I decide that it's too much, so I'll give his shirt back. I walk out to the living room and find him reclined and watching TV.

"Is it okay if I go? I have studying to get back to," I say, biting the corner of my lip.

He switches the TV off and climbs off the sofa before he calls out, "Samuel. We need to take Marigold home."

"I can grab a taxi," I say quickly, not wanting to disrupt their morning any more than I already have.

"Nonsense. I'll drive you," he says it with the commanding voice I love.

I'll admit wasting money on a taxi isn't ideal, so I keep my mouth shut and just nod.

Samuel comes running out. "Do you have to leave?" He moans.

"I'm sorry I do," I say, giving him a sad look back.

He steps forward and hugs my waist. I'm momentarily stunned. I look at Damien, who looks pale and shocked himself.

I rub Samuel's back. "What if I promise to come back one time and finish playing Legos?"

"Yes. Tomorrow?"

"Not tomorrow, but soon." Damien's voice cuts in.

I thrust out the top for Damien to take. "Here, thanks for letting me borrow it."

It was nice catching his eyes on my legs a few times. But other than that, I do not know what he thinks about me. I know he likes my body online, so it would have been nice to see his responses in real life. Would he suck in a breath?

Hiss?

Groan?

Yeah, I'd love to hear what I do to him.

"Keep it. It looked better on you."

I stare at him at a loss for words.

He clears his throat and grabs his keys.

"Ah. Thanks," I mumble, not knowing what else to say.

I squeeze his shirt in my hand and bring it to my stomach. He just gave me his shirt and said it looked better on me...what does that even mean?

I wave goodbye to Damien and Samuel, wishing I didn't have to walk away from them. Instead, I want to stay inside my bubble at their house, but reality settles in now that I've arrived at my house. It's like a cloud lifts. I need to forget the fantasy of what life would be like if Damien and I were together, because when he finds out who I am, he'll end us.

I open the door to my house with a heavy heart. When I close it behind me, a gush of air leaves my lungs. As if I closed the door on us, I drag my feet to my room and collapse onto my bed.

After a couple of minutes moaning to myself in my bedroom, I call Clara.

"Hey!" she answers, out of breath.

I sit up on my bed. "What are you doing?"

"Cleaning my room."

"Why?"

"I'm preparing to start..." she trails off.

"Oh, I get you. Do you need any help?" I ask. Even though I have to study, I know I won't concentrate if my mind is still thinking about Damien.

"Not if you don't want to," she replies.

"I want to. I need a distraction and to tell you something."

"A Damien something," she asks curiously.

I can't help but perk up; talking out loud about him makes me happy. "Yep."

"Get your ass over here and spill. But then you can't sit and watch me," she warns.

"I promise to help," I say enthusiastically.

I hang up and get dressed. Driving the five minutes to her house.

Inside her room, my eyes bulge. "Clara, this is a mess."

"I know, but I'm cleaning behind everything and then I'm moving my furniture."

I rub my temples, wondering where to even start.

"I want the camera here so they can't see my desk."

"Let's do the furniture pieces first, and then I'll help you set up the camera. Did you get new lingerie?"

This should be the perfect distraction, but it also brings up the memory of Damien and I meeting online.

I miss that.

After the sparks flying last night, I know I want to go online to see him.

"Yes," she beams. "Come look." She waves me over to her drawers.

She pulls out a beautiful blue set and I gush. "That's gorgeous," I say as I reach out and touch it. Admiring the silk and I know already I need to buy a silk set to show Damien.

"Oh, and I copied you. I hope you don't mind." She pulls out a blue mask.

"No, of course not. This is smart. Hide your identity."

"Speaking of..." She narrows her eyes at me.

"Can we at least make tea for this?" I say with a strangled laugh.

She huffs. "Okay."

We head into her kitchen. She shares this house with two roommates who are both out today.

I help her make tea rather than stand around watching. I need to do something with my hands as I tell her.

"Yesterday I went to his house," I whisper.

"What?" she screeches. And I know the shock. But also, it's not what she thinks.

"It wasn't like that. I wish," I admit.

"Ah, dammit."

We carry the tea to her table, and I clutch it in my hands. I stare down at the milky liquid.

"I cut my hand at my brother's, and it needed stitches, so he took me to his place to do that."

"The handy doctor." She wriggles her brows at me.

"He has excellent hands." I giggle.

She leans forward a bit, smirking. "And you know what they say about hands."

"I do. And I'd say they match."

"God damn. You lucky bitch!"

"Hey, you might find your guy," I say with a wide grin.

Her face falls a bit.

"What?" I ask.

"You need to be careful. Remember, he's a lot older, has a son and is—"

"My brother's best friend," I finish.

"Yes, but you're so in love with the idea of love. I feel like you could go all-in and get hurt. Again," she says with a worried look.

"I'm so bad at love, but you can't blame me for trying. Maybe an older guy is the answer," I say with a shrug.

"I wouldn't get your hopes up. He's got a lot of baggage."

"I'm already in too deep. I wanted to tell him who I was yesterday and even this morning, but I couldn't."

"This morning?" she asks.

"Yeah, I ended up passing out from the painkillers he gave me."

"It gets worse, doesn't it?" she says, shaking her head and lifting her tea to take a sip.

"I don't think it's bad. I did, however, wear his shirt this morning."

"He changed you?" she asks with a slacked jaw.

I shrug and sip my tea before answering. "No. My dress had blood on it, so Samuel found one of his dad's shirts. And then this morning, I tried to give his shirt back to him and he said it looked better on me and insisted I should keep it."

"Fuck," she mumbles, sitting back in her chair.

"I know. I know. I should've told him who I was, but I was scared," I say.

"Of him not wanting you? Man, your ex is a massive douchebag."

I laugh. "I can't argue with that."

"What about the kid? You're not even finished with school yourself."

"Sammy is so sweet. He told me no one plays with him. His dad works all the time, and his nana doesn't like it."

"It doesn't mean you need to do it. He's not your problem."

I wince. "Ouch, that's harsh."

"I'm trying not to be. More of a realist. You're always so kind and you look at life as an opportunity. And sometimes we can't fix everything."

I sip my tea, taking a moment to sit with her words. "Who in the world leaves their kid?"

"I don't have the answer, but it still doesn't mean you should dive in without thinking about the pain you could inflict if the relationship crumbles. Sammy then gets hurt again."

"Shit. You're right."

"Just go slow, and I think you need to tell him soon. Before it's too late."

"I will. I promise I was going to yesterday. Believe me, I had every intention. But when he's around, I can't think clearly."

She gets up from the table and puts her cup in the sink, and I drain my cup and follow her.

"Come on, help me finish my room. I want to do this tonight."

CHAPTER 12

DAMIEN

Wildwest25: Why did I think by being a lawyer I could change the world?

Grays_online: You will change the world.

Wildwest25: I like your optimism, but I'm not feeling it. :(

Grays_online: Would it help if I told you that was one of the reasons I wanted to be a doctor?

Wildwest25: *To change the world?*

Grays_online: *Yes. And now that I am. I do think I'm changing the world.*

Wildwest25: *Please tell me you're not full of yourself. I did like you...*

Grays_online: *I'm not cocky. I promise. And I like you too. I just love my job and I see how it changes people's lives.*

I walk back to my office from surgery the next day. My hand digs through my pocket in my scrubs to pull out my phone. I scroll through my phone, checking emails, and I notice a missed call from Elijah. I hit redial. He answers on the second ring.

"I just left surgery. I missed your call," I say as I continue moving through the corridor toward my office.

"All good. I just left your place. Your mom said you're working."

"Yeah. I'll be here for a little while longer," I reply.

"I'll see you next Sunday? Or are you working?"

I wish I was home right now. I'm spent. I barely slept last night with Marigold in my house.

"I'm off next Sunday," I reply, after checking my calendar.

"Cool. And how did Mari get on?"

I swallow the lump that's formed at the mention of his sister. My hand grips the phone tighter.

"Yeah, great. I put her in the spare room to sleep," I say as casually as I can.

I feel like I had to mention the fact it was a spare bedroom. Which was dumb because why would he think I'd let her sleep in my bed?

Because I wanted that.

But why her?

Why am I so drawn to her?

Why the fuck do I have to think about his little sister in this way? It's going to end badly.

I'm just glad we've done nothing sexual. Christ, no. That can't happen, because going deeper would give her false hope.

I can't introduce a woman to my son, especially one who's thirteen years younger than me.

Every way you look at this, someone winds up getting hurt, or my friendship with Elijah will end.

"Thanks. I really appreciate it."

He appreciates me ogling his sister.

Appreciates how I loved seeing her wear my shirt. Or how I soaked in every sliver of delicate skin on her body, admiring her freckles and the touch of her buttery soft skin as I carried her.

And then, to make matters worse, I tried and failed to jerk off with a woman online. Fuck. I'm so fucked up.

I scrub my scalp frustratedly.

How am I a doctor?

I seem to have lost all of my brain cells. Women seem to take over and turn it to mush. If I were to be with a woman, I know that I'll get hurt again, because that's what happens when you fall in love.

"Anytime," I reply.

"Do the stitches come out?" he asks.

Arriving at my office door, I yank it open and close it behind me, as I think about his question.

"Uh. Yeah," I mutter, knowing I didn't think about that when I sutured her last night. "I'll have to take them out," I add.

After how tempted I was last night, I know I'd have to remove them in my office. Away from my house. Away from the memories. And way away from dangerous territory.

"I have to drop off your birthday present on the weekend," I say, not wanting to forget. Samuel's been begging every day to drop it off. I've had to explain that we'll do it on the weekend.

His deep chuckle sounds in my ear. "Yeah, come. I don't have any plans. I'm staying low key."

I snort, taking a seat in my office chair. "Bout time."

"Hey, someone needs to have fun," he says. He's clearly making a dig at me. It's not the first time. He just wants me to live a little. It's something I'm hearing from everyone—my parents, friends and work colleagues. Everyone seems to be saying the same thing to me right now.

"I have fun...sometimes," I clip.

"Whatever you say," he mumbles. "You could come out this weekend to The Players' Club."

I've heard only great things about this club from both Alex and other friends, but the idea of going out takes time away from my son, and frankly, I don't want to pick anyone up, so I don't see the point.

"I don't know..." I say, leaning my elbow on my mahogany desk and leaning my head into my hand.

"Are you seeing someone?" he asks, amusement lacing his voice.

The internet girl...no.

His sister...no.

"No," I sigh.

"So, come. Even just for an hour," he says mischievously. He's trying to persuade me.

"It's never just an hour, though, is it?" I say, reclining back into my office chair.

"Not with Jackie and Marigold together. It will be hard to get them out of there." He laughs.

My molars grind together as he continues, "Those two are the same and when they drink, they let loose. They have every guy drooling. I'm going to have to watch them all night, so come help me."

I shouldn't care that his sister will be drunk and have guys drooling over her all night. I can't. I shouldn't. So why the fuck do I then?

Why does the very thought of her being looked at piss me off?

This needs to stop. Including this stupid boner that's tenting in my scrubs now.

"No," my voice breaks, so I clear it to add, "I already have a child, remember?"

"Touché, man. But it would be nice to have a drink together. Out. You know, away from our houses."

I know exactly what he means, but I simply can't. Between work and Samuel, I have minimal spare time, and I'm too tired to do that for fun.

I put my glasses on to check the time on my computer screen. I need to wrap up work fast and make it home before the nighttime routine is done. I'd hate to miss it.

"I gotta go. I want to finish up my notes and then head home. Mom's looking after Samuel for me, and I don't want to be here longer than I need to," I say, typing my notes to finish them.

"Alright. I'll catch you on the weekend."

I hang up and return to my notes.

After I've finished them, I send the final email. I pack up my desk, but when I go to leave, the sunset catches my eye. It draws me in closer to the window. The golden hues remind me of Marigold. I should've asked if his sister would be there over the weekend, but I probably would've made it a bigger deal than it needed to be. It's just that I don't want to fuck up my friendship with Elijah. No woman is worth that.

I made it in time to tuck Samuel in and read him a book. After a shower, I turn the TV on in my bedroom, but there's nothing interesting, so I turn to my phone and begin scrolling through social media. I spend the next hour doing that, but I'm bored again. As I flick the home page of icons, I see the Mysterious Fan app. I hover my thumb over it.

Do I?

Don't I?

I do it. Holding my breath.

Once inside, I see she's online. The deep exhale leaves my chest shaking.

When I'm about to click off, thinking this is a dumb idea and I need to stop it...she messages.

Wildwest25: *Hey! I've been waiting for you.*

I squeeze my eyes shut. She's so fucking sweet, it hurts. I'm such a miserable user. But, of course, that doesn't stop me from typing.

Grays_online: You have?

Wildwest25: *Yes. For an hour.*

At the same time, I was scrolling.

Grays_online: *Sorry...*

I trail off with nothing else because I don't know this woman and I was so close to confessing to her about my night.

My son.

I was going to tell a stranger about my son.

I've officially lost it.

Wildwest25: *You can make it up to me :)*

I hesitate. Do I want to know what she's thinking? Like, the dirty bastard that I've become, I type back.

Grays_online: *How?*

A message for a video call pops up. I pause a second, looking around my dark room lit up by the TV screen. I hit accept, unable to deny myself tonight. Maybe this will help me get my mind off Marigold.

Yeah. Anything to help with that.

When she comes into view, I see a pretty gold lingerie set against her flushed skin.

"You look breathtaking in gold." My voice is gritter than I've ever heard, and breathier. She literally stole my breath with that color on her luscious body. So unusual and yet so elegant at the same time.

"Thank you," she says with a blush that begins on her chest and runs upward onto her neck. "How was your day?" she adds, wringing her hands in front of her.

A small smile tips at the corner of my mouth. She's endearing too. "Tiring. I got called into work and it took longer than usual," I answer honestly.

It's strange for someone to ask me about my day. Not even my ex-wife asked. She only cared about spending my money. She didn't care if I was barely home, as long as I gave her the lifestyle she wanted. I felt more like a bank than a husband. And even after giving her everything, she walked away.

"Let me help you forget about it," she whispers with a knowing grin.

"What about your day?" I ask, genuinely wanting to know how her day was. It's probably unusual, considering the app we're on, but this feels like a friendship, at least to me it does. She feels less of a stranger now.

She smiles at my question before answering lightly. "I hung out with a friend and then came home to finish an assignment."

Her high-pitched tone makes me understand the importance of completing college and how proud she is of that.

"Good girl," I say with my own praise. I know what it feels like to achieve and to graduate from college, so to find her just as happy hits me differently in the chest. Like it adds another connection to this online stranger. One where work and careers are important. You're in control of your future, but you ultimately have to put the work in.

She's putting the work in. I'm proud of her.

Her teeth catch on her bottom lip. "I like being your good girl. But did you want me to show you how bad I can be?"

I sit up in surprise. The purr in the way she said *bad* has my attention.

"Of course."

A soft, adorable smile overtakes her lips. "I got you a present."

My brows rise, but I stay silent. I've never received a present from a woman. Well, unless you count when you're ten and you have a girlfriend and think she's your forever girl. So a woman buying me a present seems too good to be true.

And we barely know each other, so what could it be...

"A new toy."

That has my attention. "Yeah?" I say with a wicked grin.

"Do you want to see it?" She bats her eyelashes, totally seducing me, and it's working. Of course, it's fucking working.

"It actually matches my outfit."

My curiosity peaks.

She crawls over the bed to her bedside drawer, and my dick jerks. I get the vision of her crawling toward me.

Would she be down for that? Because fuck, that would be hot. I could ask her for it after she shows me the toy.

She grabs it and slides off the bed and comes to the screen to show me. Instantly, a deep growl leaves my chest at the butt plug. She moves it around, so I get all angles in the camera and really appreciate its beauty. The small rose jeweled end is gold. Fuck, that's hot. My dick is painfully hard now. Tonight is going to be wicked. But when she inches closer to the camera, I freeze.

Fuck, no way.

She's wearing the same purple nail polish as Marigold does, and when I catch those brown eyes, I instantly wonder how I missed them.

My stomach hardens, and I end the video.

It's Marigold...

CHAPTER 13

MARIGOLD

A few days later

"How's it feel to be thirty-five?" I tease as soon as Elijah opens his front door.

He laughs. "The same as thirty-four."

I step inside his two-story brick house. He closes the door behind us.

"Figured. It's just a number," I say, walking through the house. Damien is a couple of years older than my brother.

"I feel like I did in my twenties," he mutters from behind me.

I walk into his living room and make my way to his gray sofa. "Just with a few extra lines and bags under your eyes," I say with amusement.

He smacks his chest. "Ouch."

I shrug casually at him. "It's fine. We all get there." I take a seat on his sofa.

"You're way off it, lil sister."

Normally, the little sister comments don't bother me, but today it hits different. I want to be seen as a woman. I push the disappointment aside and pull out my phone, ready to order our lunch. "What does the birthday boy want to eat?"

"Jackie is taking me out for dinner, so nothing heavy," he says casually.

That has me smiling. I'm so happy my brother met his one. He's been career focused for way too long. Yes, he's a successful billionaire, but he's worked every day for years. It's surprising she wasn't his PA or someone that works for him. Don't get me wrong, there's nothing wrong with that. But to me, that's him finding something convenient and not finding the right one.

So, with Jackie, it was a complete surprise.

I feel like she's the sister I never had. We're so alike, it's uncanny. She used to be a bartender for The Players' Club but recently stopped. Well, I'm going to blame my controlling brother. Not that she'd have to give up her job. I don't see my brother putting too many rules in place. He can, however, be persuasive. People listen to him.

"So, things are good with Jackie?" I ask excitedly. I turn my head as he takes a seat on the other sofa, flicking the TV channel from sports.

"So far," he answers nonchalantly.

I smile. It's those minor details of knowing I don't really like sports that make me wonder what he's like as a boyfriend. He's a typical guy, so me asking too many questions will have him closing up. I pick and choose my questions each time I see him.

"I'm happy for you. I like her. Well, I'll order a sandwich from the deli. That's lighter."

"Yeah." He shrugs, not bothered.

I order our food. When it arrives, we move to his dining and kitchen area.

I'm sitting eating lunch with Elijah at his table when the door sounds.

Jackie must be here.

He pushes his chair out to answer it as I take a bite of my sandwich.

"Hey, Damo, come in," my brother says happily.

I almost choke on my food.

"Thanks. Happy Birthday," Damien replies as their heavy footsteps sound.

Coming closer and closer to me.

"Thanks man. Catching up to you in the old age." He laughs.

Damien's deep chuckle sounds.

I squeeze my eyes and scrunch my face up tight. The age topic makes me sick.

My throat tightens and I force myself to swallow the piece of bread that's in my mouth. I lower the rest of the sandwich back to my plate and push it from me. I put my hands on my thighs and rub them up and down. The butterflies somersaulting in my stomach are making me too nervous to eat.

The last time I spoke to Damien, I was showing him a toy online. A blush hit my cheeks at the mere thought.

How embarrassing.

He messaged after a couple of minutes, saying the line disconnected the other night and he said he had internet problems. So he could not get back on. But he hasn't been back on since, leaving me to believe the opposite.

Maybe I'd pushed him too far. Maybe he's not interested in different toys? Even though he initially seemed excited, he quickly became wide-eyed, and then he disappeared.

To see him today is uncomfortable. He doesn't know it's me. I've kept my identity a secret, but I know how uncomfortable I'll feel. The only savior will be Samuel. I'll just play games with him the whole time to avoid Damien.

They come into view, and my flush deepens. I focus on my brother, who sits down at the table. Then I move my gaze to Damien. He's face is hard today. The line between his brow is deeper. When his eyes catch mine, his body stiffens.

"Hi," I say in an uneven voice.

He nods. But he doesn't talk back.

"Take a seat," Elijah encourages, but he just shakes his head and stands in the doorway to the kitchen. He's refusing to sit down at the table, as if he doesn't want to be here.

What's with him today?

He's back to being grumpy and quiet. I hate it. The online version and the one I saw at his house are much more relaxed.

"Where's Samuel?" Elijah asks. I wondered too, but with the cool exterior he's giving me, I remained silent.

"He's got a cold, so my mom is watching him. I told her I wouldn't be long. Hope you don't mind."

My brother shakes his head. "No biggie. Hope the little bugger feels better soon."

"Me too," Damien mumbles, stuffing his hands deeper into his tight acid-wash jeans. The black biker jacket and his black top scream moody. It's a shame he's hot and I have a stupid major crush on him. I purse my lips and wish he wasn't frowning at me. Instead, I imagine him giving me one of those crooked smiles from our night chats. I'm coming to crave the rare smiles. Which is dumb. Clearly, he'll never be interested in me.

He has no problem replying to my brother, but with me, I get the silent treatment.

"Did you want a drink?" Elijah asks.

"No, I'm good," he replies.

"What about something to eat? We just finished lunch, but I got snacks." Elijah pushes out his chair and grabs a bag of crisps. He holds them out to Damien.

His lips twist slightly, but if you weren't watching them, you would have missed it because his mask is already back in place. "No. Seriously, just relax. I'm here to see you."

My brother lets out a sigh. "Well, sit down. You're making me nervous. Did you want to watch some of the basketball game?"

My brother moves toward the other room, but his phone rings, and he answers it.

"Hey," he talks, but the way his face wears a stupid look, I'm guessing it's Jackie. Ugh. He walks away to talk, leaving Damien and me alone.

The silence in the air is too uncomfortable. He doesn't look like he'll speak to me. His thin lips, hunched shoulders and crossed arms definitely tell me he's in a mood.

Maybe something happened with his ex-wife?

"Are you okay?" I whisper.

He doesn't answer, just stares for a moment. His gaze drops to my hands and then back up. Something is definitely up. His jaw is tight and his muscles twitch.

The silence returns, and it's deafening. I can't sit here any longer like this. I push back on my chair, rising to walk to use the bathroom.

I need a moment alone to wrap my head around this awkwardness.

The layout of my brother's house means I need to step past him. So I suck in a breath and hold it. I ignore the way my body hums being close to him and move past him.

But just as I think I'm safe, he grabs my wrist and grits out. "It's you."

Panic swirls in my gut. His angry face inches from mine. "What are you talking about?" I ask, my heart beating wildly in my chest. A sense of dread washes over me.

I want him to say the words in case I'm wrong. But of course, I'm not.

"You're Wildwest25," he spits under his breath. I drop my hand. He pushes off the frame and stares down at me with wild eyes. "Fuck, how stupid am I?" He shakes his head and drags a hand over it. "Your name, for fuck's sake. And I never realized. I must be a joke to you!" he sneers. The words drip like venom from his mouth and it tears me apart.

My heart is thumping so hard inside my ears. "No, you're not." I rush out in a panic.

"Then why trick me?" The hurt staring back at me pierces my heart.

"I didn't," I plead. My voice cracking just like my heart. I wish he believed me. I didn't know it was him. Yes, when

I did, I should have come clean. I tried to, but I just…Jesus, I couldn't do it.

He laughs, but it's scary.

"West. Twenty-five. Like fuck, why didn't I think more?" he says with disdain as he scrunches up his nose, causing a wrinkle there.

"I'm sorry," I say, twisting to walk off, but he grabs my hand and I spin back around. He leans into my hair. His nose touching my head and he sucks in a deep breath. Normally, this position is romantic, but right now, it's painful. My heart is already cracking. I just want to go and be alone to cry. I've made a huge fucking mess. And I do not know how to fix it.

"You smell like my soap," he grunts.

I shudder. Even to myself, the fact I bought his soap to smell like him is insane.

The words slip out from my lips. "I wanted to have you around me all the time," I stupidly admit.

He pulls his head back, his eyes frantically looking into my eyes. "Fuck. No. This is a bad idea," he adds, pinching the bridge of his nose.

"What the fuck is going on?" My brother's icy voice cuts in.

CHAPTER 14

DAMIEN

HER LAST NAME IS West, and she's twenty-five. Why was I so fucking stupid? I should've put two and two together. Now, with Elijah catching us, I step back. To put some much-needed distance between Marigold and me.

"I said what the fuck is going on," Elijah roars.

"Nothing," I say, keeping my cool.

"It doesn't sound or fucking look like nothing," he accuses as his icy gaze flicks from mine to Marigold's.

Marigold stays still and all the color has drained from her face. A part of me worries she's going to faint, but I'm too hurt to ask. She manipulated me. She knew who I was and kept going. I feel so fucking stupid.

"Someone better tell me what the fuck's going on. Now!" Elijah yells again.

Marigold stares at me. My frustration gets the better of me.

"Ask your sister." My voice vibrates with anger.

The fact another woman has purposefully hurt me sends me seeing red.

Her sharp intake of breath stills me. And for a second, I wince, but no, I can't feel sorry for her.

She did this, so she needs to explain.

"Eli...I need to tell you something." Her soft voice wavers from emotion.

"Both of you sit at the table now and start explaining why the fuck you two are acting like you're hooking up." He says those last few words through gritted teeth.

He turns and storms to his table, dragging the chair out and sitting down with a huff. It's not hard to know he's pissed. He's making it abundantly clear.

I still follow with heavy feet, but less anger than him.

His face is murderous, and it's all directed at me. His hand propped under his tight jaw.

I cross my arms and sit up in my chair, not sinking in from his stare. I've done nothing wrong.

Yes, my mind and body haven't been a hundred percent pure, but I never said or acted on them. I've never had feelings or thoughts about Marigold. But suddenly, they've just started out of the blue. I always thought she was good looking, but I thought nothing more of it.

The sound of her chair squeaking has his gaze finally tearing from mine.

"Start talking, Marigold." Elijah's voice is firm, but he's slightly more in control now.

"I need money for...that's not your business. None of this is so after I explain myself, don't think you can change my mind. This is my choice. You cannot take that away from me," she says.

I bite down so hard the taste of metallic hits my tongue. I hate the thought of her working online.

The other men staring at her body, her tits, her pussy. Her brown eyes looking flirty at them. Fuck, even talking to them, not even sexually...but emotionally is making my body turn to stone.

"I don't like the sound of this," Elijah warns.

She sits up and there is this powerful aura around her as the next words pour from her lips. Loud and proud. "I work online for money."

Elijah frowns. "I'm not following. How is Damien involved?"

My full name leaving his lips shows he's hiding his anger from us. Which is way more powerful than his sneering words.

"I met him online," she says, and her lip catches quickly on her bottom lip.

She enjoyed meeting me there just as much as I did. But that's when I did not know who she was. Now that I do,

I should feel regret. But I don't. Which makes me angry again, but this time at myself.

Glad it's all coming out now and this can be out in the open. Elijah will never approve of Marigold and me.

"Online dating?" he asks, totally dumbstruck. He drops back in his chair as his eyes flick between mine and Marigold, waiting for answers.

"Yes and no," she mutters, her gaze dropping to the table and I watch the wheels turning in her head. Will she say what she's been doing or won't she?

I hope she doesn't—

"It's not dating. It's an app where I get nak—"

"No!" Elijah slams his hands on the table. It's loud, and it causes me to jump, and Marigold gasps. "You do not need to do that for a job. I'll give you the money. How much do you need?"

He digs into his pocket and grabs his black Amex. He throws it at the table in front of her. "You use that. I don't care how much you use. Pay all your fucking debts. No sister of mine lowers herself—" His words catch on the last word. He's struggling to comprehend this.

"I'm not taking it. Your girlfriend worked at The Players' Club, remember? That's how you met. Don't be a hypocrite, Eli," Marigold says with anger, pushing the card back to him. Then her arms cross over her chest, and she purses her lips. Challenging him head-on. I've never seen this side of her toward her brother.

Now it's my turn to be stunned silent.

"We will talk about this later," he sneers, and then his eyes snap to mine. "You won't come out to The Players' Club, or any club for that matter, but you'll pay for her?" He flings his arm out toward Marigold.

"Don't speak to her like she's trash, Elijah. She's your sister," I say, trying not to snap. I know he's shocked and hurt. Fuck. So am I.

"She's selling herself. What would you like me to say? I'm calling a spade a spade," he argues.

I lean forward, narrowing my eyes. "No, you're acting like a fucking prick. You know Marigold. Don't be like this. You're hurt, I get it, but don't do this." My words come out low, controlled, and cold.

"You two are hooking up! That's why you're sticking up for her." He claps and lets out a strained laugh. He's being a total asshole.

"No, it wasn't like that. We both hid our identity. Well, I didn't know it was her. I swear to you, Elijah, I did not know. I'd never do that. If I had known—"

"What, you would've stopped?" He says in a disbelieving tone. His brow raised at me.

"I figured it out the other night and I stopped," I confess, refusing to look her way as she realizes what happened.

"You two did that shit the other night. Fuck you're thirteen years older. You have a kid. You're not supposed to be with my baby sister, for fuck's sake."

An audible exhale escapes me. "I get it. I'm sorry and I promise you I didn't do this on purpose."

"Neither did I," Marigold says, interrupting me.

My lips pinch together, and my chest is rising and falling rapidly.

Where do we go from here?

"I think you better go," Elijah says angrily to me.

I nod and push back my chair to stand. My eyes flick to hers briefly, and they are frightened and sad. My gaze diverts. I can't look at them anymore. I can't help her.

I don't even know what to think or feel. I'm so fucking lost. How do I move past this with Elijah?

I need to get him to believe that I never sought her out.

I walk to the front door slowly. I pull the door open and step outside. He follows closely behind me.

"I swear I want to punch you in the face right now."

I can't stop myself from smiling. "I would too, but I promise you I didn't go on there for her." Shaking my head, I wince. "I didn't know she did that."

"Then why were you on there?" he asks.

He's standing tall in front of me, his hands stuffed in his jeans, kicking the floor in front of him.

"Honestly, I'm not ready to commit to another woman. But I'm fucking lonely," I say and I expect a hit, but it never comes. I feel like I need to open up more to get him to understand and forgive me. "It's been a long time. I work long hours, and I have a kid. I can't exactly go out and meet anyone."

He stays quiet for a moment.

"It's my fucking baby sister. You two aren't even on the same wavelength in life. She's in law school and you need to heal from your ex-wife."

I swallow the hard words he delivers, and I am at a loss. What he's saying is true.

"Go back inside and talk to her. Be gentle, she might be open to you if you're not the overbearing older brother."

He snaps. "Don't tell me what to do. I know how to talk to her."

With that, I turn and leave his house, heading for the nearest bar.

I spend hours there drinking alone. Which isn't making me feel any better because on top of the shitshow already going on in my head, I feel like a shit dad. I needed a breather, so I left him with my mom and headed to this bar. Despite only having time alone at work, my guilt still overwhelms me as I drink more. I love my son. He's my whole fucking world. And I hate that I'm not there with him right now. But I need some time to think and process what I've just found out. I'm a jumbled mess.

I sit in the corner, unmoving. My head sits in my hands on the sticky wooden surface until it is time to leave. I didn't want to talk unless I was ordering another drink.

I want to drink until I can't think about her anymore. Or the mess of my relationship with Elijah. It's now fractured, and I just hope it's not broken beyond repair. I've known him for far too long for this honest mistake to ruin our friendship.

By the time I get home, Mom has put Samuel to bed. I thank her, and, of course, she asks if everything's okay. I'm sure the look on my face and the state I've come home in doesn't take a rocket scientist to figure out something is wrong.

I'm not able to speak a word about my problem. I answer with a simple, "Yes," and tell her "I'll be fine," before she leaves. After she drives away, I close the door. Then my feet move to check on Samuel. I stand in the doorframe, swaying side to side as I watch his little body breathe. He's fast asleep. And I can't help thinking how simple life is when you're five and you have no troubles in the world.

I take a few moments to soak him in before I leave his room and head to mine, where I shower and crawl into bed. I check my phone to silence it and find a notification that there's a message...

I know it's her, and I shouldn't bother reading it, but I can't help myself. I'm a sucker for her. Opening it, I read.

> **Marigold:** *I'm really sorry, Damien. I swear I wanted to tell you the time I was at your house, but I couldn't. Please forgive me :(*

I stare at unfamiliar words...

Sorry.

Please forgive me.

Words my ex-wife never said. Not even once. She hurt me, and she simply left without a care for either Samuel or me. No sorry, no nothing, just a closed door and silence ever since.

The sides of my head pound in slow beats of pain as I stare at her message. I decide it's best that I don't respond when I'm drunk, so I don't message her back. Instead, I lie my head down on my pillow and close my eyes. In my dreams, she's wearing her gold lingerie set.

CHAPTER 15

MARIGOLD

"YOU CAN'T MOPE ABOUT him and your brother all weekend," Clara says, sitting down on the edge of my unmade bed beside me.

I haven't been making my bed or cleaning my room because I don't see the point. He hasn't been online. And he never responded to my text, either.

I've had zero desire to get back online and talk to other guys. So, there's been no point in making my bed or tidying for Clara's sake. She takes me as I am.

I won't last very long because I need the money, but I refuse to take it from my brother. He keeps trying to give me the money every time we speak, so I've started avoiding his calls. I tell him I'm at college or studying.

I'm sure he sees through my bullshit, but I'm grateful he's not pushing me right now. I need to find my happy self again.

"We had this connection, I'm telling you." I sigh. She thinks I'm doing my usual fall too hard and fast, but I don't think so. I've known Damien for many years now and I trust we've always had a connection. His marriage troubles were obvious to onlookers. But I also had insider information from my brother. Damien's ex-wife sounded like a user who wanted the lifestyle and not the family. Which is a shame for poor Samuel and Damien. She left two people very hurt.

"I'm not in the mood to do anything. And I don't have money," I complain, lying back on my bed.

"I have some money. How about we drink before we go, so we don't spend so much when we're out?" she suggests.

It's not a bad idea, but I don't want to take any money from her. "I don't want to do that to you," I say, turning my head to give her a sad smile.

"I know, but I want my happy friend back. This here," she runs her finger through the air over me as she speaks, "is not her and it's dreadful to be around this version if I'm honest."

I wince, laying my hand over my chest. "Oh."

She twists further on the bed to face me properly and shrugs. "It's true. Get up and show me some outfits and then we'll go to mine and get ready and drink."

I stare at my white painted ceiling, thinking I could lie here and sulk. Or I can get up and go drink with her and forget about him.

I get up. I've made my decision. Alcohol and a night of dancing with my girlfriend sounds like the perfect way to forget about Damien.

"Yes!" She claps excitedly.

"Skirt or dress?" I ask, walking toward my closet.

"Let's go to Luxe. Less chance we'll bump into anyone we know there," she says as she stands and walks over to me.

"Dress it is," I mutter to myself, looking through each dress I own. I pull out all my nightclub dresses and put them on the bed.

Clara helps by choosing ones she likes too. We both make a pile, and after I've gone through everything I own, we then narrow it down.

Unable to decide between the last five, I take them all and two pairs of heels as options and we make our way to her house in her car. Her housemates have already left to go out to a party, so we're alone.

She orders us a pizza to be delivered while we make our vodka and soda drinks. When it arrives, we carry our food and drinks to her room and get ready. After trying on all five options, I decide on a classic little black dress. I want to keep it simple. My hair's straight and I've done a warm brown makeup look. We've had a couple of drinks, so we're slightly buzzed. Not too bad that we can't walk straight. The bouncers at Luxe are ruthless and if you're looking tipsy or drunk, they'll deny you entry.

We head to the club and don't have to wait in line for very long. Lucky it's a warm night because we didn't bring jackets. Once inside, the club's music vibrates through me. It's so loud. The dark-gray walls are softly lit by lights; 3D sculptures are popping from the ceiling. I haven't been here for a long time, but I love it whenever I come. It's nice and clean, but most of all, we always leave having had the best night. The DJ is the best in Chicago.

"Let's grab another drink and then we can stay on the dance floor all night," Clara says, slipping her arm through mine. I squeeze it and don't object because the line isn't too long at the bar, so we're served pretty quickly.

We order our drinks at the gunmetal bar, and even though Clara was hoping someone would pay for them, no rich men took the bait tonight. Sometimes these guys are the tightest people. Hence why they're so filthy rich.

But I'm not going to lie, I'd love a guy to look after me. I want to feel special and loved. I just haven't met someone who loves me back.

It's always one-sided.

Me loving them.

They always end up loving someone else.

We grab our drinks and move away from the bar to stand together and look over at the crowded dance floor.

"Cheers for a good night." Clara beams as we clink our glasses together.

"Cheers." I clink it and we both take a decent sip. I welcome the burn down my throat from the vodka. These are strong. A moment later and I'm warm again.

"Did you want to talk to me more about D—"

I shake my head. "No." I don't want to talk about Damien. I'm here to forget him. "Tell me about you," I say, giving her a fake smile.

"You sure?" she asks, narrowing her eyes at me.

"Yes," I chuckle. "Talk to me."

She steps closer, clearly not wanting anyone else to hear. "My second night of the cam girl stuff was amazing," she says with a twinkle in her eye.

"Yeah? Why's that?" I ask, knowing her first night was a little awkward. The guys were a little weird or pushy with their kinks. I've told her to only do what she feels comfortable with. It's all about us being in control. We don't have to do everything. She has more than enough rights to say no.

Boundaries are important. And if they're abusive, block them.

I have zero tolerance for that, and I want her to as well.

Our purpose for being there is to pay our bills. We don't want to be treated poorly. We didn't sign up for that.

I sip my drink as she explains.

"Last night, this guy came on and he wanted to talk. He paid me just to talk," she says, astounded. Like it was a waste of money. But when I first started and realized it was common, I understood. Some guys are super lonely. They've either lost their wives, are divorced, or their wives don't listen to them. It doesn't matter what the circumstances are; it's important that we sit and listen. Essentially be their friend. It's what they want.

"That's all?" I ask, wondering why this one seems different.

"Yeah, but it was just the way he wore his work suit. He's so hot. Dark wavy hair, honey eyes and this model-like chiseled jaw. And God, his voice was so deep, and I actually wished he wanted more than talking."

I giggle, but it turns into a sigh. I know exactly where her mind is going. "Doesn't mean you get to see him naked."

"Damn it," she says.

We laugh together.

"How did you know I thought that?" she asks, squinting at me.

I smile. "By the way you described him. Anyone would've wanted to see what was underneath his suit."

"Maybe next time?" she asks with a hopeful look. She sips the last of her drink. Her glass is now completely empty.

"When do you talk to him again?" I ask, stirring my drink with the straw to mix the last of the soda and vodka together.

"Sunday night," she says, all giddy.

I roll my eyes. "Don't fall in love with him."

"I won't," she replies in a huff like I'm being ridiculous.

"He could turn out to be your brother's older best friend," I say, teasing my own situation.

I laugh at myself. Now that I've had a few drinks, I can do it. I see the humor in it.

"Yeah, what a nightmare," she mutters. "Let's forget about the online world and go find some real-life candy."

I nod and finish my drink. I grab her empty one from her hand. After locating the nearest table, I place them on it. She grabs my hand, and we head onto the dance floor.

The music is the latest radio pop and I'm happy I came. Sitting in my room tonight with all my studies up to date would have meant I would've thought about him all night. As we dance, I peer around at the mix of guys and girls. A guy bumps me, and I turn around. He excuses himself, and I smile at his apology. He's kinda cute and definitely closer to my age, maybe thirty?

He leans into my ear. "Wanna dance?" he asks in a slightly drunk tone.

"I can't, my friend—" I cut off my words when my gaze lands on Clara, who is currently kissing a guy.

Far out, that was fast.

"Your friend seems to be having fun," he comments.

I'm still staring at her as I answer. "Seems so," I mumble.

"How about we dance?" he asks again.

I want to but also, I don't.

The only thing I want to do is try to forget about Damien. To do that, I need to push myself past my comfort zone.

"Sure," I say with a forced smile.

"You sound so enthused," he hesitates.

I shake my head. God, how awful am I that he noticed. "Sorry it's not you. You're great," I say, hoping that's true because I don't have a clue about him. Not even his name, but I'm hoping for the best.

We dance and his pine soap smell does nothing for me. His hand on my lower back doesn't send a tingle up my spine. Right now, I feel nothing, and the alcohol is wearing off. I miss the warm buzz. I want another drink.

As soon as the song ends, I look over at Clara, but she's still kissing the guy. I don't want to interrupt her, so I decide to grab another drink. Not saying bye to the other guy I was with, I squeeze my way through the crowd, to the opposite side of where the guy I was dancing with is. As I turn around, I notice him watching. I mouth, *Sorry*. Spinning around, I pinch my lips and make my way through the crowd of people. Out of the dance floor, I pass all the VIP areas and their cream chairs. I'm passing the final one, where a quiet part of the bar is, when a hand snakes around my waist.

"Oh," I squeal from the unexpected touch. My heart is in my throat, and I'm scared the dance floor guy has followed me. Shit. He was fast.

"What are you doing here?" Damien's voice grumbles in my ear, making the hair on my arms stand on end.

CHAPTER 16

DAMIEN

HER THICK HONEY SCENT hits me as I speak into her ear. The touch of her body in my palm feels incredible. I flex my hands to savor the moment before she turns. I stay exactly where I am and stare into her eyes. They're very heavy from alcohol. I grind down on my molars.

I'm here with Alex and Mike because it was for work. One surgeon is moving to another state. Alex dragged me here, bitching and moaning, but why is she here?

I hope she hasn't drunk too much.

"I'm here with friends," she says, her gaze snapping away from me to the crowded dance floor. She's clearly looking for them. My head turns and I follow her gaze, but I don't spot anyone familiar.

"Who?" I ask, knowing I have no place to ask, but I can't help myself. I want to know if there's a guy...

"Just me and Clara. Girls' night," she answers with a hiccup.

I nod. My gaze drops over her luscious full breasts that are hugged by the smallest black dress I've ever seen. It barely covers her ass. I'm holding myself back from ordering her home.

Her hand sits on her hip, and she has a challenging look on her face.

I hold back a smirk. Even when she tries to be confident, she cannot hide her kind side.

Her pure, whole heart draws me to her. She's like the sun to my darkness.

Although life has thrown me into a shitty hole, her energy pulls me out of it, and it should repulse me. But I'm not. Samuel needs more lightness. I don't want him to grow up miserable like me.

"You look..." I know I shouldn't say this, but seeing her here sets me off. "Incredible."

A small lift to her lips and a wriggle of her nose make her so damn cute I'm struggling not to cross the line. I'm holding on to the little restraint I can. Running my hand up my neck, I squeeze the tension building. I remind myself she's off-limits. Even though her brother is not here, so technically I'm safe, it still feels wrong to be talking to her behind his back. So why am I?

Because I'm fucking stupid.

"Thanks," she says sweetly. Her eyes close as she sways herself forward. I know she wants to kiss me, and fuck, I want that too, but I can't. I fucking can't.

"I need to go," I mutter to myself. Both of us have been drinking tonight, and she's wearing a killer outfit that's not helping me make any smart decisions. She's clouding my better judgment and fuck, I'm so out of control. And I like control in my life. No, I need it. It keeps me calm. Her carefree attitude rattles me.

As I turn, she grabs my wrist. I gaze down at her delicate small hand, encasing as much of my arm as she can. It doesn't close though. I'm too thick for her hand. Her fingernails catch the light and sparkle. The damn purple nail polish haunting me.

"You haven't been online," she says.

I tilt my head back and bring my eyes to hers.

I stay silent. Internally battling myself not to answer and just leave. She's holding my gaze firmly, making it impossible to walk away. Her face is so beautiful, it's so unfair.

"I can't." It falls out of my mouth in a sigh.

Her eyebrows pinch together. "Why? Are you scared?"

"Of your brother?" I ask.

She nods.

I shake my head. "No. But he's important to me and so are you. I don't want to risk it."

Her eyes flash open in surprise before a smirk takes over her mouth. "He'll get over it," she says, but it's husky with desire.

"He wouldn't. Fuck, I wouldn't," I say, inhaling deeply. "He's still mad."

"You're not him," she whispers. Her hand reaches out and touches my jaw up to my cheek, and she moves closer. My heart stops. The alcohol is definitely making her bolder tonight. But I'm not ready for a woman to be in control of me again. I can never give that up for a woman.

"He'll forgive us," she says with a voice dripping in a plea, which makes it hard to say no.

I close my eyes to gain my control back. If I look at her while I try to explain, it could undo me. "I won't forgive myself. And your brother is one part of the problem."

There's a gleam in her eyes. Or am I imagining it? "You're reading way too far into this. Why can't we have a little fun?" she says.

"That's all you want? Fun?" I ask, trying to keep my composure. Does she really believe we could just fuck once and it would be enough?

I know once I touch her, I'll want more. That's the fucking problem. I'll need her in ways I haven't needed a woman in years.

Her hand drops over my stubble jaw to the side of my neck, where she can feel my beating pulse. She comes to rest her hand on my shoulder. Her hands feel way too right on me.

"I don't get to have fun anymore," I remind her.

"Dating seems too much for Sammy," she says brightly.

The nickname for my kid sends my heart thumping. He's fond of her. The amount of times he mentioned her name after she stayed over was a constant reminder how much I might not be enough. And I'm at a loss on how to give him more. More of what I don't know.

"We're not dating. We're not doing anything. You're drunk and not thinking clearly," I reply.

Her hand drops from my shoulder over my pec and stays there. "I'm fine. Maybe you should have another drink. Seems you need to loosen up."

I don't need to loosen up. I can't think clearly; the heat of her hand mixed with her touch is too much right now. "Don't drink anymore." I grunt through my clenched jaw.

She spins around and says over her shoulder, "I'm not yours to boss around."

I'm about to reply, but she winks and saunters away before I get the chance. But how can I argue with her? We aren't together, so I can't tell her how to behave, even if I want to.

When she's out of view, I exhale a deep breath and head back to the VIP area. The group I came here with is pouring fresh drinks.

"Pour me one," I shout.

"Where did you go?" Alex asks, doing a double take.

"For a walk," I lie.

He nods, and he hands me over a fresh drink. I take a sip and stay quiet while they go back to talking about today's game. I twist my body slightly to see if I can see where she's gone. My eyes scan all the brown hair women with black dresses, but when I can't locate her, I try to engage in their conversation again.

The next hour passes slowly. I'm leaving the bathroom to wander back through the crowd when I spot her talking to a guy. Her face seems tight, as if she's slightly panicked. My spine straightens and I pause, watching them for a second. He grabs her arm. She shakes her head and says *no*, but he doesn't remove his grip. I see red and storm over, yelling, "Get your hands off her."

"Who are you?" the guy asks when I approach him. The prick wears a smug smile, and it pisses me off further.

"None of your fucking business, but if you want to keep your face intact, wipe the smirk off your face and remove your hands off her. She doesn't want you touching her. You can clearly see that. And did she not say no?"

"She didn't say no earlier," he replies.

I stiffen.

"What are you talking about? We danced for one song," Marigold argues.

I'm breathing so hard, my nostrils flare. I'm trying to rein in my anger. His dirty hands on her. I fucking can't think about it.

"You two are weird. You're too old for her, you creep," the guy slurs.

My jaw ticks with annoyance. He's either drunk or high and calling me a creep adds more fuel to the fire.

"I'm warning you, if you say one more thing, I will not hold myself back."

I can't believe I haven't hit the smug prick. The only thing stopping me has to be how I'm trying to teach Samuel how to deal with problems, and fists aren't the answer. Even though he's not here, I feel like I owe it to him and myself not to do things I don't want him to do. This guy isn't worth it.

The dickhead says nothing. He just drops his hand and walks off.

I look at Marigold, who's shaking her head. She doesn't seem bothered now, but I still can't help it. I need to know.

"Are you okay?" I ask, stepping closer to her, close enough to hold her gaze.

There's no reply from her. She just blinks up at me in a daze. She's definitely had more to drink. Which irritates me.

"Marigold," I call out louder.

"Yes." She closes her eyes before opening them with a huff. "Will you ever call me Mari? I don't like Marigold."

"No. I don't like Mari," I answer honestly.

I never thought it suited her. It's tacky. She is anything but that.

She opens and closes her mouth repeatedly before saying, "Of course you don't." She giggles.

"Why are you laughing?" I say, frowning at her amused face. Nothing is funny right now.

"Nothing makes you happy. Yet..." she says, tilting her chin up defiantly. She steps toward me, closing even more distance between us.

"Online, you seemed happy," she says, and her breath tickles my face.

I groan, embarrassed.

"You were, weren't you?" A flicker of fear stares back at me.

"Yes," I reluctantly admit.

Why is it so hard to admit that? Because I've told myself, I won't go there with her. Yet, she's making it impossible not to want her.

"I knew it. But I wanted to hear you say it," she says with a full smile.

I rub a hand over my face. "Why do you want me? Fuck, Marigold. I'm old, grumpy and a single dad. You don't want this life."

She looks down briefly before looking back at me from under her dark lashes. "I've never felt so attracted to someone like I do with you. I looked forward to our chats, and you're obviously hot."

I shake my head. Not obvious to me. I don't see what's good about the gray flecks in my hair or the hard lines in my face or the tiredness I feel. I don't have the same energy she does.

"Chats? I'm not a talkative person," I say, confused.

"You have slowly opened up every time. With you, it takes time. It takes trust. I'm also not going to give up on you. I've finally gotten those nervous butterflies in my stomach that every movie talks about."

The words coming out of her mouth. The way she's breathing. All the words have left my lungs as I gaze down at her with wonder.

She won't give up on me.

I'm overwhelmed by her beauty. I'm done fighting.

Under the club lights, she glows, and I can't seem to stop myself from crushing my lips against hers. She gasps and kisses me back fiercely. Her body climbing mine. Her hands skim my chest, over my neck, and up through my hair. She pushes my head down toward hers. I grunt from her apparent desire. I've never felt a woman want me as passionately and obviously as she does. It's like she can't get enough of me. And that spurs me on.

My hands slide over her hips and down over that ass I've jerked myself over and dreamed about even more. I give her round ass a rough squeeze. I push her hips against mine. She gasps in my mouth, and I swallow it. I know she can probably feel my erection that I've had since I spotted her stalking across the dance floor in that tight black dress.

Our lips move in a frantic rhythm, and I press my tongue against her soft lips, needing more. She instantly parts them, and I slip in my tongue and taste her sweetness. A deep groan leaves my chest. Our tongues glide over each other, exchanging breaths. Her hand curls tighter in my hair, gripping me hard so I can't move. Her hips grind up and down over me and fuck, it snaps me back to the present...to what we're doing and where we are.

I pull my mouth reluctantly from hers. She flutters her lashes, and her heavy lust-filled eyes stare back in confusion.

"We shouldn't." I sigh.

CHAPTER 17

MARIGOLD

HE STEPS BACK ABRUPTLY. "Fuck, this is a mistake," he mutters, closing his eyes and pinching the bridge of his nose.

"Why?" I ask, stepping forward to reach out and run my hand down his arm. He watches the movement but says nothing.

"Didn't you enjoy it?" I ask, staring into his eyes. They're so full of the same longing and lust I feel, but his swirl with so much pain and torture. Is this all because of my brother?

"Of course, I did. Doesn't make it right," he mumbles. "And what your brother said to us is true."

Disappointment floods me, and I drop my hand to hug myself.

I'm so done with the whiplash. He's ruining my night. I'm here to forget about him. So, I need to do just that. I spin around and keep my head up as I storm out. It's time to go home and sleep.

I squeeze past all the people in the club to make my way to the exit. I pull out my phone to text Clara and let her know I'm leaving and if she wants to come too, she needs to meet me outside.

I'm shaking, but it's not from the cold. It's all because of him.

"Wait," he calls out.

I know it's him because his voice cuts through any noise and silences it.

I keep going without stopping. As soon as I pass the bouncers and step outside, I suck in a deep lungful of air.

My overheated body welcomes the chill of the night air. The streets are lit up by all the buildings and lamps.

While waiting for a message back from Clara, a hand grabs my arm. I jump from the sudden touch. But the spicy pear scent surrounds me again, so I spin on my heel and stare into Damien's hard gaze.

His eyes show a mix of torment and confliction, which adds to the hardness in my stomach.

"I said wait," he grumbles. Clearly unimpressed.

"I didn't tell you to follow me," I argue.

His other hand grabs the back of my other arm.

He exhales a deep breath. "I know it's just—"

He looks away for a moment. Probably to gather his thoughts, but it annoys me.

"Just what? You're hurting me. I can't deal with you kissing me and then pulling away," I say.

His hard features soften. "I'm sorry. I don't mean to be like this. This isn't how I usually act. You seem to bring this side out of me," he says.

"It's not a very good one," I mutter, letting myself admire his lips that I kissed moments ago.

I've dreamed of us kissing for a very long time. Now that we have, I want to do it again. His stubble is rough and sexy against my face. My lips swollen from our rough and passionate kiss. The way he sucked in my breath made me believe he wanted me just as much as I want him. Like he wanted more, too. Until he snapped back to reality and pulled back. I feel like a joke. As if he's treating me like a child and I'm not having it. He has to make a choice. Either we do it or we don't because these games hurt. I don't want to keep letting people walk over me. My past relationships hurt me, and I refuse to keep the same cycle going. The online job helped me feel empowered. I wish I'd use it more offline.

How I wish I didn't need to be loved. But I love the all-consuming feeling. And as I stare at his full, kissable lips, it reminds me of how it feels to like someone. The beating of my heart when I can't get enough of them. I want to talk to them and be with them as much as I can. And with Damien, I want all of that. But he's not showing he wants it too. And if he doesn't, I need to accept it and find a way to move on. But if he does, then he needs to give us a chance. And no more push and pull.

His hands on my arms drop to catch my hand. The movement causes my eyes to peer down and watch him hold my hand in his.

He does the same and our faces are so close; he leans his forehead on mine and we stay like this for a beat. I soak in the city's noise from the traffic and the drunk patrons around us. But I cherish this moment of us holding each other.

"I'm sorry," he says, moving his head off mine and he lays a single kiss on my forehead. I expect him to end us.

"I can't let you go. I fucking should, but I can't. There's this ability to trust with you that I haven't truly felt in years. And I'm not ready to leave it before it's began..." He trails off.

My heart thumps so hard I can hear it in my ears.

"So, you're going to give us a shot even though my brother will kill us?" I ask, my voice shaking. But I need to confirm it before I get excited about the possibilities. I need to be on the same page as him.

"I think we need to sleep and talk about Samuel and Elijah tomorrow. You've been drinking and I want to discuss this when we're both clear-headed."

I grumble loudly. I don't like the sound of it because I just want to jump in his arms and sail off into the sunset, but what he's saying makes sense.

I need to think about Samuel and Elijah. And then we both need to discuss how it's going to go.

"I'll call a cab after I see if my friend is leaving, too."

My phone chimes when I take it out. I see it's a text message from Clara.

Clara: *I'm having fun and I want to stay. Come back in.*

I quickly type out.

Marigold: *I'm out of here, but I'll speak to you tomorrow. x*

"Is she leaving?" Damien asks.

"No, she's staying. I'll call a cab now." I swipe my thumb over the screen, but that's as far as I get before he removes my phone from my hand.

I tip my head back, frowning. "Hey, why'd you do that?"

"You're not grabbing a taxi."

"No?" I ask, totally confused.

"You're coming with me, and my driver will drop you home." He grabs my hand, and he walks us toward a side street.

I curl my fingers tighter, enjoying the way his hand feels in mine.

We walk to a black car that's parked waiting. He opens the door and I meet his eyes in a silent thank you, before ducking my head and getting inside.

He sits down beside me and buckles in. I sit nervously beside him. As if sensing my uneasiness, he grabs my hand in his and I tilt my head to look at him. Seeing a hint of a smile on his usually tight lips makes butterflies return to my belly.

We drive off and I ease back into the black leather and enjoy the radio tunes while he directs the driver to my house.

The drive isn't long and when we park outside my parents' house, Damien gets out to open the door for me. Standing outside the car, we both stare at each other.

His gaze drops to my mouth, and I wonder if he's going to kiss me, but when his eyes lift to the house, I know he doesn't want to.

But I don't care what anyone thinks. I meant it when said I was all-in. Well, it's not like anyone's awake at one in the morning.

"Do you want me to walk you to the door?"

"Depends," I challenge with a smirk.

His head quirks. "On?"

"If you'll come inside," I ask, but I know he'll turn me down before he even says the words.

"No chance. You live with your parents, and I'd like to stay alive."

I giggle. "I live in their guest house."

My hand lifts to his face, needing to touch him as a reminder he's real. The mix of scruff and soft skin is beyond delicious.

"They won't care. I promise. Elijah will, but we'll deal with him," I plea.

He drops his chin with a groan. The movement makes my hand slip from his face. I hold my bag instead, to give my hands something to do.

"It'll be fine. Stop stressing," I say.

"Is that the answer?"

I nod and step closer to him, so my open-toe black heels hit his black dress shoes. I press my chest against his and he sucks in an audible breath.

"Marigold," he growls.

I press my index finger to his lips. "Shhh, unless you call me something else." I ignore the excitement my body feels when I have my finger on his lips.

But I don't let him utter another word because I close the distance between us. There was no way I was walking inside without another kiss before bed. This is my dream coming true.

This kiss is just as frantic as the first, but the fact my bed's not far away makes me hornier. The bed he's seen in my videos.

I pull back, breathless.

"We'll talk tomorrow," he says, his voice husky and interrupting.

"What time?" I ask.

"I have to work, but after that?" He kisses my lips for a moment longer, prohibiting me from speaking.

I bite the corner of my lip. "Yes. I'd like that very much."

"Okay, Goldie, get upstairs and dream of me." He winks. I don't know if it's the alcohol or the high of us that makes him carefree right now. But I'm loving it.

"Not full of yourself, are you now?" I tip my head back and laugh. His mouth moves to my exposed neck, and he kisses the sensitive flesh there, which causes me to erupt with a loud moan.

"Shhh," he mumbles into my neck.

I pinch my lips together.

When he pulls back, I hold his gaze. "You called me Goldie."

"I did," he replies matter-of-factly.

"Why?" I breathe.

"You really want to know?"

I roll my eyes and shove his chest gently. "Duh."

He shakes his head. "You can find out tomorrow."

I groan and get annoyed. "Unfair."

He chuckles before stepping back. And I know it's time to end tonight.

He pecks my lips and I go to head off, but he grabs my hand and I frown, confused.

"I'm walking you to the door."

I want to argue and let him know it's only a few steps away, but the other part of me loves him caring for me. Making sure I'm safe. So, I nod.

We wander over until I get right up to my parents' wooden door. I grab my keys and unlock it. When I'm inside, he walks back to the car and waits beside it until I close the door. I rush to the living room window and push back the curtain to look out. He stands beside his car door with a smug expression. It's as if he knew I would do it. I feel like a princess in a castle, looking out at this grumpy dad who is turning out to be my knight in shining armor. I wave and he blows me a kiss and mouths, *Goodnight, Goldie.*

CHAPTER 18

DAMIEN

> **Marigold:** Thanks for the best kiss of my life.

I BLINK. SURELY NOT. She's just trying to make me feel good about defying her brother and giving into the kiss we both have been longing for. I text her back.

> **Damien:** You can't be serious.

> **Marigold:** Deadly. No guy has kissed me the way you have. Like you were destined to kiss me.

I stare at her words. How true they ring. I'm addicted to her. One taste wasn't enough. A twenty-five-year-old woman who's my best friend's little sister is totally consuming any rational thoughts when I should be fucking disgusted with myself. Yet I already long to hold her in my arms and kiss her again.

And I type out the words like a confession.

> **Damien:** I was. Even though I shouldn't.

Her brother was there for me when my wife left. He helped me pick up the pieces and now I want his sister. Fuck. I'm addicted to her. Like messaging now, I can't stop myself.

When she walked off in the club, I couldn't help myself. I had to go after her. Consequences be damned and I've now said yes.

Marigold: We should…

> **Damien:** In secret?

Marigold: Is that the only way I can have you? Because that's unfair. I'm not a dirty little secret.

She's right; it's not fair, but I can't sing it from the rooftops when people could get hurt, if and when she leaves. Because what if we're not really a match? We're better off as friends?

I selfishly ask her...

> **Damien:** Just for a few weeks?

> **Marigold:** And then we tell him?

> **Damien:** Then we tell all.

I bought myself a few weeks. She'll probably get sick of me by then. But if not, it gives me the time to figure out how to tell her brother and enjoy some alone time with her with no outside noise.

"I've been sick all morning," my mom coughs down the line. "I can—"

"No," I say, cutting her off. "Stay home. I'll figure something out." I run my hand through my hair aggressively, trying to figure something out quickly. I'm meant to be in surgery in a couple of hours.

I hang up and call work to reschedule as much as I can.

I receive a message and it's Marigold. It gets me wondering...

Marigold wouldn't mind, but I don't want to.

Fuck, I can't ask this of her...Can I?

I lean back on my kitchen counter and read her message.

> **Marigold:** Hey handsome, what're you doing?

"Dad, can we go play some basketball out back?" Samuel asks, coming to stand next to me in the kitchen.

I lower the phone to the countertop to talk to him.

With a heavy heart, knowing I have to say no, I gently explain. "I've gotta find someone to look after you. I'm supposed to be working soon."

"Nana will come," he replies.

I shake my head. "She can't, bud. She's sick."

"What about Mari? She was heaps of fun," he says, nodding excitedly. The way his face lights up makes it hard for me to ignore the obvious.

What's the harm in asking? She can always say no.

"I'll ask her." I suck in a breath and pick up my phone.

> **Damien:** Any chance you're free today? I need a favor.

> **Marigold:** What type of favor? ;)

I pinch my lips together, knowing where her mind is going. And as much as I want to touch her again, I have to get to work.

"Did she say yes?" Samuel yells, walking off to the toy room.

"I haven't asked her yet," I call back.

With the clock ticking and no other options, I type a reply.

> **Damien:** My mom's sick and I need to go to work in two hours.

> **Marigold:** You need me to look after Sammy?

> **Damien:** I don't want to make you do this. We're only just seeing each other. You didn't agree to this. But I'm des-

perate. I've canceled and rescheduled as much as I can, but I'm stuck with a few hours of work. I can't move. It's an emergency.

Marigold: *I'd love to.*

Damien: *Seriously?*

Marigold: *Seriously. Sammy and I will have the best time.*

Damien: *Thank you. I owe you one now.*

Marigold: *You can owe me…*

Damien: *What are you thinking?*

Marigold: *Something fun for me, but torturous for you.*

> *Damien:* I don't agree!

> *Marigold:* You won't have a choice.

> *Damien:* Payback will be twice as hard, Goldie.

> *Marigold:* I'm twitching thinking about it. Who said mine's dirty? I could make you drink tea with me.

> *Damien:* Not happening.

"Is she coming?" Samuel asks again.

"Yes, bud." I say, and the way the corner of my lip lifts tells me I'm in trouble. Not only is my son obsessed, but I am too.

"Yes!" He claps. "Now?" he asks.

"Very soon."

> *Marigold:* Dirty is better, then?

> **Damien:** *Way better than tea.*

> **Marigold:** *What time do you need me to be there?*

> **Damien:** *Latest, two hours.*

> **Marigold:** *I'll be there in an hour.*

I tuck my phone away and head to my room and get dressed for work.

An hour later, the doorbell rings and Samuel sprints to the door.

I open the door when Samuel pounces on her.

"Mari, I've set the Legos up. Come play." He grabs her hand and pulls her along through the house.

My throat constricts at the sight. He's so at ease with her.

"Hang on a sec. Meet me there. Let me talk to your dad before he leaves."

"Don't be long." He gives her a sad look and I shake my head. He's so much like me it's scary.

"Samuel, she'll be there when we're done," I say with my low and controlled dad voice.

He runs off.

"You're such a wonderful dad." She smiles.

I look at her, frowning before blurting, "Me working on a weekend and calling you to babysit doesn't seem good to me."

I'm not used to compliments about me being a father. I try my best and give Samuel everything I can. She wouldn't fake the compliment, though...would she?

"You're a single father who needs to work. There's nothing wrong with that," she replies with a shrug.

"You're too nice."

She wiggles her brows. "Not a bad thing."

"People can take advantage of you," I mumble.

"Like you?" A wicked grin appears, and I can't help but grin back.

I lean forward in her ear. "You have no idea. The things I want to do to you."

Her whole body shivers before she clears her throat.

"You owe me."

"Mmm, and?" My mouth moves slowly toward hers.

"I might not want that." Her voice cracks, betraying her.

My eyes drop to her full breasts and hard nipples. "Your body says otherwise."

"I can say no."

"Is that a challenge?" I ask darkly.

I may not have been with a woman in a while, but it doesn't mean I don't know how to pleasure one.

A challenge with her would be fun. The way we met online was part of the spark. Speaking of buying her outfits and toys...my body hums with desire.

She sucks her lip into her mouth while my head stays close to hers.

"I need to go," I whisper.

I hear a whoosh of air leave her lungs.

It snaps something in her. "Yep, I'll go to Sammy," she says in a prominent voice, walking away from me.

I stay like that, and when she turns to look over her shoulder at me, she finds me staring back. She dips her head and walks into the room and out of my sight. I'm in over my head with her.

I need some thinking space, so I grab my keys and walk out of the house.

This is the first woman, other than my mother, that has looked after Samuel all on their own since my ex left.

What's strange to me is that there's no panic or fear pulsing through my veins. Only excitement for me to get home to them.

Six hours later, I finally arrive home. I'm beat. When I step through the door, I'm hit with a smell. I frown, strolling through the hall, and when I enter the kitchen, I'm surprised to see she's cooked. Except for the mess. Walking around, I grimace at the state of the counter. There are splatters and dirty dishes. Despite the shitshow it is, I try to figure out the sweet and sour smell. My mouth waters and my stomach grumbles, remembering I haven't eaten since lunch. I tidy the counter and stack the dishwasher. Her soft voice talking causes me to pause my wipe down of the counter.

I try to return to cleaning, but I'm too distracted. I need to know what they're doing.

I quietly head toward Samuel's room. It's seven thirty and I'm surprised she knew to put him to bed. I failed to tell her what time he goes to bed. Somehow, she just knew.

I stand in the doorway, admiring her lying beside Samuel, reading. His big, heavy lids drop every so often. He's tired. But also, stubborn. He'd happily fight to go to bed. So how did she do it? Or is he being good because it's her?

I do hope they had a good time...

"Are you going to come in and say hi or just watch us?" She taunts with an amused expression.

"Dad. Hi," Samuel's excited voice calls.

I move to his side of the bed to give him a cuddle.

"Hey, you're in bed?" I say, surprised.

"Mari said I should get some sleep and that she'd read me books until I fell asleep."

In the corner of my eye, I see her sitting up and swinging her legs off his bed.

"I need a shower. Did you want Mari to finish reading the books while I do that?"

He nods excitedly.

She swivels and kicks her legs back up. I catch her button nose turn slightly pink, but I don't ask why.

My phone rings, and it's the hospital. I say goodnight to Samuel and then walk out of his room to answer it. I wander through the house, giving the nurse phone orders. When I get off the phone, I kick off my shoes and strip.

I turn the shower hot and stand under it. Enjoying the way the heat melts away my tension. A creak of a door has me tipping my head forward and swatting away water from my eyes.

I wipe my eyes again, thinking I'm seeing things.

Marigold leans against the bathroom counter, watching me. She's flushed in the face, and I haven't moved.

I have so many questions.

"What are you doing?" I whisper-shout.

"You owe me," she says with a mischievous expression.

My jaw drops. Marigold was always the good girl. But this new side I keep seeing is bolder. More direct. Pure dynamite.

"I do. This is an easy repayment. I'm going to hope Samuel is asleep."

She dips her chin. "Out like a light." She clicks her finger.

"How?" Mom and I always struggle. He fights for at least half an hour, but more like an hour. Marigold did it in ten minutes? How?

"Back tickles," she says proudly.

"He's going to expect that every night now," I grumble, shaking the water from my face.

"Stop being such a party pooper. If I want to do it, let me. Or are you jealous because you want some?"

"No one would ever turn down back tickles."

"You already owe me..."

"I'm paying for it now. You're watching me."

"That's not enough."

A brow lifts. "What do you want?"

"I want to watch you jerk off," she says with such ease.

I shake my head. "Come in here and join me. Make us both feel better."

"No. You gave me a challenge and I will withhold until I've claimed my prize."

I'm stunned. I didn't think she'd stay true to her word, but here we are.

"I haven't done this before," I mumble, grabbing the conditioner. "Sure you can't help? You're going to get too excited."

"It's okay. It's the same as if you didn't have me watching."

"But I do..."

"Don't worry about me." She waves her finger over my lower body. "Get pumping."

"I can't believe you're not helping me," I mutter.

She crosses her arms over her chest. "Stop whining. You'll sleep like a baby once you come and I tickle your back."

I hum. "That does sound good."

"But you're not horny?" I ask curiously.

"I'm wet and achy for you, but I have control."

My dick jerks at the knowledge she's needy for me. "So do I. I have the best control. Well, normally I do. With certain situations, though, you seem to break down that wall."

I hate that I'm losing control and it's even worse now that I know I can't stop it. I'm fighting a losing battle. The way Marigold has a hold on me is unlike anything I've ever felt before. It's a mix of relief and anxiety. Will giving her control end up with me getting hurt?

"I know. I'd say I'm sorry, but I'm not. In all aspects of your life, you're in control. Hence why I want to control your actions now."

I stay silent and read her face. My dick has been hard since the moment I spotted her in here.

I lather the soap on my hand and lower my hand onto my throbbing dick. I hold her gaze the whole time in hopes she'll crack and join me in here, because surely, she will.

CHAPTER 19

MARIGOLD

MY EYES SOAK IN every droplet of water running over his naked body. It's erotic and I've never done this before...seen a guy bring himself to pleasure while I watched.

I feel naughty, but I can't stop...

His solid chest is bigger than the videos and his dark hair is short, and it sticks to his chest. That wide chest would feel nice to lay my head on and have his strong arms wrap around me.

As I think of all the possibilities, his abs contract, pulling my eyes lower. I follow every muscle in his stomach until I stop on his hand. Which is wrapped tightly around his thick cock and he's pumping slowly.

I fix my gaze on his movements. That it takes a moment to register he's talking to me until he repeats his question.

"Did you want to join me?" he rasps out.

"You owe me, remember? And I don't see how me getting in there will end up in my favor." My voice is weak and breathy.

"I can give you the best orgasm," he tries to coax me.

That I can guarantee.

He's already shown he could definitely blow all my previous sexual experiences out of the water.

He screams experience and pleasure.

Definitely the second.

His happy trail of dark hair from his belly button to his dick is my favorite part. It's like an arrow to his cock. As if anyone could miss it.

He's also the biggest I've been with, which sends my nerves up.

"I know you can, but you could give yourself one." I jut my chin out toward his stroking hand.

"I intend to. If you don't want to help."

"I do, but I want to watch you more," I admit, feeling my cheeks turn pink.

"You like to watch," he states. It's not a question, more an observation.

"I do."

"Are you wet?" He grunts out.

I nod and bite down on my lip. "Yes."

"Good girl. Did you want to come together?" His voice is thick, and it sends a shiver down my spine.

"I told you—"

He cuts me off. "No. I mean, you stay there and touch yourself while I touch myself here."

The tingle between my thighs is too much to bear. "Sure."

"Touch yourself and tell me how tight, wet, and warm your cunt is."

My lips part and the steam of the bathroom and how horny he's made me make this room combustible. I can't breathe when he talks dirty. It's such a turn-on. A part of me wants to say no. To push back, but I can't. There's something about him telling me what to do that leaves a promise of an orgasm.

And I want that.

I want that so badly.

My sex pulses at the thought of a hard orgasm.

I keep my gaze on his dick as I slip my hand in my jeans, but I struggle. They're too restrictive.

"Take your jeans off," he barks, as if annoyed by them.

I unbutton and wiggle as I slide the jeans over my hips until they pool at my ankles. I kick them away, then I peek up at his face and whimper at the sight.

He's breathing rapidly with his brows furrowed and lips parted. Droplets of water run over his lips. I lick my own as I imagine kissing the water off his full lips.

"Get rid of the panties. I want to see all of you."

I push them down easily and now I'm naked from the waist down. I stand staring at the God-like man in the shower. His eyes on my pussy. He stares like he wants to feast on me. If he didn't challenge me, I'd let him.

"Touch yourself," he instructs with a growl.

I slip my hand down to my pussy, feeling my wet, swollen bud and causing me to moan. I close my eyes and enjoy the way my fingers draw circles around my hot clit.

"Tell me what you're doing." His guttural voice causes me to flutter my eyes open.

I look at him in a daze.

"I...I touched my clit," I stammer.

A rumble in his chest sounds. "Rub it in hard circles."

I do, and my body suddenly feels heavy. Leaning back on his bathroom counter, I welcome the support as I widen my legs.

I'm panting as I feel the ache increase. I need more.

My fingers touch my soaking entrance.

"Put your fingers inside of you and fuck them," he says, as if reading my mind.

I let out a relieved breath and enter two digits inside and move them in and out.

"Faster," he yells out.

My eyes snap to him and he's fucking his fist so fast that the sight unhinges me, and I meet his pumps with my own. Both of us are chasing a release. I want us to come together.

The tingles in my sex tell me I'm close. I'm gasping for more air and a release.

I do as he asked and I'm fucking my fingers hard until the pressure becomes too much and my legs quiver.

"Come now." He groans.

My eyes drop from his heavy lids to his flexing bicep and tight forearm, all the way to down to the tip of his dick, where I watch the stream of his cum burst onto the shower floor and over his hand.

"Fuck." He grunts loudly.

I moan and come apart. My whole body shakes from the intensity.

The water turns off. I peel my eyes open and he's rubbing his body roughly with a towel.

His head quirks. "You want more?"

"Not yet," I reply, but it's more like a pant. I'm still coming down from the high.

He smiles. "Soon?"

"Definitely, I just need a second to recover."

He steps forward, closing the distance between us. All the air leaves my lungs. I'm face to face with the chest I've been dreaming about, that I've only seen on camera.

I drop my gaze to his chest, watching my hand touch his warm body. The softness of his chest hair against the hardness of his chest is incredible. I curl my fingers, enjoying the feel of the hair between them. His pec moves underneath my palm. I gasp and retract my hand.

"You're even better than the video," I breathe, staring into his heavily hooded eyes.

The air is still thick and wet from the steamy long shower, but also filled with the soap that I now use on my body. But it still hits differently when he wears it.

"If you don't want me to fuck you right now, you need to stop looking and touching me like that," he rasps out.

My skin prickles with excitement, but I don't get to speak because he adds.

"But don't get me wrong. I love it. I must admit, it's a little strange to hear." He sighs and steps back.

Immediately, I miss his body close to mine. But his words confuse me. He's withdrawing. "Why?" I ask.

He runs his hand through his damp brown hair. "My ex and I weren't very..." He clears his throat and his forehead creases. "Close sexually."

My mouth drops. "Oh."

I'm taken aback. How could she not want to have sex with him every chance she got?

"Me and my body repulsed her." He looks down at his body.

I throw my hands up, completely lost. "You must be joking."

"I wish I was." The pain etched in his dark eyes crushes me.

"Her loss," I say with a small lift of my shoulder.

He stares at me so intensely and his nostrils flare with every exhale that I feel like I've upset him.

"How could I be so lucky? Why would you want an—"

I cover his mouth with my hand. His eyes widen with shock at my response.

"Don't talk badly about yourself. You're a catch and I'm sick of the ex-talk. Fuck her and her dumb ass."

I feel movement behind my hand and his eyes soften. I drop my hand slowly away from his mouth and he grabs my head, slamming his mouth on mine. He kisses me with such hunger that I can't help but match the ferocity. I grab his head and wiggle my ass so I can sit on the edge of his bathroom counter.

"I believe you said you needed time..."

"You can't blame me," I say between kisses. "I need you."

He pushes his hips into my open legs. His hard dick hitting my aching pussy.

His white fluffy towel has long gone somewhere on the floor. My fingers grip his damp hair, tugging his head closer to me as he rewards me with a grunt.

My legs lock behind his back, and I grip him tighter to me. My pussy and his dick flush against each other.

"Dad, I can't sleep." The door rattles, but thankfully, it's locked.

Samuel's voice sends a panic rushing through me, and our lips instantly pull apart.

"I'll be right there. Just got out of the shower," Damien says calmly to him. I don't know how he did that; I'm still shaking all over.

Our position remains unchanged. We haven't moved yet. "Okay," Samuel's footsteps patter away. He's gone back to his bedroom. I let out a deep exhale, full of relief.

Damien holds my eyes again and leans forward to whisper over my lips. "I'll tuck him back in. Wait for me in my bed. Please don't go." The last three words are hoarse, like it was painful for him to say.

"Of course." I peck his lips and watch him step away, his bare ass walking into his closet. I slip off the counter, turning around to look at myself in the mirror. My face is flushed with arousal. I wash it under cold water to cool myself down until a smack to my ass has me jolting and standing back up to see a smirking Damien.

He whispers in my ear, "I'll be back."

I stand and dry my face and then I step out of his bathroom and slip into his bed, and I hold back a moan. His bed is soft, but the way I can smell his scent everywhere feels so heavenly, and I just want to sleep here tonight.

Not wanting to put the TV on and make noise, I turn on the bedside lamp and wait.

When he walks in ten minutes later, I can't help but feel giddy.

He dives toward me on his stomach. With his elbows propping him up, he looks at me. "He wanted more of your tickles," he grumbles, but I see a hint of a smile.

"Are you jealous? Do you want some so you can see why they're the best?" I ask.

"What makes them so good?" he asks with a scrunch of his nose.

"My nails," I say, wiggling my fingers in front of his face.

"You know, that's how I knew it was you."

I frown. What's he talking about?

"Your purple nails. You wear the same color." He lifts my hand and threads it through his, staring at our interlocked fingers.

"Maybe I should change them," I say as I look at the purple sparkling in the warm lamplight.

"No. It's you. Girly, sweet and fun."

My heart skips at how he can say the nicest of words to me when no one's around.

I run my hand over his shoulder. "Come closer. I can't reach your back."

He shuffles up the bed. And his head lies down on my stomach, and he drapes his arm over my legs.

I run my nails over his back, and he sinks further into the bed. "Incredible."

I continue moving them across his shoulder and back. Enjoying the planes of muscles there. His breathing slows as he groans here and there. "Fuck. I love your nails."

I dig harder and he grunts. "Mark me, Goldie."

He sounds delirious. But I draw over his back repeatedly. Words like I like you. But, of course, he doesn't get it. I'll have to tell him with words. Even if it may seem too fast to Clara.

This is me.

I don't want to change.

"So now you'll have to tickle Sammy to sleep. Now you know how good they are."

Silence.

I lean forward and take in his beautiful face.

He's fast asleep.

I look over at the time on his alarm clock and I realize I have to go. I've got classes tomorrow. Reluctantly, I slip out from under him and slide off the bed. I walk over to his side and bend down, kissing his lips softly.

"Goldie, I need you." He muffles into the blanket.

I freeze. My heart is beating frantically.

"Shhh. I'm here," I hush into his ear and tickle his back again. He goes back to sleep. I slip out of his room and into my car. God, how I wish we were out in the open and I could crawl into bed with him and sleep over.

CHAPTER 20

DAMIEN

"DAD, AM I GOING to school today?" Samuel's voice pulls me from my sleep.

I rub my face into my pillow. A soft honey scent makes me sigh.

I lay my head to the side and see Samuel standing over me. He's watching me. I jerk in bed. It scares the crap out of me.

"Yeah, bud, just give me a second and I'll get up and get you breakfast."

A sudden thought hits me. I frantically look around the bed. Is she hiding out in the bathroom?

I scramble out of bed and usher him out of the room. I rub my hand over my face, move to the kitchen, and see the time.

Double fuck.

Did I sleep in?

I never sleep in. My natural lack of sleep means I haven't used an alarm clock in over ten years. And yet today, I slept in. I don't even have time to think about what this means and why this happened. I just know I need to get him to school and my ass into work.

"We don't have much time, so you need to be fast like Superman today, okay," I say, trying to get him to move faster without him panicking.

I grab his breakfast in record speed.

"Here's your cereal. I'm going to have a quick shower and then I'll get you dressed. Stay here and eat."

I rush off to see Marigold in the bathroom, but when I walk in, it's quiet. "Marigold?" I whisper-shout. No answer.

I walk into the closet and it's dark and empty. There's no sign of her here.

Did she go home last night?

She left in the dark and drove home. What if something happened to her? I wouldn't have known.

I walk to my phone that's on charge and swipe it open.

A message sits there.

But when I open it, I sigh. It's not from her. Mom texts to say she's still off.

My day is going from bad to worse.

I run a hand through my hair and wander to the bathroom and text her.

> **Damien:** Did you get home safe?

Despite my desire to wait for a text, I don't have the time to check my phone. I shower as fast as possible and get dressed. I start with my boxers and socks, then my white shirt, and finally my navy suit pants. I multitask by checking my phone while fastening my buttons.

She texted back. I tuck my shirt in and zip, then button up my pants and read it.

> **Marigold:** I did. You were out cold. I didn't want to wake you.

I type out a response.

> **Damien:** You should have woken me. I don't know how I didn't hear you. I'm normally a light sleeper.

I put the phone on the counter and walk back into my wardrobe, grabbing my jacket and shoes. Before slipping them on, my phone dings again. I pick it up.

> **Marigold:** *It must've been those back tickles...*

I can't help but wear a stupid, lopsided grin.

> **Damien:** *Those nails are a good and bad thing.*

> **Marigold:** *Just like me.*

> **Damien:** *Just like you. A lethal combo for me.*

Why is she so different? What is it about Marigold that makes me feel something new? Is it because we've been around each other for years that I feel comfortable with her? Fuck, am I settling for a woman who's giving me the attention my ex never gave me? I hope fucking not. Surely, it's because we're attracted to each other, even though we're so opposite. It just seems to work.

> **Marigold:** *You're perfect for me, too.*

I brush my teeth and style my hair. I'm leaving my bed unmade because my maid will be here soon. I get out to Samuel and hurry him along. I don't want to hire a nanny. My goal is to fulfill both the mother and father roles to the best of my ability. It feels like he deserves that, at the very least. I'm just wearing myself down little by little, but it won't last forever. He'll grow old and not want to know me, so I'll enjoy this for as long as possible.

I drop Samuel at school and drive to work. When I ride the elevator to the hospital, I text her back.

> **Damien:** Are you talking to anyone else online?

> **Marigold:** No. I haven't responded to anyone else since I met you.

I read her message and grip my phone tighter. A mix of happiness and jealousy pulses through me. On one hand, I'm grateful it's just me, but on the other, I'm hating the knowledge she was speaking to other guys before me.

> **Damien:** Do you miss it?

Marigold: Miss what?

I open my office door, walk straight to my seat, sit down, and text her back.

Damien: Being online?

Marigold: I haven't really thought about it. I need to get a job soon, though.

I stare at the words, and I know I can't have her with anyone else. She needs a job. Maybe I could give her two?

Damien: I have a proposition for you.

Marigold: I'm listening…

I turn my computer on and rub my jaw. I should think about this. Can I ask for both? Is this a good idea?

I put my glasses on and stare at my screen. I can't concentrate on a single word. Not when I need to answer her text. Fuck it. I'll ask her. The worst that can happen is she says no. Emails can wait. I won't be long.

Damien: First, we could do a night a week where we go online. I pay you as normal, but I'm your only client.

Marigold: I feel like there's an and...

Damien: There is. Could you babysit Samuel when my mom can't? I don't want to hire a nanny; I don't know. I want to be there for him as much as possible, but Mom's still sick and it made me think about how I have no backup. Would you be interested if I get stuck?

Marigold: You'd pay me to do both?

Her message seems like she's not keen on the idea. I quickly type.

Damien: You don't have to do either. Don't feel obligated to say yes.

I don't hit send because a message comes through from her first.

Marigold: It sounds too easy.

Damien: But is it too much with your studies?

I know how important college is to her. She went online because of that.

Marigold: But why online when you can have me in real life?

I think about our time in my bathroom last night. Her fingers were deep in her pussy, fucking them until we both came. I've never come as hard as that. Watching her come apart from looking at me fuck my fist. I think I've found something I enjoy. To have her come undone from my words without a single touch from me was incredible. The power it gives me is something I crave. It makes me feel desired for the first time in a long time. Deep in my gut, I feel true want, genuine desire, and a deep need. And fuck, every time we do something together, it's hotter than the previous time.

I want her every way I can. One way is not enough. I'll take everything she's willing to give me.

> **Damien:** I want both.

I'm addicted to her in every way. And why choose one when we can both get off when we're together and when we're apart? I still connect to her when we're online and we can play.

> **Marigold:** Oh.

> **Damien:** I love watching you. You're sexy and confident on camera, but I love how you submit to me when we're together. It's the best of both worlds. What do you think?

Marigold: *Deal. What night is the online chat?*

Damien: *Eager? To come or for me?*

Marigold: *I miss you.*

Those three words make my chest tight. No one misses me. Well, except for my parents and Samuel. A knock on my door breaks me from my bubble of lust.

"Doctor Gray." My nurse comes in and drops off a list of typed patient notes and new charts for me to look over. We talk for a couple of minutes about a patient, and I explain I'll be there to visit the patient soon.

"Thanks," I mutter and pretend to be reading an email on my computer. As soon as she leaves and my office door closes, I grab my phone and type out a quick response. I need to get back to work. Marigold's totally consuming my every waking moment.

Damien: *Wednesday? Get me through the week.*

Marigold: And I'll be with you this weekend?

Damien: Exactly. But mom's still sick tonight. Any chance the babysitting can start today?

Marigold: You owe me again.

I smile as I reply.

Damien: I'll make it up to you tonight, I promise.

I know exactly what I want to do to her tonight. My mouth is salivating, thinking about it.

Marigold: Like, fall asleep again?

I chuckle to myself. The sound leaving my throat and that feeling of warmth spreading across my chest are unfamiliar. Yet, it's a feeling I want more of.

> **Damien:** *Cheeky! Just don't tickle me.*

> **Marigold:** *Deal.*

> **Damien:** *I'll see you at about six. Here is the code to get into my house 1234 and Samuel's school is on Bell's Road. He finishes at three. If you need anything, call me.*

I get to answering all of my emails while I wait for the patient to come in. But before I do, I tuck my phone into my desk drawer, so I don't get tempted to message her again.

CHAPTER 21

MARIGOLD

I'M WAITING TO PICK up Samuel from school. I get a few odd looks from the other moms. Their eyes scan my black leggings and crop sweater. I'm sure they are comparing me to their designer pants, tops, and bags. They even look like they have stepped out of the hair salon.

They whisper into each other's ears. I manage to catch a few words.

"Who is she?"

"She's young."

"Surely not a girlfriend?"

"Must be a new nanny."

"To whose kid?"

I internally roll my eyes as I kick the ground in front of me. They're all so cliquey. I thought high school was over.

I guess not.

Adult women seem to be worse.

I've been feeling extremely insecure since he messaged. His offer for me to do one online worries me he just wants sex. Maybe all he wants is the online fantasy girl. The one he can control. He can pay for. And maybe he isn't ready for a relationship. I've always been a little this way because of my past boyfriends.

How can I not?

Being cheated on, or not being fully committed to, wounds me a little.

So, in the back of my mind, a warning bell is going off. But I forget about it the moment I see Samuel exit the classroom.

"Mari," Samuel yells. He comes running over and cuddles my legs with such force, I almost topple over.

"Hey, Sammy. Are you ready to grab an ice cream or cookie before we go home?"

The shriek of a woman near me pulls my attention. I peer up and find her horrified expression. I remember I said home. It didn't even cross my mind to say his house. It slipped out naturally. I'm sure I'll be the talking point of the women now. Great...

"A cookie?" he asks, his face lighting up with pure excitement. I forget about the moms and focus on Samuel.

I squat down to his level and speak. "Yeah, and then we need to do homework while I cook some dinner. I might grab some items from the store."

"Okay," he says, but he's lost the spark in his voice.

"What's wrong?"

I want to know what I said that seems to have upset him. It won't make a good impression if I upset his son.

"I wanted to play Legos," he mumbles.

I smile, understanding his mood shift. "Oh, we will. First, we need to get the cookie, then do the boring but super important things like homework and dinner, but the quicker we do them, the quicker we can play. Does that sound like a deal?"

He frantically nods.

"Let's get the cookie first," I say as I grab his bag and sling it on my back. He grabs my hand and I look down and see his smiling face.

"My dad says I shouldn't have too many sweets," he says as we walk along holding hands.

"Why's that?" I ask.

"He says it's not good for me."

"He's a doctor, so I guess he would want to protect you."

"That's boring," he mumbles.

I try not to laugh at his words. I agree it's not fun, but luckily, Damien didn't tell me I couldn't give him sweets.

"It is, but I'm sure he'll be fine with one cookie if you eat your dinner. And maybe if we buy him a cookie, he won't be so grumpy."

"Good idea," he replies excitedly.

"Who can be grumpy when you eat a cookie?" I add as we walk into the shop.

Fifteen minutes later, we walk out with many cookies because Samuel couldn't decide which one to pick. It was difficult for me to choose one for Damien, too. I don't know what flavor he would like. I'm a little embarrassed, I don't know. But all the times I've seen him at my brother's place, I've never seen him eat sweets. My mission tonight when he gets home is to find out what his favorite flavor is.

At eight o'clock, I tucked Samuel into bed already. Checking my phone, Damien still hasn't checked in. Where is he?

I'll give him until 8:30 and then I'll message him. Luckily, I brought my studies. I spread out my work over his coffee table with the TV on. I find a lamp to turn on and begin. I don't know how long I'm there for, but when the door clicks, my body jerks up. He's home.

My eyes train on the entry to the room. I wait for him to come to find me. The thrill of that is something I've never felt before.

The keys drop to the bench and his loud feet stomp down toward this room.

His large body stops in the doorway, his hands deep in his pocket. "Hey, is the little man asleep?"

Damien's silhouette is huge and the way the lamp hits him, I can see his brown hair is free of his usual styling gel. He's clearly had a rough day. His hands have been raking through it.

I nod and stand up with a struggle. My legs are numb from being in one position for too long. I need a study break. I've been going hard since Samuel went to bed.

"He sure is. Out like a light. Let me heat you some dinner," I whisper, coming toward him and pausing in front of him to meet his dark and curious eyes.

"You cooked for me?" His face softens as his hand reaches out at the same time to trace a finger lightly along the side of my face.

My heart beats wildly from the awe in his eyes. "Yeah, it's no big deal. Just tacos," I reply.

He leans in and kisses my lips. Completely surprising me.

He pulls back an inch and breathes. "Thank you."

I lick my lips, savoring his taste. I take his hand in mine and drag him into the kitchen and get him to sit down on the stool.

I lay out the taco shells, chopped lettuce, tomato, cheese, salsa, and a clean plate. I heat the meat and let him make his own. Then make one of my own.

"You haven't eaten?" he asks, as if he's angry at me for waiting.

"I did with Sammy, but I only had one so I could eat with you."

He stares at me oddly. "Where did you come from?"

"I've been around you for years. It's only now that you've taken notice." I wink.

"Hard not to when you masked up and seduced me," he teases. Then takes a bite of his taco.

He moans like he hasn't eaten in years.

"I didn't plan for it. But I'm glad it happened. I'm glad you went on."

"Guess I've got to thank my buddies for peer pressuring me."

"To be on the app?" I ask.

"No, for pushing me to try dating."

"Oh," I mumble.

"Yeah, they know nothing about the app."

"I see." He's naturally always been quieter, like my brother. Not sharing much.

I want to hear about what happened tonight and where he was.

"How was work? I'm assuming bad if you're coming home late," I ask as I take a bite of my taco.

He wipes his hands of crumbs. "It was. I had an emergency surgery."

The mix of conflict and pain written on his face tells me something isn't good. I keep quiet to let him know I want to hear more when he's ready.

"I don't normally talk about my day. Good or bad, and today was definitely fucking bad."

"I'm here. And I want to hear about your day every day." The corner of my lip pulls up in a half smile.

He stares at me for three seconds with trepidation before sadness washes over him, as if getting pulled back to work. "The surgery was on a child who had been bitten on the face by her family dog."

"What?" I choke. I can't imagine what's running through his head as he performs those surgeries.

He looks down at his plate and spins it, speaking to it rather than to me.

"It was awful. She's seven and now needs multiple surgeries for the rest of her life."

"Christ, I can't imagine," I mumble as I reach out to cover his hand with mine. His gaze fixes on it and we stay silent.

Staring down at the hands that help others, I can't help but admire him more.

"How was your day?" he asks, the question surprising me. And I'm sure an unusual question to ask anyone when he gets home. I'm sure he's used to only asking Samuel how his day went, so to ask an adult, a woman, I'm sure is unusual. It is for me. But I surprisingly like it.

"I think you have a few fans," I say as I remember those women today. The whispers, the outfits, and God, when they registered I was there for Samuel. I can't help but laugh.

"What do you mean?" He tilts his head, meeting my gaze with a wrinkle on his forehead.

"You should've seen the whispers I got picking up, Sammy. I think they thought their shot with you was over."

He grimaces. "I'd never touch any of them. And half of them are married, anyway."

"Are they?" My eyes widen with horror, and I add, "I didn't check for wedding rings."

His eyes darken. "Were you jealous?"

"No. I was more worried about you. They look like they might hit on you."

"They do and I run away every time," he grumbles.

I try to imagine the scene in my head. What they would look like flocking around him and him trying to escape. A deep scowl in place as he grabs Sammy and runs.

"Did he have a good day?" he asks.

"Yeah, Sammy said he's got show and tell this week."

"I'll have to text Mom and remind her."

He goes to make another taco.

"Save room for dessert. We bought you a cookie today. Sammy will be sad if you don't have it. Speaking of, what's your favorite flavor?"

He pulls his hand back and doesn't make another one. Instead, he gets up to take his dirty plate to the dishwasher, but he stops behind me. He leans in and breathes. "The only flavor I want is yours. I know that will be my new favorite." His voice tickles my neck. And his words send a tingle running from my head to my toes. It's not a flavor I want to say, but my imagination runs wild with the vision of his hungry mouth on me. I can't think clearly when he oozes confidence and talks about sex. It has me wanting it even more.

I go to get up and make some tea, realizing he doesn't have any, and I forgot to get some at the store. I'll have to remember to bring some next time.

But will there be a next time?

I need to remember I'm only filling in while his mom is sick.

"Were you looking for this?"

He opens a cupboard above the kettle, and my mouth drops open at the sight: a mass selection of every type of tea imaginable.

"You bought the entire store."

"I didn't know which flavor you liked, so I got one of everything."

CHAPTER 22

DAMIEN

AFTER SHE DRINKS HER tea, I come to stand beside her and reach for her hand. She slips off the stool and stands face to face with me. Right now, I don't even know my name. I've been dying to have her. I've thought of nothing else.

I lock my eyes on hers. She emits warmth that has me lost. I inch forward. Our lips are almost touching. Our breaths tickle each other's mouths.

"I hope Samuel doesn't wake this time," she breathes.

I suck in air, desperate for my next breath.

"Same, because the things I want to do to you requires no interruptions."

The quiver in her chin makes me close the distance between us. As soon as our lips join, she grips me with urgency. I groan and kiss her back with equal passion. I'm so different with her. More desperate.

"It's not my birthday yet. For this thing you want to do to me," she rushes out between our kiss.

"I'm going to have to think of a birthday gift," I mumble between peppering her with kisses.

"Just come to my dinner. That will be enough."

"No, that's not a gift. That's a given. But what are you going to say when your brother asks about us?"

It's probably unfair to ask her to do this, but it's either that or this ends. And I don't want this to end yet. We've only just begun.

"Lie." She moans.

"Good girl," I say and kiss her.

She pulls back, her lashes fluttering open. I gaze down at her adorable face, waiting for her to express her thoughts. She's so easy to read.

"I wish I didn't have to. It's only a dinner with my closest friends and family," she says.

It makes me reach out and stroke her face. I wish I wasn't so fucked up and could give her what she wants now.

"I know, but it won't be forever. Just until we figure us out."

She opens her mouth, but I can't give her anymore, so I selfishly shut her up with my mouth. I run my tongue over her bottom lip. She parts them easily. I want to be tender, but I also want to ravish her like a starved man. Which I am. I haven't had a woman in a long time, especially one that cares for me and my son. Well, I'm fucking desperate for that.

I pull back and suck in a deep breath as I stare at her. I know I'm going to have to beg her to stay. And fuck, I'd just do that if she wants to leave my house right now.

"My bedroom?" I rasp out. Unable to hide my desire.

"Is that a trick question?" she whispers.

"Don't be cheeky. Meet me in my room in five. I want to check on Samuel...Say goodnight."

I felt like I owed her a reason for not throwing her over my shoulder and into my bed. But even though I want to be a caveman, I haven't seen Samuel since this morning and even sleeping, I just need to check in on him. And after today's case, I just want a moment where I sit on his bed and look at him and count my lucky stars that he's here and healthy. And how lucky I am and how sorry I am for being late tonight.

That part sucks, and it's also time I can't get back, but I also can't throw away my job. It's what keeps me feeling in control and provides his education. He can do whatever he wants to do with his life, and I love how I can provide that for him. My parents could do that for me, and I want to do that for him.

Marigold kisses me, and I watch her stroll toward my room. My heart is so full right now. To have someone in my room waiting for me. Who wants and needs what I can offer?

When I can't see her anymore. I head off toward Samuel's room.

Inside, I take the moments I need there before walking into my room. The instant I see her in my bed wearing one of my white work shirts with the light of the lamp highlighting her, I almost choke on my tongue.

She's delectable, and I never want her to wear anything else.

"Is something wrong?" she asks with a wicked smirk. She knows exactly how hard I am. And I know how ready she is for me. Her tight nipples evident through my shirt.

"You know damn well there's nothing wrong. Everything is right." I close the door softly behind me, locking it, and then walk over to her.

She's grinning sheepishly at me.

"This shirt is yours. It looks way better on you." I reach out and touch the collar of the shirt, feeling the heat of her skin. I trace my finger from her neck down to her collarbone.

Her breath hitches. And it makes my dick jerk. I love all the sounds she makes.

I drop my hand on the blanket and rip it off her. I lick my lips as I take in her bare legs uncovered by my shirt.

"Are you wearing any panties?" I rasp.

She bites her bottom lip and shakes her head.

"Fucking perfect. You know how to please me."

"Yes, sir."

A deep grumble leaves my chest. I haven't heard that word since we met online. And I love it. I've never been called it before, but it's so hot coming from her lips. And with her, it feels special.

"Good girls need to be rewarded."

She nods frantically.

I crawl between her legs. Her eyelids heavy as she watches me come toward her. I hope it's as hot as she looked crawling over the bed that day online. And one night I'll get her to do that. But tonight is all about her. I'll crawl to her any fucking day. When I reach her, I push her thighs apart.

She hitches a breath.

"I've got you," I say, as if to remind her. Promising only pleasure.

She sinks back into the pillows. She looks so dreamy in my white plush pillows.

I settle my body between her legs. My fingers skim over her thighs. They prickle with goosebumps, and I don't stop even as I watch her clutch the blanket beside her.

It excites me, and as I push her shirt up, I growl.

"You're dripping. Fuck, Goldie, so wet so—" I run my tongue over my teeth and move closer, my hands gripping her thighs. Unable to speak anymore. I just need to taste her already. Unable to hold back, I lean in and take one large swipe of my tongue over her opening and up over her swollen bud. Her back arching and her mouth moaning.

Her hands clutch my head and I open my eyes, watching her face light up in ecstasy.

My tongue enters her slick opening. I feel her tighten and I can't help but fuck her with it. Slowly at first, but then, she tips her head back, exposing her neck, and the fast beat of her pulse on the side of her neck spurs me on to fuck her hard.

She rewards me with a clench of her thighs, and I let her do what she wants with me. Suffocate me with her delicious pussy. I'd happily die this way. Her thighs are tight on my head as her ankles cross on my shoulder blades and she rocks her hips up and down. And I'm officially the hardest I've ever been. I can feel precum leaking from my tip without a single touch. I'm on the verge of coming in my pants if she doesn't come soon. She rides my face faster and harder. My name leaves her lips, and this is heaven. She's heaven. The taste of her pussy. Her clutching at me as if I'd come up for air.

I don't let up as she writhes on the bed as I try to go deeper. She continues to arch into my face, and I keep my eyes trained on hers. Lost in the moment. It's incredible.

"If you don't stop, I'll come." She struggles for air, and it's hot as hell hearing her try to talk.

"Come. Come on me. I want to taste what I do to you," I say that to her between her bucking her hips. It's muffled by her pussy encasing me, but I don't care. I don't want to move until she comes apart on my tongue and with that, she lets out an, "Oh my god."

And I know she's close. I thrust my tongue in harder and fuck her with it.

She moans and comes hard on my tongue. Her whole body shudders beneath me. When her body relaxes, her thighs dropping away from my head, I slowly withdraw my tongue and sit up to hover over her. With my hands on either side of her head, I take in her flushed post-orgasm face. Her eyes flutter open, and she stares at me with adoration, making my heart pound harder. As if it wasn't already beating madly from the thrill of pleasuring her. I stare at her intensely with hooded eyes, her brown eyes a lot brighter now.

"You're so beautiful when you come."

I'm so ready to just hold her. Something I've never wanted to do before; yet, right now, I want to wrap my arms around her and sleep.

CHAPTER 23

MARIGOLD

I SAW STARS. THE intensity of my orgasm sedates me. The lust staring back at me when I open my eyes makes my heart pound.

He crawls up over my body and licks his lips, and the sight is my undoing.

He lies beside me, and grabs hold of my waist. Then pulls my body in front of him. The hardness between his thighs alerts me to an important fact. "You didn't come."

"Later, Goldie, for now, you need rest, and I just want to hold you."

We haven't had sex and I'm worrying why? Old demons come up.

Am I not enough?

His arms tighten around me and I don't want to be insecure and drag the night down by overthinking. So, I snuggle my head into him with a sigh. He lays a chaste kiss on my cheek and then props his chin on my head.

The closeness I feel is something I've not felt before. I'm wondering if he was like this with his wife.

I don't think so based on what he's told me.

The thought makes me sad.

Don't you go into a marriage for love? I've always loved the idea of getting married and wearing a big poofy princess dress. With a sequined bodice with so much tulle, I look small in comparison.

I want to look like a real-life princess. I've always wanted a big wedding. And as I close my eyes, I get lost in a dream that Damien is waiting at the end of the aisle with an actual smile. No scowl, just utter longing and awe.

A deep exhale in my ear and the heaviness of his arms tell me he's fallen asleep.

After his day, I can understand. I need to leave in five minutes; otherwise, I will fall asleep. Samuel isn't supposed to know about us. At the moment, no one's meant to know.

The tug on my heart hurts. I hate this secret. I get it, but I don't like it.

I just need to remind myself it's not forever. He just needs a few weeks.

I soak in the last couple of minutes of cuddling him. I finally find the energy to slip out into the darkness, making my way to my cold bed, wondering if he'll notice I've gone. Secretly, I hope he does.

∽

"You look like shit," Clara announces the next day as I step into her apartment. The smell of baked goods hit my nose.

"Thanks," I reply with a sarcastic tone.

"What? I'm just telling you what I see," she says, closing the door behind me.

Walking into her kitchen, I scan the counter. I spot the bread cooling on the wire rack. I take a seat, ready for a cup of tea, and to talk her ear off about Damien.

I need some neutral advice.

She doesn't ask if I want tea; she just goes about grabbing out cups.

"Tell me what's wrong," she encourages, while dropping a bag in each cup. Then fills them with water and cream.

I push the humiliation away and speak. "I went to help Damien out with Samuel again because his mom's still unwell. And when we went to bed that night, he didn't want sex."

"At all?" she asks, bringing the cups to the table and sliding mine over toward me.

"Thanks," I mutter and grab the handle, but don't sip yet, knowing it'll be too hot.

"No. We...sorry." I shake my head. "He did stuff but not that," I say, hoping she won't ask exactly what the stuff we did was because I'd rather not say. That's just between him and me.

"And you want to have sex with him?"

"Yes," I say quietly, "But it's more the fact I worry he doesn't want me sexually, and it's messing with my head."

"When are you seeing him again?"

I blow on the tea, trying to cool it before I take a sip. Enjoying the warm, sweet liquid. Comfort in a cup. I take a moment before I answer. "So, we agreed we'd do an online chat during the week and on weekends, I'll go over to his house. I'm due to see him online tonight." I explain and sip my tea again.

Clara gets up and opens her cupboard and pulls out some homemade cookies. She returns and slides the plate between us. "Maybe ask him tonight."

"I want to, but then I say it in my head, and it makes me sound crazy. I'm too scared I'll sound stupid."

She grabs my hand and squeezes it. "You're not stupid. Guys have mistreated you in the past, so you're needing extra reassurance. A real man will give you that."

Oh, he's a real man alright. There's nothing unmanly about Damien.

"And another thing," I say, "Something about being online with him feels off. It's less exciting now."

"How come?" She asks, puzzled.

"I want him in person. Not online."

She lifts a brow.

"Don't give me that look."

"What?" she fires back.

"Yes. I'm comparing him to my exes. Totally unfair, but I can't shake it. I just want to be with him. Talk to him. Hang out with him. Normal relationship stuff. Online makes me feel like he isn't really into me. Like he's only into the other version of me."

Why was that so hard to admit?

She bites into a cookie. I follow her lead and grab one, taking a bite of the white chocolate chip cookie, enjoying the butter taste on my tongue.

"Yeah, I guess I can see that. But online is fun," she adds with a smug grin.

"It was fun until I had it in real life. Now I want him offline every time."

"I need to take note. Never meet a guy offline."

I nod. "Exactly. Well, how's it going? Are you enjoying it?"

"Yeah, it's good. I've been talking to this one guy a lot."

I sip my tea. "Don't meet him," I add too fast.

"Jesus, woman, say it, don't spray it." She wipes her face, laughing.

"I didn't spit," I argue, feeling heat tickle my cheeks.

"You did. Anyway, I get it. I don't need complicated anyway, so online works for me." We drink our tea before she speaks again. "What are you wearing for your birthday dinner?"

I groan. I'm not as thrilled to go, so I haven't given it much thought. "I don't know, but he'll be there. And so will my brother."

She whistles. "Well, this should be interesting."

"Yeah, we're keeping it quiet for a few weeks. Trying to get to know each other. We still need to figure out the best way to tell Eli and Sammy."

She snorts, but then it turns into a laugh. "Good luck with that. Not Sammy, I mean your brother."

I grumble. "I wish I could sit next to him and be a couple at my birthday dinner."

She offers me a sad smile. "Maybe you should make it difficult for him."

My eyes brows pull together. "What do you mean?"

She leans in. "Let's go find a new outfit that's sure to piss him off."

A part of me likes the idea. Make me too tempting to resist and see what he'll do.

"I can't spend money."

She eases back into her chair, frowning. "Isn't he paying you?"

"Too much," I mutter, remembering the money that he transferred into my bank account for looking after Samuel.

"What do you mean?" she asks.

"He transferred one thousand dollars," I admit reluctantly.

"Are you kidding me?"

I shake my head. "Nope. Ridiculous right."

"Ridiculously good. If I got that for babysitting, I'd do it all the time."

"I know it was a shock to see it in my savings this morning."

"Well, let's go spend a little on an outfit. Treat yourself. Make him struggle all night. Or better yet. Have him hard all night. Payback's a bitch. I bet he'll take you back home and you'll get the sex you want."

I stare at her, contemplating her offer. My brain is trying to think if there's any other way. But when I realize there isn't, I answer her with a sigh.

"Why not?"

It's our Wednesday night online date. And I'm nervous.

Why? It's not like I haven't done this with Damien before. Hell, I've come on camera for him. Then why can't I shake the flutters in my stomach away?

I decide to take a photo and send it to him. With the hope it makes me feel more comfortable before we start.

I turn my lamp on and light a candle that I love and then slip the new baby blue lingerie on. I pose in the mirror, so my body is hiding any insecurities, and snap a photo and text a message.

> **Marigold:** *I'm ready, sir.*

Before I can over-analyze it, I hit send, not wanting to attack any of my flaws.

I don't have to wait longer than a minute to get a reply.

> **Damien:** *You're incredible. I'm going on now.*

I swallow the lump in my throat and wait for him to come on the app.

When he comes on screen, I can't help but give him a small smile.

"Hey," I whisper.

"What's wrong?" he asks, not even waiting a full minute.

"Nothing." I wave it off, not wanting to ruin the start of the night with my concern. I wanted to bring it up in the end. Or better yet, on the weekend when I see him. I wonder if I'll see him after my birthday dinner this Saturday.

"It's not nothing. You've lost that sparkle in your eye and you're not smiling the same."

I swallow hard at his keen eye. Am I really less smiley today? It's sweet he notices these parts of me, but I really don't want to confess the silly, childish thought. I think deep down it's because I want confirmation there's nothing wrong with me.

I've been obsessed with this man for so long, I don't want to screw it up now. I need to keep my mouth shut. Let him change the subject. Or better yet, distract him so he forgets. Maybe after tonight, I'll feel better. I'm probably just in my head.

"It's nothing," I whisper, running my hands over my exposed skin, along my stomach and the curve of my hips. My movements are slow and controlled. I'm trying to tease him and turn myself on. "So, you like the blue?"

"I love it," he replies.

On his bed, he looks effortlessly handsome. It helps me to get in the mood a little more. His eyes drinking me in. His upper body is naked, hard and hot. No shirt, just a pair of gray sweats. He loves my body just as much as I adore his. We could get lost in each other's bodies for hours.

My fingers continue to skim over my feverish body. His chest rises and falls the longer I tease. I imagine it's his fingers trailing over my skin. Not mine. I close my eyes and allow my head to roll onto my shoulders. The teasing of my warm, soft skin helping ease the tension. I trail my finger to my bra strap and push it off my shoulder. My pebbled nipple is now exposed to him. I part my lips, and my tongue skims my bottom lip. My fingers move to the other strap and push it off.

When I open my eyes to see him, his parted lips and messy hair make me want him more. I can't get enough of him. But in this moment, my façade drops and his face changes into a tortured expression.

"Goldie, please," he murmurs.

The endearing name and the plea are hard to ignore.

I sigh heavily and wander toward the camera. I lift the straps back onto my shoulders to recover myself. My fingers are twisting, but my eyes are trained on him.

He's now sitting on the end of his plush mattress. A bed and a room I remember so well.

His top is still off, but he's closer in the viewfinder. It all makes me wish I was beside him...or better yet, on top of him. His arms around me, holding me and then pleasuring me.

He noticed I'm not feeling this, so I should feel satisfied, but I'm consumed with stress. Why does he have to read me so well? Even through the damn camera, he knew I was faking enjoyment. I tried too hard.

"Why won't you have sex with me?" I ask quietly.

"Is that what's bothering you?"

I tug my lip into my mouth and nod. "I know it's lame, but I can't help it."

He sits up in his bed. "Hey, listen. I definitely want to have sex with you."

"You do?"

"Of course." He gives me a sexy smirk. "It's just…to be honest, it's been a long time since I had sex. I want to take my time and savor all these moments between us. Rather than rush in and do it all quickly."

I think about what he's saying, and it's more thoughtful and sweeter than I realized.

But while I'm being honest, I want to get everything off my chest. "So, it's got nothing to do with me?"

"Of course not. You please me so much."

My body relaxes for the first time tonight. A small smile appears on my face, knowing it was the right decision to admit my concern.

"How about tonight we just talk for a while?" he says.

My heart thunders in my chest. "I'd like that very much."

I don't change. Instead, I stay in my sexy blue set.

He leans back on one elbow. "You should've seen the moms at school today."

My lips twist into a full smile. "What did they do now?"

He shivers visibly, and I giggle. Whatever he's about to say clearly is in the forefront of his mind in a disturbing way.

"They surrounded me and fired me with questions about you."

"Yeah?" I smirk, picturing the scene in my mind.

"Don't smirk. You're the cause."

"I am. They think I'm competition."

"They're dreaming. I only have eyes for one woman."

"Really."

"Yeah, she's five-four and fucking edible in baby blue."

My finger runs along my lip. "What else is so good about her?"

"She's intelligent. Studying law."

"And that helps how?"

"Good lawyers always want to be on top of things."

I roll my eyes and laugh at his dirty joke. "I do."

"But the worst was Samuel. He comes running out after the school bell with the words 'Where's Mari?'" he explains, running a hand through his hair. "And I said it was only me and the cheek on him to tell me 'Oh, I miss Mari.'"

"You're not his favorite anymore. That's gotta hurt," I tease.

"I can't blame him. You're too..." He trails off, as if not knowing the word. "Adorable."

As dumb as it is, I needed to hear those words. I should be content with how our relationship is progressing, but the little voices in my head were there with my ex too. I ignored them and look where that got me. No, this time I want to ask the questions. As difficult as they are. I may have fallen fast again, but this time, it's different. I've known Damien for years. Everything with him feels different—including me.

We spend all night talking about a variety of things, from his work to Samuel, then life in general, and my classes. Even the moments of silence are relaxing and I'm glad I asked the burning questions. And I'm happy we did nothing sexual tonight.

After, I say goodbye and get changed for the night.

I walk out of the bathroom when my message tone goes off. I reach over, thinking he sent me a text, but it's the money for the online chat. Staring sadly at the screen, my heart feels heavy. He's paid me for tonight. While I stare at the money in my bank account, I realize I don't want that. I want the feeling that he's falling for me, because my crush has turned to me falling for him.

I need the money, and we agreed. But something about this makes it seem more like a transaction. I'm going to have to tell him on the weekend I can't do the app anymore. That it doesn't sit right with me.

Chapter 24

Damien

I walk into The Guild Restaurant searching around in the dim lights for those brown eyes. It's Marigold's birthday dinner and I can't shake the sudden nerves. I know I'm going to have Elijah drill me with questions. Every time we've spoken, he asks me elusive questions, which is his way of checking to see if me and his sister are still hooking up.

And every time I lie through my teeth. I need to figure out a plan soon. It'll be worse if he finds out by walking in on us again. God, I can't even imagine how he'll react.

The restaurant has a mix of dark brown leather chairs and booths with dark wooden tables. It's the opposite of how Marigold is. This is moody and dark. The only commonality is that the darkness adds sexiness, and she has that in abundance.

As I'm waiting to be served, it's as if everything disappears and it's like a spotlight shines directly on Marigold.

All the air has left my lungs and I force myself to move. I stride to the table. As I come closer, I see her family and friends have already sat down. Checking my watch, I'm on time—just. I had to wait for my mom to come and watch Samuel before I could leave.

My eyes drop over her outfit. She's wearing a black satin V-cut dress that makes my mouth dry. It molds perfectly to her body in the most delicious way. The sexy slit in the already short dress makes me think how easy it would be to rip that dress in two.

As I've been strolling closer and soaking in all her beauty, I've found myself in front of her.

"Goldie, you look breathtaking," I say hoarsely.

She bats her lashes and gives me a sweet smile. "Thanks." I don't miss the way her eyes run over my black suit and my heart beats faster, hoping she likes it. I bought it just for tonight. Just for her.

"You look handsome," she responds, her eyes gleaming with happiness. Her hand reaches out to run her fingers over my black checkered tie.

Feeling eyes on me, I clear my throat and hold out her gift. It causes her to drop her fingers away from my body. "Happy Birthday," I say with a hint of a smile.

"You didn't have to," she replies with a grin, but takes the bag and the touch of her fingers feels all too much, but not enough when they leave. I push my hands inside my pockets and watch her peek inside the bag.

"Don't open it here," I whisper as I lean in so no one else can hear.

She closes the bag and peeks up at me from under her black lashes. "Now I really want to know what it is," she whispers back.

"Later," I say with a wink.

Just then, one of Marigold's friends comes over to join us.

"Hey, I'm Clara," she says, sticking out her hand.

I dip my head and shake her hand softly. "Damien."

"Oh, I know who you are," she deadpans.

A sense of dread hits me.

What has Marigold been saying?

I look around and I've got two choices: either I go to the table, or I go to the bar, and see if I can get five minutes more without seeming suspicious.

"Let me buy you a drink," I say to Marigold.

"That would be amazing. We just finished our drinks," Clara interrupts. Even though I want Marigold to myself, having Clara there might look better to the other eyes. Mainly Elijah.

Marigold's sympathetic eyes meet mine. I dip my chin and stroll to the bar. The click of their heels tells me they're following.

When I reach the bar, I rest my elbows on top. I tilt my head, and I'm relieved to see Marigold next to me. "What are you girls drinking?" I ask.

"Grasshoppers," Clara calls out.

I frown, thinking of the bugs. "What are those?"

"They taste like a thin mint cookie," Marigold says and the way her gaze drops to my mouth, I can't help but lick my lips.

When the bartender arrives, I order two of those and an old-fashioned drink for me.

"I wish I could kiss you," Marigold breathes.

I look back at her friend, finding her busy talking to another friend at the bar. I'm relieved because I can talk without worrying about Clara overhearing.

"You have no idea how much I want that too," I say in a low voice. My eyes stare at her plump, glossy lips. Before I bring them back to her eyes.

"I have to admit something," she says, looking away from me.

"Mmm. What's that?" I probe with a little concern at her uneasiness.

"I don't want to be online anymore."

I sigh in relief. "I'm not going to complain. The thought of sharing you makes me murderous."

She's about to reply when the drinks arrive, and she picks hers up and takes a sip while I pay.

I pick up my glass and raise it to hers. She copies. "Happy Birthday, Goldie. May your wishes come true."

We clink glasses. Our eyes never leave each other's as we both take a sip of our drinks.

"My wish came true," she says as she lowers her drink.

I lift my brows. "Oh, really."

"Mm-hmm. I finally got you," she says with a wide smile.

I'm stunned. No words are forming. She must see it, so she asks an unrelated question.

"Do you want a taste?" she asks, holding out her cocktail glass. My mind wants to say yes from your mouth, but it's not an option. Even though I wish it was.

"No thanks. I've got mine," I murmur, holding up my glass as I take a drink. "Do you want a taste?"

She screws up her face. "I don't know. That looks strong."

"It's alcohol," I tease.

"Duh. I know that. But I'm a lightweight. I also have had little to eat tonight," she admits, taking the glass and wincing as she sips. "Ah."

"You don't like it?" I hold back a laugh.

"No, it's foul. I'll stick to this." She sips her green cocktail, clearly trying to wash away the taste of my old fashion.

"You need to eat if you're drinking," I say.

"I don't want to bloat. This dress isn't forgiving." She drops her hand over the front of her stomach.

I groan. "Are you serious? You're the most beautiful woman in the room."

She blushes. "Thanks."

"It's true. Listen to me." I reach out and grab her chin and lift it with my finger. I want those shimmering eyes on mine as I speak. "Do not worry about what you look like. To me, you're perfect. Hot, smart, and kind. Every guy in this place has looked at you at least once tonight and is probably jealous of me right now." I reluctantly drop my hand from her face.

"Except my brother," she adds.

I grimace. "Yeah, minus family. But every other guy has wished they were with you and that's only from the outside. If they knew you in here," I touch her chest briefly, "they'd want to date you."

She doesn't speak for a while. She just blinks.

"I don't want to date anyone else," she replies.

"No?"

She shakes her head. "No. The one person I want is you."

Bold Marigold is so hot. I stare wordlessly at her, trying to figure out a response. We're still a secret, so is that dating if no one knows? I don't think so. She deserves better, but I'm selfish and I can't fucking let her go.

"Going back to what I was saying. I didn't mean just with others…" she trails off nervously.

I go to reach out with my hand to touch her arm, but I curl my fingers back in and grab my glass. Hopefully, it will prevent any additional near misses. I need to keep my control in check. Otherwise, Elijah will breathe down our necks or cut my dick off.

"I don't want to do the online night with you on the app anymore," she deadpans.

My jaw slacks. "You don't?"

I almost want to say you don't want me anymore, but I am quick to close my mouth.

She moves her head and her perfume from her hair hits me, causing me to suck in a deeper breath. I notice she still uses my soap, which is adorable.

"I want you in real life. It wasn't the same the other night," she adds quietly, as if embarrassed.

"Did I make you uncomfortable?" I ask, trying to think back. I never asked her to do anything sexual. We just ended up chatting for a couple of hours.

She shakes her head. "No, never. It's just now that I've had you in real life, that's all I want."

My chest expands from her words.

"What about your college bills? How will you get by?" I ask worriedly. "Are you going to take the money Eli offered you?"

"No way. I'd never take his money. I'd feel like I owe him something. Life is about opportunities, and I'll see when the next one comes along."

I take a sip of my drink. "No plans will lead to failure."

"Listen, I'll figure it out. You don't have to worry about me," she replies with a hint of frustration in her voice.

Is she joking?

"I do and I always will," I say.

She stares at me, bemused. "See, so online doesn't work. You act protective and yet we're a dirty little secret. We need to come out and tell people."

I exhale a heavy breath. "Soon, I promise."

A wave of disappointment hits her face. But she picks up her drink before I can speak again. "I better get back to the table." She saunters off toward her family and friends and since I can't ogle her, I turn back to the bar and sip my drink, lost in deep thought.

CHAPTER 25

DAMIEN

AFTER ORDERING ANOTHER OLD-FASHIONED, I wander back over to the table.

"Hey. Over here." Elijah waves me over. I nod and approach the empty chair beside him. I lower my glass to the table and sit.

"Hey, Jackie," I say, tipping my head. It's hard to miss the large dimple on her cheek when she smiles, and her youthfulness reminds me of Marigold. Probably because they're similar in age.

She finishes sipping her drink to say hello. Her cheeks have a new flush, probably from the alcohol.

"Nice for you to finally come over and say hi," Elijah says, squinting his eyes at me. He's pissed.

"I had to say happy birthday," I reply.

"And you came with a gift," Jackie adds. I don't miss the twinkle in her hazel eyes.

"I did," I answer.

"What is it?" Elijah asks. "Ah. What did you do that for?" Elijah rubs along the side of his navy suit.

Jackie glares at him, wearing a scornful look. "Don't ask him that. It's rude," she replies.

I exhale a sigh of relief. I didn't want to lie to him about what I bought her. It's not something he'd appreciate.

"Sorry," he grumbles.

Well, this is new.

Elijah apologizing and following a woman's orders. Here I was, thinking he'd need a feisty woman to keep him in line. Turns out we both have a soft spot for sweet, young, and determined women.

They quickly share a private conversation, making me feel like a third wheel.

I turn to grab my glass, but I pause it midway to my mouth. Marigold is sitting directly across from me. And I have to swallow the groan bubbling in my throat from the way the boning of her dress pushes her beautiful full breasts up.

My erection is becoming harder to handle. I'm sitting next to her goddamn brother hard as a rock. I have no control over my body when it comes to her. It has a mind of its own. And right now, it wants to be buried deep inside her.

Her eyes flick to mine when she grabs her drink before turning to her friend and whispering something. She gets up and walks off alone, and I follow her with my eyes. Enjoying the way her hips sway with each step.

I lower my glass and stand.

"I'll be back," I mumble to Elijah without looking at him and walk off in the same direction Marigold went.

I peer around the dark hallway and see no one else. Before I'm noticed, I slip inside the bathroom. The door closes with a thud behind me, causing an echo inside the bathroom.

Inside, a door is moving, so I step closer and hold my hand out. I catch the door before it closes. She gasps when I push it open before she can lock it. The fear instantly drops from her face the second she realizes it's me. Now there's the sexy as fuck challenging look. Since we've hooked up, she's found her voice. Less of the quiet, scared Marigold. Now she's the woman she wants to be.

Confident, empowered, sexy, and downright irresistible.

"What are you doing here?" she asks, lifting a brow. "It's the ladies' bathroom. The men's is next door."

I close the door behind me as I smirk at her smart-ass comment and stalk closer to her. She steps back until she's backed against the stall wall. She sucks in a breath. Her reaction to me is clear, and I have to control the ache in my chest.

I dip my head, bringing my face to the side of hers.

"Damien," she pants.

I run my nose from her ear to her collarbone, whispering over her warm skin. "I know exactly where I am. And I know you wanted me to come find you. Didn't you?"

She nods lazily. "Yesss."

"You wear this short, tight, barely there fucking dress for what? To get my attention?"

"Yes. I wanted to drive you crazy."

"It fucking worked. This dress. Fuck, this dress shouldn't be seen by anyone else but me. But fuck, I love it. I love it so fucking much." I lay a kiss under her ear, feeling her pulse beating wildly against my lips. "So now you've got me. What do you want, Goldie?" I ask against her skin before pulling back to stare into her magnificent eyes.

She exhales with a shudder. Her arms trail up over my arms, all the way up over my neck until her fingers grip my hair tightly. She brings those plump lips to my ear.

"I want you," she purrs.

My dick strains against my pants and I can feel precum leaking from my cock. I want her so badly.

She blinks slowly.

"What part of me do you want?" I ask.

"All of you."

I swallow hard, knowing her lust-filled brown eyes are telling the truth.

"You want me to fuck you here in this bathroom and not romantic on a bed?"

She nods her head with a cheeky smile. "Yes. I'm sick of waiting."

"Are you wet right now? Are you making a mess in your panties?" I ask, as my hand drops to her ass and then to the tops of her thighs, where I pull up her dress and find her bare pussy.

"I'm not wearing any—"

She's too fucking hot. I can't hold back any longer; she's making it impossible.

"Fuck! Goldie. Tell me you really want this here and now," I beg.

"Yes! Fuck me, Damien. Fuck me so hard, I'll walk out of here feeling sore. Every step reminds me you were there," she says huskily.

A growl rumbles from my chest. I snap. My mouth comes down hard on hers and I kiss her with all the night's worth of pent-up passion. Fuck, her lips. They feel so soft and plush against mine. I've missed this. Missed her.

My tongue touches hers and a deep, guttural growl leaves my chest. She's so fucking perfect. I'm trying to ignore the gnawing ache in the center of my chest. This is too good to be true. People like me aren't worthy of a woman like her. She's kind, pure and intelligent. When she figures it out, she'll leave me, but right here, I'm savoring this moment.

Our bodies tangle in limbs going everywhere. I push her dress up to her hips as she fumbles with my jeans, belt, and button. When her hand dips in with no warning and grabs my length, I choke on my breath. "Fuck."

I grab both of her legs and lift her by her thighs. I push my erect cock over her wet pussy and roll my hips around. She tips her head back and a loud moan leaves her chest.

I bury my face into the base of her neck and rasp, "Shhh. Otherwise, someone might hear you."

She hums. My lips trail up her hot neck, nipping at it until I reach the shell of her ear. Enjoying her heavy perfume. She shivers under me. "Your brother will kill me if he finds my cock buried deep inside you," I add.

"Oh." She whimpers as I rub my cock through her pussy. "Please, Damien."

I'm so hard for her. I've never wanted anything as much as I want Marigold right now. The online foreplay, the desire of her body and this new intimacy we share, they all make me excited to have her shatter on my cock.

"Condom. Hang—" I say, pulling away. Her legs drop from my waist so she's standing again.

"No! I'm clean. I want nothing between us. I want to feel all of you," she cuts me off, gasping. Her hands grabbing my shoulders. Yanking me back to her. She's desperate and so fucking sexy.

"Fuck, Goldie. You're too fucking good for me."

I want to tell her I haven't been with anyone since my ex, but I don't want to bring up her name and ruin the moment.

My hand grabs the side of her face, the other gripping her hip. With our eyes locked, I ask, "Are you sure?"

She answers me by trying to grab my cock. But I'm quick and I grab her hand, lacing our fingers and pinning them to the wall. "Don't move them."

She closes her eyes, expecting me to kiss her, but I bend down and lick up her neck, over her beating pulse. Her head falls to the side until my mouth lifts off her skin. I grab her hips again and lift her, so her legs wrap around my back.

Her warm heat is at the perfect angle now. Her breath quivers.

I line up my cock and slowly enter her. The tightness steals my breath. "You're so tight. Fuck."

I slide in and out of her slowly, stretching her.

"You're big," she says with a pinch to her tone that has me pausing.

I stare at her. "Are you okay? Do you want me to stop?"

"Don't you fucking dare," she replies.

I close my eyes briefly and my grip on her tightens with approval.

"I better give the birthday girl what she wants. And it sounds like she wants to be fucked hard."

I slide farther in until I'm buried as deep as I can go. Her head drops back and her parted lips gasp for air. "Yes."

When I thrust the rest of the way in, I still, waiting for her to adjust and then when her body softens, I fuck her hard. My lips return to hers in a punishing kiss.

The way her walls tighten tells me she's close. She pulls her lips away and cries out as she orgasms. My name leaving her lips in the sexiest pant. I feel the way my climax hits me, and I can't form the words to tell her to be quiet. I don't think I could. The way she looks shattering on my cock is hot. Her body sags and she whimpers. We both are breathing heavily as we come down from the high. She was better than I could've imagined, responsive, eager, with the most perfect pussy. I just wish I wasn't here right now so I could hold her.

"You're exquisite," I rasp, enjoying the way her cheeks are a darker shade of red.

She smiles groggily back at me, unable to answer. She's still riding high from her orgasm. It reminds me of her statement earlier about lack of eating.

"When we get back out there, you need to eat something. You need your energy."

She nibbles her lip. "Why?"

"Because I want to fuck you again, but this time, I want to take my time, and in my bed, where you can scream as loud as you want."

"I love the sound of that," she replies.

"So you'll eat?" I ask.

"Yes, sir." She gives me a smug look.

"Fuck. I love it when you call me that."

"Good to know." Her eyes have a mischievous look about them. And I want to ask what she's thinking. But I'm aware of the time and that we both need to get back out there before they notice she's missing.

"I better get back out there."

"Yeah," she replies, the same disappointment lacing her voice. We both don't want this to end.

We redress and then I lay one last lingering kiss on her swollen lips. They're extra pink from my five-o'clock shadow, which is hot. I can't stay, so I reluctantly drag myself out of the bathroom and back into the hall. Marigold is back at the table, so I head to the bar.

I'm waiting to order a drink when Clara's voice sounds behind me.

"You know she's falling, right?"

I turn my head to see Clara moving closer to me. She mirrors my stance on the bar. Her grasshopper cocktail in front of her.

"Sorry?" I ask.

She rolls her eyes. "She's falling in love with you."

"She is?"

She sighs heavily. "This is what she always does. She falls too hard, too fast, and then the guys don't feel the same."

Her eyes twitch and I can see she wants me to talk. Only I'm not a talker. Well, normally, I'm not. Unless it's Marigold and I can't seem to stop talking. Our conversations are always so effortless. Different from anyone else.

"Okay." I'm at a loss for words. What else should I say?

I'm not falling in love with Marigold.

I can't.

"So please, let her go if you don't feel the same. I can't see her in pain again. If you break it off now, it won't be as bad."

My mouth opens and closes, but no words move past my lips. She takes that as if I've given her an answer.

"I thought so. Do the right thing, Damien," Clara adds, picking up her drink and walking off. She leaves me there goggle-eyed and open-mouthed.

If I don't love Marigold, I have to set her free, because she's already fallen?

I rub my hand over my face. I can't even think about this right now.

No.

I'll talk to Marigold later.

I'm sure she hasn't fallen, and Clara has it all wrong...right?

I walk back to the table and sit.

"Where'd you go?" Elijah asks.

"Bathroom and then to the bar," I reply.

Elijah is about to speak to me. "Where's your dr—"

My phone vibrates in my pocket. Slipping it out, I look at the caller ID. Fuck!

It's work. I can't ignore it.

"Sorry, it's work. Let me grab this really quick."

He nods. I slip out from the table and walk away to answer it. Five minutes later, I'm walking back to the table with my head hanging low. My eyes catch hers and I see the concern etched on her face.

"Everything alright?" Elijah questions. "Is it Samuel?"

I sigh. "No, it's work. I've been called into the hospital for an emergency."

"You'll miss a good night, but with the way she's looking at you, I think it might be for the best."

I don't have to look very far to know he's referring to Marigold.

Has she been watching me all night?

We've held each other's gazes a couple of times, but that's it. However, I guess Elijah would be watching us closely.

I'm glad he didn't catch us in the bathroom a couple of minutes ago.

I'm reluctant to leave. I don't like the fact we just had sex for the first time, and now I'm running away. I feel like a dick. Maybe she could still come by after I get off? But when her friend brings her another cocktail, I'm reminded that it's her night. She's here with friends and she'll be drunk later. I grind my teeth, hating her drunk and out of control at God knows where they end up later. I imagine someone taking advantage of her, so it's difficult for me to leave now. I just want to...watch her?

Fuck, seriously, what's wrong with me? No, that's not fair. I have to trust her.

"I'm off, but have a good one. Sorry I had to skip out early," I say to Elijah and shake his hand.

He slaps my shoulder. "Don't sweat it. It's your job."

I walk around the table and stand behind her seat. She stands and I'm well aware of Elijah and Clara's eyes on us.

There's a decent amount of distance and I keep it that way.

Marigold's cheeks have the cutest shade of pink. I wonder if it was the mind-blowing bathroom sex or the alcohol.

I hope it's the first reason.

"I've been called into work. I'm sorry, I've gotta leave your dinner early."

Why is it so hard to say the words?

Maybe because the way she looks at me with sad doe eyes makes me feel remorseful for leaving.

A strand of hair is in her face, and I clench my hand to refrain myself from tucking it behind her ear.

"Oh right. Work. I get it," she replies with a quiet voice. "Thanks for coming," she adds, forcing a smile afterwards.

Fuck, if I didn't already feel horrible for leaving, she goes and kills me with one look. The alcohol is not masking her feelings.

"I'm sorry," I whisper.

"So am I."

I stand there gobsmacked at this beautiful woman whose birthday dinner I'm leaving.

CHAPTER 26

MARIGOLD

WATCHING HIM WALK AWAY was hard. As I stare toward the exit, I swallow the disappointment.

It's my birthday, and he left for work. I know he works hard, but damn, on my birthday, that sucks.

I know it's not his fault and the work he does helps so many people. It just hurts when it affects you. Like we aren't even able to spend as much time together as it is.

"He's not coming back," Elijah deadpans coldly.

I tear my gaze from the exit and face him.

"I know." My voice cannot hide the disappointment.

"You're not still fixated on him, are you?" he asks. I take my seat again.

Jackie tugs on his arm. "Don't do this here."

"Exactly," I reply, avoiding his comment because I'm not just fixated. I'm utterly obsessed and head over heels for Damien. I don't think he'd want to hear that, though.

His lips thin, but he says nothing else, thankfully.

I turn to Clara. "I need another drink."

"Yes, you do!" She squeals.

We stand and amble to the bar. Where we order our grasshoppers.

"You seem down," Clara states with a curious expression.

"I am. We hooked up in the bathroom and then he left," I murmur, so no one around can hear.

Her eyes widened. "You mean hooked up, hooked up?"

I nod. "Yep. It was incredible. I've never been with any guy that's made me feel this good."

"I can hear a but coming."

I huff, knowing she's right. "He left and I feel a mix of dirty and bummed. He said I was going to go back to his place. But then work called."

The bartender arrives with our drinks. After paying, we clink our glasses together and take a sip.

"You're not going back to his. We're gonna go dancing until we can't feel our feet anymore."

I giggle and it helps lift my spirits a little. "You know what? I don't want to feel down. I want to still have a good night. We're dressed up and I will not waste it."

"That's the spirit. Let's drink and play nice until the party leaves and then let's head out."

I lift my glass to my lips with a wicked grin. I love how Clara knows me so well. Maybe better than I know myself.

I'm ready to have some fun. Even if I wish I was going back to his place, I know Clara and I can still make this a great night.

The next morning, I wake with the worst hangover.

"Fuck, my head feels like it's going to explode." Clara rolls in bed beside me.

I check the time on my phone and see a message. My head feels just as bad.

"I'll order some MacDonald's. I need greasy food stat." I groan.

"Mmm. Good idea," Clara mumbles.

I prop myself up on pillows and order some food quickly as Clara rolls back over to go back to sleep.

I can't sleep, so as I wait for the food to be delivered, I open the message. It's from Damien.

> **Damien:** *Finally made it home. My bed feels empty without you. How was the rest of your night?*

He messaged at 4 a.m.

I don't know what time we got home, but I didn't see this message.

Marigold: *Sorry, I just woke up. I must've passed out last night.*

Damien: *That's okay. I didn't get home until late. How was it?*

Marigold: *Great. We went to Luxe. I drank and danced until I don't know what time. I'm paying for it today.*

Damien: *Did you eat?*

Marigold: *No, sir.*

Damien: *I told you to eat.*

Marigold: *I didn't feel like eating.*

Damien: *Why?*

I kept my feelings to myself about him leaving and feeling hurt and angry, so I change the subject.

> **Marigold:** *Thanks for my gift. It's too much though, I can't accept it.*

I snap a pic and send it to him. But I cut out my head because I look like a hot mess. I need to shower after I've eaten.

> **Damien:** *So beautiful. And it's not too much. I should've done something better. I just know you aren't into materialistic things. Which makes it hard to buy you a gift.*

> **Marigold:** *These are perfect.*

I stare down at his white shirt and touch the gold G necklace. G and gold. Fitting for the nickname he uses for me...Goldie.

> **Damien:** *Are you mad I left?*

Here's my chance to admit how I honestly felt. Normally, I'd want to be the happy-go-lucky partner and not say anything to make the guy mad, but with Damien, I feel like I can be myself and maybe he won't run.

> **Marigold:** I understand it's your job, and it's important, but I'm sad you left. It was my birthday.

I hit send and wait to see how he reacts. I'm proud that I expressed my feelings without toning them down. This is another step in striving to become the newly empowered Marigold. I've always toned myself down for men and look where that's left me.

> **Damien:** I'm so sorry. I'll make it up to you, I promise.

I don't know what to reply. So when the door sounds, I rush to it and grab our food. Along the way, I get some painkillers for our pounding heads.

I return and lower the food on the bed. Straight away, grabbing a fry and chewing it. The salt is exactly what I need right now. My belly is churning from finally getting food. I definitely should've listened to him and ate something and I definitely would've if I didn't feel sick when he left.

My phone chimes and I see it's another text from him.

> **Damien:** What are you doing this weekend?

> **Marigold:** I'll be doing assignments or studying. Why?

> **Damien:** I'm taking you away. You can bring your books with you.

> **Marigold:** Is this to make up for leaving?

> **Damien:** Yes. I fucked up big time. Let me make up for what I did. I'll give you just-me time all weekend.

God, I want that so much. Before I can type a reply, he sends another text.

> **Damien:** *I should've made other arrangements.*

I'm not fighting this offer. I'm desperate for alone time.

> **Marigold:** *I'll pack a bag. What's the weather?*

> **Damien:** *Bring a mix. I want to surprise you with the destination.*

> **Marigold:** *So many surprises.*

> **Damien:** *You have no idea.*

It's finally Friday. I go straight home after college. I have been adding items to my open suitcase as I think of them. With us not doing our Wednesday night video chat, it means I miss his face and voice more than normal. We still text, but that's it for the week. So, I'm excited to have all his attention on me.

I pull all my clothes onto the bed and begin with the lingerie when I hear a knock on my door.

"Come in," I call out.

"You told your mom you're going away with me?" Clara announces as she wanders into my room.

I wince at her from my kneeling position on the floor. And with an apologetic smile, I say, "I'm sorry. I just can't tell them it's with Damien, they'll tell Eli."

"Why does he have a problem with it?" she asks.

I shrug. "He thinks Damien needs to heal from his ex, and I need to focus on school."

She shoves clothes aside from a section of the bed, so she can take a seat.

"Listen, I'm not a huge fan of this. I worry if this is really what you want?" Clara says, which totally surprises me.

"Him, of course. He's different," I reply.

She purses her lips. "I'm not sold."

I huff. Emotions bubble through me. I feel like I'm on the verge of crying. How can I convince everyone he's not like any of the 'ones' before him?

"Why?" I ask.

"He's older and a single dad. He's set in his ways. You're a carefree, single young woman, living the best years of your life. Whereas he's living a quiet and busy work and dad life." She leans her elbows on her knees.

"I know we sound so opposite, and yes, I've seen his hectic life and his controlling ways, but I've found my voice with him. I've started speaking up. That's something I've never done before. Have I?"

She shakes her head. "No, but I don't want you to change for him."

"I won't and if I'm changing, it's because I've found myself and my voice. If things don't work out, I'll deal with it then, but at the moment, we can't officially date because so many people frown upon us. Our relationship with strangers commenting will be hard enough. I need support right now."

She stands up from the bed and drops to her knees in front of me. "Don't think I'm not supporting you. I love and care about you. Since I've been through a few breakups with you, I just want to protect you."

"I get that, but sometimes I need to be hurt to grow. And I've gotten stronger. I finally realize my worth."

She hugs me and asks, "How can I help you?"

We break out of our hug, and I turn to the mess on the bed.

"Could you pass me clothes and tell me yes or no? I have to take a bit of everything because he won't tell me where we're going."

That's what's adding to my nerves. I wish I had an idea if it's cold or hot. Jackets take up way more room than thin summer dresses.

"You have no idea?" she asks.

I shake my head. "Nope."

"Okay. Well, that's a bit cute."

He's more than a bit cute.

I exhale a breath. "Let's start with lingerie, socks, bikinis."

A new knock sounds at my door.

"It's open," I yell out.

The door opens and closes. Footsteps come until my mom appears in my room.

"Marigold, this just arrived for you."

I stand and grab it from her. "Thanks."

"Do you girls need anything?" Mom asks.

I shake my head. "No, thanks, Mom. We'll be over at the main house soon for a cup of tea."

She smiles. "I baked a chocolate cake, so that will be good timing."

I nod. She closes the door as she leaves.

I open the package and laugh. Bikinis.

"He just gave away that he's taking me to somewhere warm!"

I pull it out and she laughs.

"Guys are so dumb sometimes," Clara adds.

I giggle. "But so thoughtful. Him buying me stuff is odd. I'm not used to it. Is it bad that I like it?"

"No, silly. It makes you normal. I'd like it if a guy did that for me," she admits with a long sigh.

"What's happening with the online guy?"

"Still good, don't get me wrong, he's hot. But he will not be taking me away. And if he buys me a gift, it'll be dirty, not sweet." She laughs and I laugh too.

"I guess a gift is a gift," she adds.

"That's true. And are you still enjoying it though?" I ask.

"Yeah, I like the extra confidence it brings."

I smile at the memories. "That's what I loved."

"Do you miss it?" she asks.

"Not at all. I just worry about money, but I'll figure something out."

I don't know what yet. But I'll need something soon.

CHAPTER 27

MARIGOLD

LATER THAT DAY, I step outside, where I expect a taxi to be waiting. But I falter mid-step when I see an older gentleman in a black suit standing beside the same black car as the night after Luxe.

"Miss West," he asks.

"Y-yeah," I stammer.

What in the world is going on?

"I'm here to take you to the airport." He steps back, pulling open the door for me to go in. "Mr. Gray is waiting," he adds.

Excitement bubbles inside me at the thought of Damien being inside.

I'm moving quickly now. I duck my head in and look around for him, landing on his awaiting gaze.

"Hi," I say, trying to ignore the butterflies in my stomach.

His eyes are brighter, and he's wearing a sexy grin. I can't help but smile back. I take my seat next to him.

"Goldie, come here," he says, patting the seat beside him.

His deep, smooth voice runs over my skin, warming me up. I dip my head and move. When I'm close, he wastes no time locking his lips onto mine. The touch of his heated skin on mine causes my sex to ache.

"I've missed you," he adds between kisses.

I whimper as he nips on my lip. It sends desperation through me. There's a privacy screen between us and the driver. I climb onto his lap, and he grabs my hips roughly. He pushes me into his groin. I don't miss the hardness in his pants. I rock my hips over him, and he grunts.

My hands grab the sides of his face and I hold him tight and kiss him hard at the same time as I rock my hips. I tell him with actions just how much I've missed him, too.

I know he's allowing me to control what we do right now.

And he does nothing when I run my tongue over his, tasting him. He explores my mouth just as hungrily.

Inside I'm building and I increase my speed to chase a release. His fingers dig harder into my hips, and I love how much he's enjoying this.

"Use me. Get yourself off," he rasps between kisses.

I rock faster and grind down harder.

"Oh, Damien." I moan.

"Leave a stain on my pants, baby. Let everyone know I'm yours. That's what you want, right?"

I clench at his words. My pussy is so hot, and I feel my lower back tingle.

"Yes. You're mine," I choke out.

"And you're mine," he says with such a deep, low voice, it sends me over the edge.

I shudder as the orgasm rips through me.

I collapse in his arms.

He catches me, and I suck in deep, heavy breaths. I soak in his spicy pear smell. It's comforting. His warm arms hold me and his scent relaxes me. I feel as if I could drift off to sleep. I was too excited to get much sleep last night, so I'm paying for it today.

One of his hands moves up over my back, where he rubs up and down in a soothing manner. He encourages me to stay right where I am.

His cock is still hard, and I make a note to help him as soon as I've recovered.

I just want to stay in the bliss of my post-orgasm state. Even though I can't believe I just dry-humped him like a teenager, but honestly, I'm not even sorry. He let me take charge and use him. And I know that's a big step for him. Control is something he likes; yet, he let me. No. He assisted me in controlling what I wanted.

That's why I know deep down we have something special. That's worth fighting for.

We stay like this for the entire drive. With me safely in his arms and the car in total silence.

The car stops, so I reluctantly pull away from his body and gaze into his soft brown hues. Something passes between us. I lean forward and peck his lips. "Thank you," I breathe.

"What are you thanking me for?" he asks.

"Being you."

We exit the car when we arrive at the airport. I hitch my handbag higher on my shoulder. As we walk in, he taps my tricep and I tilt my head to the side. He's waving his hand near mine. My pinched brows drop. He wants to hold my hand.

I try not to react too much on the outside, even though inside I'm dancing.

The walls are down now. We're away from home. This will show me exactly what he'd be like as a boyfriend. And maybe after this trip, I can convince him to be exactly that.

With our fingers interlocked, we waltz through security and to the gates.

"Let's grab snacks." I tug him along to the shop before the gate.

"You want snacks before boarding?" he asks, puzzled.

"Why do I get the feeling you've never had airport snacks?"

"Probably because I haven't."

"Ever?" I ask, mortified.

He shakes his head and says, "Nope. A couple of times when my flight got delayed, I grabbed a coffee, but that's it."

"Well, I'm about to blow your mind."

His brows rise. "With sugary, unhealthy snacks."

"Mm-hmm. Don't knock it till you've tried it." I playfully poke out my tongue and add, "The doctor cannot come along on this trip."

"We'll see about that. Lead the way."

My heart swells. The way he just allows me to choose what I want to do without a fight. I'm trying to wrap my head around why he's been single for so long. But then I remember his usual cold, quiet stance with others is to protect himself. With me, he doesn't hide away. I don't even think he's realized; it's just happened naturally.

I stand in front of the chips, grabbing a few Doritos and Pringles and then move to the chocolate and grab an Almond Joy and Reese's.

With snacks in toe, we move to the gate, and the first class is already boarding. Before I get to sit down on the black leather airport seat, he's pulling me. "We have to go board now."

"But that—" I trail off, my mouth wide open as I realize he's paid for us to fly first class.

"Seems I'm about to blow your mind." He smirks at my stunned reaction.

"My snacks seem stupid compared to this...this is too much, Damien," I mutter.

As we step onto the plane, the flight attendant offer refreshments and I take the champagne because I need something to kill the nerves.

"Nothing is too much for you. It's your birthday."

I look at him with a frown. "You've already given me a present." I touch my necklace as if he needed a reminder.

He sighs, and a tight expression sits on his face. "I left your night early and I hate that I hurt you."

"I-I..." I stumble, trying to talk.

What should I say?

His desire to make it up to me after hurting me makes me feel appreciated. However, this is way more than a simple apology and trust me, I'd have forgiven him with that.

I'm totally overwhelmed by this.

I peer around the space. There's so much leg room. My own TV and being waited on, this is seriously a pinch-me moment.

"Where are these snacks?" he asks, pulling me away from my first-class inspection.

"Ah. Here." I pull the bag up from the floor.

Once the plane's completely boarded, the pilot talks and mentions Santa Barbara. I knew it was warm but I didn't know the exact location.

"Are you kidding?" I whisper, turning to face Damien. His brow knits. "Never been?"

"No. But I've always wanted to," I admit.

"I can't wait to take you then," he replies, grabbing my hand in his and squeezing it.

"So you've been?" I ask.

"Yes, once with my family, but I've always wanted to come back with someone."

The way he says it with a gleam in his eye makes it obvious he means me.

Getting off the flight feeling refreshed is a novelty. I could get used to it. Once again, we're hand in hand and walking to get our bags.

It isn't long before we're ushered into a private car and on our way to our hotel.

But when the car pulls into this large house, I wonder exactly what we're doing. Lush landscape surrounds an old Victorian bed-and-breakfast. It gives me a warm and inviting feeling. Pure relaxation, and yet again, I'm surprised he's taken me here.

When we check in, it makes me feel like royalty. The service is unlike anything I've experienced. We're shown around privately, and I try to absorb everything that I'm seeing. Then they leave us alone to explore.

"Wow." I exhale. "This place is beautiful."

He kisses my temple. "We have this whole place to ourselves, so you can choose whichever room or cottage you want to sleep in."

"You rented this whole place?" I ask, perplexed.

I don't even know why I did because I know the answer before he says it.

"Yeah. I wanted us to spend time alone. I want to block out the noise for a while and just be with you. Spend time with you for a couple of days."

"You could have done that with one of the private rooms."

"No. I want you alone. I'm selfish." The deeper tone hinting at exactly where his mind was. It sends a shiver through my body, causing all the hairs to stand up on my body.

I try to ignore my body's reaction and focus on walking through the gardens. Admiring each cottage. First stop, we walk into a more traditional cottage room. Then an orange painted one, followed by one with crazy green and white patterned wallpaper. The last one is simple in fresh white paint. All the rooms have a king-sized bed and a fireplace.

I'm unsure which one to choose because of how unique they all are. I want to stay in them all. The last few are nice too, but the cottage that catches my eye has a traditional four-foot bath and a four-poster dark wooden bed.

"This one." I turn to him.

"It's nice. What part do you like most?" His voice is low and thick.

He likes this one too.

"Ah. The bath and the, um, the bed."

"Mmm," he mumbles as his hands grab my waist. He turns me around to face him. His eyes are darker. He dips his head and kisses me. I sink against him, feeling his hard muscles against the softness of my breasts. He grabs my ass in a hard squeeze, thrusting my hips into his large, hard erection. I moan into his mouth, reveling in the feel of him. My palms move from his chest to his cheeks, enjoying the roughness of his beard against my hand. Our tongues tangle in a hard kiss. He tastes of whiskey and peanut butter from the plane and it's delicious. I can't wait to have him in every way tonight. To taste him and have him deep in my mouth. I've not done it before and the thought of me bringing him to his knees at the sight of me on mine is a dream come true.

"Definitely this room. I can tie you up and fuck you hard before getting in that tub and soaking in it for hours with you in my arms."

"Oh, Damien," I rasp against his lips. That sounds like heaven.

My grip is tighter on him, and he edges me back to the bed.

"You'd like that, wouldn't you?"

"Yes," I choke out.

"The thought of you spread out on that bed, unable to move your arms and at my mercy, is so fucking hot."

"Oh God. Please, Damien," I beg. Not caring how desperate I sound. I want that now.

"Please what? Tell me what you want," he rasps.

"You," I beg.

"You have me."

"I want you to tie me up and fuck me," I admit.

"Fuck, those words leaving your mouth are sexy. And fuck. Get on that bed now!"

With a grin, I step back and obey his commands. I kneel on the bed in my sweats. I wonder if I should remove them or leave them.

"Good girl." He steps toward me.

I'm about to take my gray sweater off, but he shakes his head.

"Leave it on. I want to peel the clothes off you. It's like a present to me. Your body is mine." He grunts, all his control disappearing.

The sound of his phone ringing breaks our moment. He runs his hand through his hair. "Fuck," he spits, pulling his phone from his pocket. He checks the caller ID, his eyes softening, and then glances back at me with an apologetic face.

"I better grab this. Mom is trying to FaceTime. I have to take it."

I nod. "Of course. I'll have a quick shower."

But as soon as I slip off the bed and he turns to answer it in the small living room where the fireplace is, I can't help but admire his firm body. I'm all hot and bothered.

I smile as an idea hits me. His hands and mouth are busy, but mine aren't.

CHAPTER 28

MARIGOLD

"WHAT ARE YOU DOING with Samuel today?" he asks his mom.

She thinks he's away at a work conference and I told my family I was going away with Clara.

I amble closer. His brows pinch; he's probably worried I'm going to say hello, even though I know I'm still a secret. I don't dwell on that now. Right now, I want to control his pleasure. When I stand in front of him and unexpectedly drop to my knees, his eyes widen.

He braces his hand on the back of the large armchair in front of the fireplace. As if he needs the support.

I've taken him by surprise.

I'm about to see how controlled he can be.

I shuffle my knees closer on the cold wooden floor until my face is at eye level with his bulge.

Reaching out, I unbutton the top of his pants. I keep my innocent eyes on his hungry ones. I can see his breathing quicken, but he doesn't remove his eyes from me. My fingers push his pants and briefs down at the same time until they pool at his feet, leaving his big, hard dick exposed.

"O-Okay," he stumbles, trying to answer his mom. "The line's terrible. I gotta go. I'll phone you right back," he adds, throwing the phone to the side.

"Oh God," I mutter as I take in his muscular thighs covered in that same dark hair and make my way to his dick and stare at it. He's huge. I don't know how my hand will even wrap around him, let alone how much will fit in my mouth, but I'm going to try. I'm eager to try it. I flick my eyes up at him. His wide, dark brown eyes fix on me, and I can't help but lick my lips. I'm excited about doing this. The thrill is becoming too much to wait. I'm salivating.

He swallows and I watch the bob of his Adam's apple. "Fuck. You're eager to suck me, aren't you, Goldie?" He grunts.

His thumb reaches down to rub my lips roughly. I tip my head back and hum in response. My core aches. I'm savoring the way he looks at me with adoring eyes. As if he can't quite believe this is happening. Hell, I'm the one that's dreaming. I've wanted this for so long. And it's finally happening.

My lips part, and I open my mouth wide. He guides his thick cock to my mouth. But instead of pushing his dick inside, he traces my lips in a tease. My tongue darts out to try to catch him.

"Fuck." He chokes out as a drop of precum leaks and I lean forward, catching it. I swallow the unique salty taste.

Another hum leaves my chest.

"Those noises you're making are killing me. I need to fill your mouth and hear what sounds you make when your mouth is full of my cock." His voice is husky. It makes me desperate, to the point I'm almost feral with the need for him to come undone. To make his knees buckle and quiver as he comes just from my mouth.

He guides his dick into my mouth, and I wrap my lips eagerly around him. Loving his hot skin and more of his salty taste on my tongue. A hiss leaves his mouth. His cool composure is falling.

He likes it, and it encourages me to keep going. I twirl my tongue around the head of his cock and then suck hard, hollowing my cheeks. I'm moving my head slowly up and down his cock. Holding onto the base of his thick cock with one hand and gripping his ass with the other, I'm in control. A hand touches my hair and I peek up from under my lashes to see his heavy eyes watching me.

"Keep your eyes up. I want to see you."

I do. Not only because he tells me, but because of the way he's staring at me. I'm in control of him and I think he needs this. I need to take more control and he needs to give in. The perfect combination.

He's growing thicker in my mouth, so I try to take more of him. He thrusts his hips at the same time I take him down my throat. I'm loving the fact that he's really close right now. He fucks my mouth like an unhinged man.

I don't want this to end. His fingers curl in my hair, and I try to suck back, but he holds my head still. I flutter my lashes as I see him close his eyes and his dick jerks and hot cum spurts down my throat. I try to swallow as much as I can, but some leaks out of my mouth. He drops his tight grip from my hair, and he pets my head in a silent thank you.

"Better?" I ask.

He brushes his thumb over my lips and then cheek. "Yes. Thank you," he whispers hoarsely.

I sit back on my heels, my hands on my knees, staring up at him as he looks down in a daze.

He holds out his palm. I put my fingers in his and push up to my feet. My hands land on his solid chest. His heart beats wildly under my hand. I'm grateful I'm not the only one rattled by what just happened. It was better than I could have imagined. I feel powerful and unstoppable.

He presses his lips to mine. We kiss until I need air.

"You better call your mom back." I wink.

He looks down at his pants and briefs still around his ankle. "You're something else, you know that?"

"I'm yours," I say, biting the corner of my lip and strolling toward the bathroom. My jaw is aching in the best way. It's a reminder for me. I just gave him the best blow job I've ever given a man. I take a peek over my shoulder to find his eyes on me. A wash of disbelief and awe.

Inside the bathroom, I turn on the shower and shave and refresh my body. Then I step out, finding a robe, and slip the white fluffy warm robe on and walk out. He's on the phone walking around half-naked, so I go to the white-sheeted bed to enjoy the show. I'm probably going to pay for earlier, but the thrill of his punishment makes me wet.

A few minutes later, he's saying goodbye, and his eyes hold mine. He stalks over to the bed. I'm propped up on pillows with the soft sheets under me. My pulse speeds up with anticipation growing.

"Was that fun?" he asks with a voice still full of arousal.

"Yes," I breathe triumphantly.

"Did you enjoy sucking my cock?"

I nod. "So much."

He removes his shirt, tossing it to the floor.

He's standing completely naked. I was going to ask if he enjoyed it, but he beats me to it.

"That was the best fucking blowjob I've ever had," he says, climbing onto the bed and crawling to me. The way his biceps flex with each movement causes a whimper to leave my parted mouth.

"Really?" I say coyly, fluttering my lashes because I know full well he loved every second.

"Yeah, really. Watching you take me deep into that tight mouth and then eagerly suck me until I came down your throat was fucking hot." He looks at me with delight. "But I should punish you for trying to give me head while on the phone with my mother."

I drop back on the bed when he gets closer. "How?" I whisper. My brain went blank at what he could do to punish me because tying me up and fucking me are things I'm craving right now. There's no punishment in sex.

"How about I bring you so close to the edge of orgasm but then don't let you come?" he says, looking torn. His gaze drifts seductively down my body as if he doesn't know where to start. When his gaze holds mine, I lose my breath. There's so much desire and lust swimming in his eyes, but his words finally hit me. Sinking in.

What?

I gasp. "No!"

"But then that would punish me if I was to do that," he murmurs as he touches the tie holding my robe together.

"I want to feel you come apart from my cock being buried deep inside you."

He yanks at the tie hard until it comes apart and the robe opens. The middle of my body on display for him.

"You're naked," he mutters in fascination. His eyes drop hungrily over me. It makes me feel adored.

"I had a shower," I reply.

His finger touches my stomach, and I shiver from the rough pad of his finger. "Without me."

"Sorry, sir." I whimper.

My nipples tighten to hard desperate peaks. He trails his finger up to my mouth in a straight line, avoiding my begging nipples. He traces slowly down. I arch into his tender touch. He doesn't stop until he touches the top of my mound.

"Are you wet?" he asks in a gravelly tone.

I close my eyes briefly and nod. "Yes."

His gaze is dark and hot on my core while my gaze is on him. His fingers slide down over my swollen clit to my opening.

I moan.

"You're so wet for me, Goldie." He growls. "How am I so lucky? Is this all for me?"

His finger strokes over my clit in lazy circles. Slow at first, then circling a little faster.

"Yes. Damien." I pant.

"Damien?"

"Yes, sir."

He grunts. "Better."

My core muscles tighten in response. The heat between my legs is becoming an inferno with every slow stroke.

"Oh, God," I mumble, desperate for his thick fingers to enter me. And it's as if he can read my mind because he eases his fingers inside me. Moving them in and out slowly. I moan loudly. My walls tighten around his fingers, encouraging him to go deeper. He doesn't need help to find the spot. He knows exactly where it is. There's no need to introduce him to a woman's body. No, he reads my body so well. As if my pleasure means more to him than his own.

His fingers feel so good. I never want this to end.

"Yes," I breathe. "Just like that."

Our eyes meet and I swallow a moan at the mirroring sight. His gaze is full of arousal.

He adds another finger and more pressure to my clit at the same time. The pleasure building inside me is almost too much.

"Don't stop," I cry out.

"Never." He growls. "I'm going to make you come like this. And then again on my cock."

"Yes." I whimper loudly.

His thumb rubs at me harder as he keeps a solid pace. My core losing control and my orgasm pulsing through me in hard, delicious waves.

I blink, trying to focus on him under the post-orgasm haze.

He's breathing hard when his hand pulls on the robe. "I need to see all of you. Take this off."

I slip off the bed and drop the robe, then turn to face him. He's lying on the bed with an elbow propping his head up. "You're so beautiful. Come here."

As I do, my phone rings this time. For God's sake, will the phones stop ringing? I want to ignore it, but I need to see who it is before I turn the stupid thing off.

"Elijah," I say, showing Damien my phone with my brother's name flashing across the front.

"Answer it," he says with a sexy grin.

I don't have time to ask him what the looks for, otherwise, I'll miss the call.

"Hey!" I answer.

"How's your trip?" Elijah asks.

"I just arrived, but the place is—"

"Is what?" he pushes at the same time Damien picks me up.

"Breathtaking." My voice wavers from the nerves and excitement running through it.

"Where did you end up?" Elijah asks through the phone.

I stare down into the wicked brown eyes kneeling between my thighs, and I clear my throat to talk.

"Santa Barbara. I thought I told you," I lie. Since I did not know where, I kept it from him.

"You didn't, but it's a brilliant spot for a few days. How are you paying for this? I thought you weren't online anymore."

I squeeze my eyes shut. This trip and this moment are too precious to be ruined by my brother. "I'm not, but I'm about to have lunch. Can I talk to you after?"

He grumbles, clearly not happy with my answer, but I speak before he can. "Okay good. I'll call back soon. Bye."

I hang up and toss the phone. I'm met with Damien's dark eyes.

"The only person eating lunch is me," he says with a wide grin as he spreads my legs.

Suddenly, I'm shy about him going down on me. I've showered and shaved; yet, I feel nervous.

He leans into my pussy and inhales. "God, you smell incredible."

My heart is beating wildly in my chest. He kisses the top of my apex, and the sweet gesture is too much to bear. I close my eyes and tilt my head back.

"Don't be nervous. I'll look after you. Open your eyes as you watch me enjoy every inch of you."

I open my eyes and meet his head on. I ask the question playing havoc in my mind. "How did you know?"

"I'm good at reading people. You're not relaxed at all."

I suck in a deep breath, trying to calm my body down. "Guys don't like to do this."

The last time Damien went down, I didn't have time to stop and think. But today is different and I'm feeling vulnerable. My exes hated going down on me.

"I'm not all guys. And I fucking love it. You'll see. I'm already painfully hard from the smell and sight of your pussy. One taste and I'll have to hold myself from coming in my pants like a teenager."

My sex clenches and my fears trail off when I feel that first lick of his tongue on my pussy. And that one lick causes me to cry out with need. He continues to lick and fuck my pussy with his tongue, making these sweet grunting noises from the back of his throat.

"More," I beg, forgetting about everything other than how this feels.

"Your taste is addictive," he says, barely removing his mouth from me so it's muffled.

He circles my swollen clit with a swirl of his tongue, and I whimper.

"This is so good." I pant. He sucks on my clit hard, and I buck my hips. "Ah." My fingers slide through his brown hair, and I push his head to my pussy, not wanting him to stop. The building intensity in my lower body becomes unbearable. I buck my hips again when he circles his tongue, fucking me hard with it.

"Damien!" I cry out. My orgasm slams into me.

He doesn't stop devouring me until I'm completely spent. When I sink further into the mattress, I try to catch my breath. His body moves to lie beside me. One of his arms grabs my waist to hold me tight. We both lie there naked, totally exposed, yet closer than ever.

CHAPTER 29

DAMIEN

I LAY A KISS on her forehead, soaking in the scent of her shampoo. "I'm going to run a bath for us."

She moans in pleasure. I hold her in my arms, but struggle to let her go. I know I'm becoming addicted, and I don't see how this weekend will not have me craving her more.

I reluctantly pull away and walk toward the bathroom. I wonder if we'll venture out of this house in the next forty-eight hours or if we'll stay here ordering food in.

I wouldn't say no. The thought of waking up, fucking, eating, talking, and relaxing with her is the perfect break.

Come to think of it, when was the last proper break I had?

I have an annual vacation with Samuel during spring break, but one-on-one with an adult...with a woman. Never.

Now I want to plan another trip as soon as I get back home.

I switch on the faucet on the bath, then look around to find bath salts and rose petals. I put a scoop of the salts in the water, then sprinkle the roses around the bath.

The room is full of steam, and I walk back into the bedroom and pause. Marigold is lying naked on the bed. My gaze runs over her curves. The ones I touched recently and I'm currently obsessed over. She's stunning as always, but there's a sparkle in her eye that makes her a whole other level of incredible.

"Don't look at me like that. Bath first. Food and then sex," she mutters.

"How did you know?" I ask with a crooked grin.

She goes to sit up, but I move closer to the bed and scoop her up in my arms. I don't want her to walk.

Her arms come around my neck and gently hold on as I wander into the bathroom.

"The look in your eyes."

I remember I asked how she knew my mind was on sex.

"What look?" I ask.

"They dilate and the brown is almost black. Like you're—"

"Hungry," I finish her sentence. "I'm more than hungry. I'm famished."

Her breath hitches and I lower her into the white tub. She grabs the sides of the bath and looks up at me. I go to pull back when she speaks.

"Aren't you coming in?" she asks with a disappointed tone.

My lips twitch at her eagerness. I kiss her briefly. "I'll order us food and then I will. I wouldn't miss this for the world."

No. The way her body looks submerged in the water and her doe eyes look at me with a silent beg. I wouldn't miss one second.

Fuck. I need to feed her before I fuck her and God, I want to fuck her again.

"What do you want to eat?" I ask, squatting beside the tub. Leaning my arms on the side. My chin resting on my hands.

Her head drops back to lean against the white edge.

"Noodles or a burger," she replies after a minute. Her eyes try to suck me in, but I stay strong.

"Alright, let me see what I can do." I rise halfway and kiss her lips before walking out of the bathroom.

I find a noodle bar not too far away. "What noodles do you like?"

"I'm easy. Surprise me," she calls out.

I read the menu and find something with beef, and it sounds somewhat healthy, so I order that and a chicken dish, just in case she doesn't want beef.

"What did you want to drink?" I ask, moving to the bathroom. I find her totally relaxed in the bath with her eyes closed.

"Pepsi," she replies.

I screw up my face. "That stuff is bad for you. It's full of chemicals," I argue.

She tilts her head and opens one eye. "But it's also tasty," she says with a smile before closing her eyes again.

I order her a Pepsi and myself water.

"Dessert?"

"Is that a trick question? Of course, I want dessert."

I shake my head. "What artery-clogging item do you want?"

She shakes her head. "You need to live, Doctor Gray. You're way too serious."

I stay silent for a second before I lift my eyes to her soft facial features. Admiring how brutal honesty just rolls off her tongue.

I swallow hard because fuck, I know I'm set in my ways. Health is my life. But it's also stopping me from enjoying it too. And that's a tougher pill to swallow.

"That wasn't the question," I call back as I scan the menu.

"Fine. Give me ice cream or pudding. Yeah, yum, chocolate pudding." She moans.

I rub the side of my temple as I read over our list before I hit order and pay. It'll be here in thirty minutes. Plenty of time to bathe together and with those noises and sinful curves, I want to soak in our time together every spare second I can.

I put the phone away and then move closer to the tub.

"It says it'll be here in thirty."

A smile plays on her lips, and she shuffles in the bath. "Well, what are you waiting for?"

"Nothing. You've been a good girl. Patiently waiting. You deserve a reward."

I carefully get in behind her. There's not a lot of room for both of us when I lie down but having her on top of me was the plan, anyway. My fingers automatically grab her waist and lay her on me. Enjoying the way she fits perfectly in front of me.

"Are you always hard?" she asks, obviously feeling my semi on her back.

"I can't help it. You're naked in here and the soft touch of your skin against mine is too good. I want more."

"Well, we can fix that," she says as she tries to spin around. Her ass grinds along my cock. I swallow a growl and tighten my grip on her so she can't move. "No, let's stay here. You need to eat first." I say it out loud to remind myself that she needs food for energy.

"I am pretty hungry," she teases.

I chuckle. I know exactly where her mind is, but I need to care for her first. "I'll be happy to fuck your face after you eat. Which means you'll have plenty of energy for sex and you'll need it."

She twists her head and lifts her chin to look up at me as she drawls, "Oh, really?"

"Mm-hmm," I mumble, pulling her close again, not leaving any space between us. My hands fold over her waist. "Yes. All fucking night. But for now, let me hold you."

"I can't argue with that," she whispers, lying her head back on my chest. Her whole body relaxes on top of me. Our relaxed state causes me to close my eyes and rest. Something I do with her. From someone barely getting a full night's sleep to nodding off in a bath, who am I?

The buzz of my phone wakes me. Food's here.

"Let's get out and eat," I whisper into her ear.

"Mmm. I am getting wrinkly skin on my fingers from being in the water too long."

I release a deep laugh and whisper in her ear, "I love your wrinkly skin."

"I love your wrinkles too." I know she genuinely is speaking about the lines on my face. The fact she loves them soothes the worry I'm feeling about our age gap. The fact she knows we are so different, yet she still wants me, makes my chest swell.

She peels herself away and gets out of the bath, and I follow her.

We eat our late lunch in silence. Now we're both dressed in robes. I can't believe I'm wearing a white bathrobe. I've never worn one of these in all my hotels and holiday stays.

Yet here we are, matching each other like an old married couple. And that thought should send me running for the hills, but it doesn't.

"What did you want to do before dinner?" I ask when she's finished her bowl of noodles and Pepsi. As much as I'd love to lie around in here, I also want to check in and see what she wants to do.

This trip can't just be all about me.

Her comment about me living a little has been playing on my mind since she said it.

"Let's go for a walk. The gardens here look beautiful."

She tucks her legs up onto the chair and hugs her knees.

"Are you planning to garden?" I tease.

A light giggle leaves her. "No, but it would just be nice to go for a walk around here with you."

She gazes away from me, but I get out of my chair and grab her chin softly. I gaze into her soft eyes.

"I'd love to do that, but, also," I lean in to kiss her lips, thinking of a great idea, "did you want to watch the sunset?"

Her eyes flutter open, and she gives me a giddy smile. "That would be nice. I'll see if I can find a picnic blanket or something we can sit on."

I kiss her lips again as if it would never be enough. Then I step back. "I'll get changed and flick through the information booklet and see what trails I can find." I walk toward my bag to grab a change of clothes.

"No. Let's just walk and explore. No thought-out plan. Let's just see where we end up."

"I don't like that. What if we get lost?" I ask, horrified. This property is enormous, and we could easily get off track.

"What if we don't? You're so controlled and organized. Why don't we just relax here?" She sighs.

"We don't know this place. If we get disorientated..."

She quirks her eyebrow at me. "What? What are you gonna do?"

The humor in her face makes me laugh out loud.

"Nothing," I say as I walk over to her and kiss her again. "Nothing at all. I guess if I have you, I'm not lost, am I?"

"Exactly, Mr Cute. Let's go on an adventure." She beams.

"You realize I'm thirty-eight and not eight?" I tease.

"I'm well aware of how old you are. That's the difference between guys I've been with previously."

"I don't like thinking of you with other men. It pisses me off," I grumble, pulling her up into my arms and holding her tightly.

"We all have a past..." she adds.

"I'm well aware." Not wanting to talk negatively about my ex right now, I steer the question around. "What's the difference with me?"

"So much. I'll start with the fact you're generous, kind, thoughtful, and sexy. Oh, and you know your way around a woman's body. No need to tell you what I like. It's as if you can read my body better than I do."

"I love your body and the way it responds to me and my touch. It's addictive. Your body is beautiful. I can't get enough." The tone in my voice drops.

"Nah. Ah. Mr. Gray, we need to get ready to explore." She wags a finger at me and steps out of my reach.

I grumble. "I'll be happy to explore you."

"You're insatiable." She shakes her head as she spins to open the cupboards, and I turn around to get changed. I can't believe I'm about to go out there without a map.

We step out of the cottage and into the cool air. Wind gushes and she quickly zips up her jacket before I grab her hand.

"Which way?" I ask, taking in all the trees and flowers. A lot of it looks so alike, I try not to worry about getting astray and finding our way back in the darkness.

"This way. I want to see the flowers with the light we have left."

We amble through the garden, which is surprisingly fun. Seeing many flowers and trees I've never seen before. The way Marigold's face lights up with a flower that's unique makes me want to plant all of them in my yard. Her radiant face deserves to be there all the time.

"What would happen if your ex-wife wanted you back?" she asks in the dead silence of our walk, which takes me off guard.

I grind down on my teeth. The mention of Lucy irks me. But it's not Marigold's fault.

"No chance," I say through gritted teeth.

"For her or you?" she replies.

I stare out into the greenery, soaking in the peaceful place. The sounds of bugs and nature puts me at ease. Or is it her? Because isn't she always the thing that grounds me?

It's why I'm sneaking behind her brother's back. I know I'm doing something forbidden in his eyes and maybe everyone's eyes, but I can't help it. She draws me in with her whole being. I just want to stay close to her warmth. I'm pushing aside how fucked I'll be when Elijah finds out. But as I think about my ex and then Marigold, I see how vastly different they are.

"I begged her to not leave me...us," I exhale, unable to believe I'm spilling it all to her. "But she didn't choose us. She chose herself."

It's silent for a beat before she asks, "Did she cheat?"

"I don't know. Well, I should say not that I'm aware of."

She touches an orange rose. "Ouch." She winces, shaking her finger where a thorn has pricked her.

Immediately grabbing her hand, I turn it over, and blood is trickling. I suck her finger and then look at it in the crappy night sky. It looks okay, but I need to ask her to be sure. "Better?"

"Ah. Yeah," she breathes. "How do patients not hit on you?"

I chuckle. "Oh, they do, but I'm very firm about my no-dating rule."

"You've never dated a nurse or staff member?"

"No, remember I have an ex-wife..."

"Yes, but between her and now. You have needs," she adds, in a tone that's a little unsure.

I stop in front of her and lean forward, rubbing my thumb over her bottom lip. "I do. But you fulfill them perfectly."

She opens and closes her mouth. And I can see her struggle to form words.

"Why don't you believe me?"

"You're hot and a doctor. I just assumed."

"Wrong," I add.

There's a softness in her face and a lift in the corner of her mouth that tells me she enjoyed hearing that.

"Let's set up the blanket and look at the stars."

She scrunches her face up. "Why do I feel like there's something I'm not getting?"

I shake the blanket in a hidden spot that gives the best views of the garden and the sky. The moon is so bright tonight.

I move closer to her and run my finger over the zipper on her jacket. She sucks in a sharp breath.

Her eyes widen. "Here?"

"Yes. Here. I want to fuck you under the stars. So every time I look up, all I think about is you."

CHAPTER 30

MARIGOLD

I DON'T SPEAK. WORDS aren't forming. Only a sudden swelling in my chest from his words. I clutch his head in my hands and reach up on my tiptoes, smashing my lips and body to his. He grabs my ass with a firm squeeze and a deep grunt. His hard erection hits my stomach. In a frenzied mess, I run my hands down to push his sweater up. He breaks our kiss to help lift it over his head. I stare at his white shirt that fits tight over his muscled chest. I'm quick to remove that, too. He tosses it on the grass, and I soak in his familiar muscles. I reach out to touch him, enjoying the feeling of his hot skin on my hands. I make my way down to the top of his sweats. He grabs my hands and lays them on either side of my thighs.

"Let me peel these clothes off you. I want you naked on that blanket now."

His hands expertly remove my clothes in no time. Leaving me panting. There's something about the way his eyes watch me that makes my core ache.

"Lie down."

I don't hesitate, fearlessly lowering my naked body down. I want this more than I want my next breath. The cold blanket on my feverish body is a welcomed surprise. My nipples are tighter buds as I stare up at his broad frame hovering over me. His aftershave fills my nostrils with a familiar warmth. A promise that I'll remember this moment for a long time.

"Stunning," he rasps with a look of adoration. It's always something I've longed for, and I see it in his eyes whenever he looks at me. He lays a kiss on my neck. "You're so beautiful," he adds, kissing down to my chest.

He moves to kiss my nipple with an opened mouth and a sweep of his tongue. It's warm and wet with added pressure that has my back arching for more.

"Oh." I gasp, clenching my thighs together to ease the tension that's becoming borderline painful.

He moves his mouth to my stomach, continuing to lay hot kisses over my body. With the cool night air and the warmth of his breath, I shiver. When he drops to his knees and lays a trail of kisses from my stomach to the top of my mound, I moan from the intensity. My eyes never leaving his. Seeing his large frame between my legs is something I'll never get sick of looking at.

"You ready?"

I nod frantically. I want his mouth on me again, but I also just want to be fucked under the stars like he promised. But the slow way he's kissing me tells me he's not rushing tonight. Even though the thought drives me to the edge, I want him whatever way I can get him, because I know I'll love every second.

With a firm grip on my hands, he spreads my legs on the blanket. "Keep them open."

I don't answer. My words get lost when he pushes his sweats and briefs down and then off and I get to see his thick cock sitting hard and ready between his thighs. My fingers twitch to lean forward and grab him, but he crawls and hovers over me. His hands settle on either side of my head. I'm sitting with my legs wide open and he's kneeling between them.

Looking at his face and then between our bodies, I see how close his thick cock is to my opening. I rock my hips up, trying to get him inside me.

"You're eager tonight."

"I need you, Damien," I reply desperately. Unbothered, I'm doing so. My gaze returns to his lustful ones.

"Fuck. I need you too, Goldie, so fucking much."

"D—" but the words fall from my lips when he enters me.

The tight way he fits inside me steals my words.

"You're pussy fits over my cock so perfectly. Do you see how well we fit? Look at us," he commands.

I lift my head and look at where his cock enters me. And Christ, it is perfect.

"It's made for me. This pussy is mine to take as hard or as slow as I want."

"Yes. Don't stop," I breathe as I drop my head back down.

"Oh, Goldie, I don't plan to. I'm about to fill you so full of my cum that it will drip down your legs on our walk back."

"Yes-s," I stutter. His filthy words are everything I've wanted.

He wants me. This is not a one-sided relationship. The knowledge sends another flutter in my heart.

There's sweat forming on his brow as he thrusts his hips in and out in a deliciously slow rhythm.

He fills me all the way as deep as he can go and then pulls all the way out just so his tip is in. It's a lot and yet I need more.

"Harder," I cry out. I grab his shoulders and tilt my hips up as he enters me, trying to get more friction. He must read me because, on his next thrust, he slams into me. The tingle in my lower body lets me know I won't last much longer.

"Yes. Don't stop."

"This pussy is so greedy for me," he says with a grunt. Slamming even harder into me. Our skin slapping together is the only loud sound to be heard. It adds to my growing orgasm.

"I'm so close."

As the words leave my lips, the ripple of an intense orgasm slams into me. I cry out into the still air. My toes curl until the wave of climax eases. I sink back down into the blanket and watch his hard face turn to pleasure as his own orgasm takes over. I feel the jerk of his cock, knowing he's coming hard, and I enjoy every minute.

Afterward, he stays inside me, sucking in deep breaths of air as he stares at me, bewildered.

"Incredible," he says as if he's shocked it keeps getting better too.

"You're probably going to have to carry me back. I don't think I'll be able to walk."

He chuckles. "I like the sound of that. As long as I can fuck you again later?" he adds, licking his lips.

"You're serious?"

His eyes roam my body. "I'm already half hard again."

"Seriously?"

"Yeah. Your body is addictive. I can't get enough."

"I feel like a teenager."

He pulls out and aftershocks have me shuddering. I'm spent. "You're all woman to me."

He lays a kiss to my lips and then my temple before he lies beside me, and we hold each other. Our heavy breathing in sync, I stare at the stars and thank them for bringing him to me. I'll never look at the night sky without thinking of this special night.

Even if we're not boyfriend and girlfriend yet. Well, we can't be until we're not a secret anymore. Despite that, the way he shows me he cares is keeping me hanging on. Our connection is real. These moments are glimpses of what I know could be our life together. They are everything and yet more than I could have ever asked for.

A cold, wet droplet hits my face. It's raining.

"Are you ready to sit by the fire and study?" he asks as more rain sprinkles down on us.

I twist in his arms to face him. He pecks my lips.

"That sounds nice," I reply, picturing the evening snuggled up together, listening to the rain outside.

It sounds relaxing and carefree. So different from our lives at home.

He stands up and holds out his hand. I grab it and stand up. Ignoring the heavy, cold splashes hitting me. He grabs the blanket and folds it.

"I should've checked the weather," he complains.

"Why? It's nice feeling the rain on my skin."

He blinks, and a pinched look hits his face.

"What?" I ask.

"You're unlike any woman I've ever met. And in my line of work, I've met a lot."

"Don't remind me," I mumble as I peer down at the grass.

He lifts my chin to bring my eyes back to his. He strokes my cheek with his thumb in a reassuring way. "Don't be jealous. They don't hold a candle to you."

"Are you saying I don't need any work done?"

"Never. I wouldn't touch you. You're perfect the way you are."

"But I like the look of fake bo—"

"No," he cuts me off.

His free hand touches my breast and squeezes. I moan. The unexpected touch stirs me up again. "These are the right size and feel. I don't want plastic. I love how real you are."

"Are you just saying that to get into my pants?" I grin in the darkness.

He chuckles lightly. "I've already been in them tonight."

"True. You love your job, right?" I ask as the rain comes down harder on us, but we don't walk any faster. Instead, we keep the same pace.

"I do. I've always wanted to be a doctor and then I became fascinated with plastics."

"You've done nothing else?"

"No."

"You don't want to?"

He's quiet a second longer this time before answering. "No. And enough about me, it's your turn."

I bump my shoulder into his arm. "You never want to talk about yourself."

"I did for what felt like the last ten minutes."

"Fine. Ask away,' I reply.

"Have you thought about what you'll do after college?"

"You mean other than get a job," I tease.

"Cheeky."

I blow out a deep sigh. "I want to work with one of the top three firms in Chicago."

My voice lacks conviction, and of course, he doesn't miss a beat.

"But..."

I look down at the paved path as we stroll back to our cottage. I explain my fear. A fear I've told no one. Not even Clara.

"I don't know if I'm good enough."

"What makes you say that?"

A jerk on my arm spins me. He stopped walking.

I frown, not understanding.

He tugs on my hand, and I move closer to him.

"Tell me. Why don't you feel good enough?"

His brown eyes glow in the night. The warmth of his body radiates through me.

"I wasn't accepted for a scholarship, and I believe in signs. This feels like just maybe I should choose a different career path."

I bite down on my bottom lip nervously.

The gentle stroke of his finger around my neck pulls me closer and he whispers across my lips. "You're more than deserving. It's a business, remember? If you didn't qualify for a reason, it's because of their rules. They aren't signs; I promise. A sign. You want to know a fucking sign?"

I nod.

"You were on Mysterious Fan the night I joined. Of all the people I met, I met you. My ray of sweet golden sunshine."

I can't help but smile widely. "It was a scary coincidence."

"It was destiny, and I want you to never doubt yourself. I know what it's like to feel unworthy."

And before I can ask him why in the world he would ever feel unworthy of love, he brings my head closer to his to kiss him. He makes me forget my name. His kiss is so strong that the rawness of opening up pours through my lips. As the rain continues to pour down on us.

CHAPTER 31

DAMIEN

I WAKE TO THE shallow breathing of the brunette lying next to me. A soft curve lifts on my lips as her honey scent lingers. I snuggle her closer to me. My morning wood pressing into her side. I can't get enough of her; I seem to have a constant erection.

I wish we didn't have to leave today and go back to reality. But that's in fact what we have to do in the next two hours. Even as I lie here after a night full of sex, studying, and a sleep-in I never had. The thought of the amount of work that's piled up since being here makes me not want to return.

Rather than focus on the negative, I kiss her cheek and try to wake her gently. I want to soak in this time before we land back in Chicago and go back to barely seeing each other.

My fault. I know.

She's made it clear what she wants and that it's me who needs to pull the trigger and make us official and fuck the consequences. But the fear of losing my best friend is what's holding me back. I've been risking it ever since Marigold and I began hooking up. But telling Elijah, when I know he's already warned me away from her, is tougher than I thought.

I run my fingers over her delicate, warm skin. Starting from her hand to her shoulder in soft, lazy strokes. The purple on her fingernails is so soft and feminine...so her.

I drag my lips along her neck and onto her cheek where I lay a kiss on the side of her face and she rolls over. The morning sun glows on her. Like a spotlight. My Goldie.

She's not ready to wake up. I'm the eager one. She's flicked a switch in me and made me find extra energy. It's as if I'm twenty-five again. So, I slip out of bed, go to the bathroom, and then go search in the cupboards for breakfast.

Minutes later. I'm buttering toast when a warm body comes up behind me. Marigold's arms circle around my waist. My abs contract from the touch. Her head lies on my back as she cuddles me from behind. "Good morning," she mutters in a sexy morning whisper.

"Morning, how'd you sleep?"

"Mmm. Really well," she replies.

"Not too sore?" I ask eagerly, lowering the knife when I finish buttering.

Her head lifts from my back and her arms drop. "Tender, but not sore. Did you make this for me?"

I twist to face her. She scans the tea and toast before glancing back at me with wide eyes.

"I fucked it up, didn't I? I was supposed to dip the tea bag in and throw it out. Stupid Google said either that or leave the tea bag in. I left it in." I run a hand through my hair, frustrated.

"No, I'm shocked because you made me tea." She smiles, stepping in to hug me. "And you haven't complained that it's not coffee and how I should be drinking that."

"There's still time," I joke, as I wrap my arms around her and kiss the top of her head.

She tips her head back to look up at me. "But no, this is great. I love my tea strong. Thank you."

I kiss her lips in a slow I-can't-get-enough-of-you kiss. "Anything for you."

She opens her mouth but then closes it.

It's been a long time since I waited on a woman, but for her, I'd do it every day. I'd do anything to make Marigold happy. I make coffee as she lifts the cup to her mouth and blows on the steam.

My phone rings and it's Mom, so I know it'll be Samuel. I miss him. I know this break is good for me because I haven't had one since Lucy left. Any time my mom has cared for him, it's been for work. Never for pleasure. And here I am, away for pleasure. I try not to drown in the guilt because if I do, I'll close back up on Marigold and jump back on the plane. I need to remember taking time away will make me happier and a better parent. He can spend some special time with his nana, making memories he'll treasure forever. I swallow the lump of guilt and answer the call. I take the brown chair in the lounge room and talk to them for a few minutes.

After I get off the phone, I see we have two hours before our car comes to take us to the airport. I walk into the kitchen but find it empty. The dirty tea cup and empty plate are making me twitch. I should clean it.

"Goldie?" I call out.

"In here waiting."

I frown. Waiting? For what?

I step into the bedroom and fuck. She's standing at the foot of the bed waiting for me. She's wearing the same outfit I saw her online in. My favorite one. The gold lingerie that made my mouth water and is again. I don't miss the gem she's holding. The same one I saw on that video.

She bites her bottom lip. "You're staring."

"Goldie. Fuck, you're so beautiful," I say as a groan slips out. I can't believe she's so giving to me. Am I worthy of her and how perfect she is? I can try. Fuck, I can try right now.

"Yeah?"

"Mmm, so sexy. And I saw you brought the plug. Do you want to play?" I ask hoarsely.

She nods with a wicked smile.

"Have you used a plug before?"

She shakes her head softly. I don't miss the way she flushes up her neck and onto her cheeks. Her brown hair flows messily over her shoulders with the movement.

"Lets warm you up first then. I don't want to hurt you." Those words ring true in so many ways.

"I brought lube." Her teeth catch on her pillowy bottom lip. The way she wants to try this new thing with me is hot. She trusts me. What is strange about that is...I trust her too. I haven't trusted a woman in forever. But with Goldie, I openly trust her, and it doesn't even scare me.

I smile. "Good girl. But come here." I curl my finger in.

She takes a step.

"No. Stop." I hold up my hand, still wearing a wicked smile. "On your hands and knees. Crawl to me."

Her face transforms and her lips part. She's eager and I bet already fucking dripping wet.

I'm hard as stone watching her move slowly, purposefully, licking those pouty pink lips.

"Fuck. Goldie. You're so sexy. You like this, don't you?"

She nods slowly.

"Yes, sir." She pants.

My cock jerks and I'm already leaking. "Jesus Christ," I mumble under my breath. She's going to be the death of me. And if I'm not careful, I'll be coming way too fast and I don't want to. I want to enjoy fucking her with the plug deep inside her. Even the thought is driving me wild. I'm going to come so hard inside her.

She stops at my feet and sits back on her heels. Looking up at me with heavy, longing eyes.

"Are you wet?"

"Yes-s," she stammers.

"Show me," I say in a controlled voice, even though I'm shaking from holding myself back. I'm not touching her until she begs.

"Slip your fingers into that thong and show me how wet you are." My eyes lock onto hers. My fingers twitching to touch her. But I can't. Not yet.

She follows the command, and her slickness covers her fingers.

I suck in a sharp breath.

Fucking hell.

"Taste it. Tell me how sweet you are."

She doesn't hesitate; instead, she keeps her eyes on me and her wet, pink tongue slips out and she licks at her wetness. Her eyelashes flutter, and she moans. "Mmm."

I'm throbbing with need. But she has to come at least once first.

"Do you taste good?"

"Hmm-mm, so sweet."

I lose it. "Don't tease me."

Her eyes open wide, and she gives me a look. "Sir, do you want a taste?" she purrs as her hand lifts toward me.

I don't want just a taste; I want to devour her.

She knows exactly what she's doing, but I'm in charge today. I want her to have all the pleasure.

"Soon. First, I want you to get on that bed, spread your legs and fuck yourself with two fingers until you come all over your hand."

Her brows pull together. "What will you do?"

"Watch."

She hesitates, wondering if she can walk or if she has to crawl.

"You can walk," I say and hold out a hand, which she takes and then walks to the bed.

"Do you want my thong off?"

"Yes," I answer in a low growl. I stand at the end of the bed perfectly between her spread thighs and Goddamn. Her beautiful pink glistening center is too much.

"You're soaked."

"I'm horny," she breathes, biting down on her bottom lip as her hands slide over her stomach and slip through her wet pussy. She circles her clit with her two fingers and moans.

This is torture. I want to fuck her already. My eyes are locked on her slow and controlled movements. It's hypnotizing.

"Are you hard?"

"So hard, Goldie, it hurts," I answer honestly.

"Let me help you." She begs in that seductive tone. Killing me more.

I shake my head. "No. Fuck your fingers now."

And she does. She slips two fingers deep inside her pussy and I lose my breath. She fucks them slow at first and then she picks up the pace to where her toes curl, her neck on display, because she tipped her head all the way back. I know she's close.

She continues pumping until the words, *I'm coming*, fall from her lips.

My heart is hammering inside my chest. "Good girl. Come for me."

"Ahhh." Her body shudders in shock waves as she comes hard.

I move and then crawl until I'm hovering over her, breathing hard and fast. "Incredible."

"Now roll over. Let me warm your other hole up."

"Oh," she flips over eagerly.

I unclasp her bra and skim my hand over her back down the dip just above her butt. Her skin erupts in goosebumps.

I touch her full ass and smack it gently. She moans. I love how fucking responsive she is to me. Both my words and touch make her putty in my hands.

I enter her pussy with two fingers.

"Ah, Damien. Yes."

She's so fucking wet.

"Is this mess all for me?" I ask hoarsely.

"Yes," she pants.

I move my fingers and when she tightens her walls against them and her breathing picks up, I slide her wetness up over her tight hole.

I press a single finger inside and she cries out. In a feral way. A mix of a moan and pain. Her puckered hole so hungry for me.

"Are you okay?" I ask, holding back how hot this is making me.

"Yes. Don't stop." She whimpers.

I'm going to come apart inside her when it's my turn. I can't wait.

"I can't wait for your ass to take the plug."

"Yes-s," she stammers again.

"I'm going to stretch you first. You like this, don't you?"

She nods.

I move my finger in and out. When she takes it easily, I ease a second one in. She moans more. "Do you like the way this feels?"

"Yes. So much."

I move my fingers in a rhythm that has her wriggling and writhing in pleasure.

"Fuck!" My dick jerks just from watching how much she loves this. I love this.

She's ready...

"Where's the plug and lube?"

"In my bag."

I remove my finger and she groans.

I smirk. "I'll be back."

"I got the smallest one," she answers in a hurry.

"Goldie, relax, I won't be long. You need the lube, even if it's the smallest size."

She exhales and slumps down as I quickly grab the plug off the floor and the lube from her bag.

I climb back on the bed and open the lube and squeeze a generous amount down her crease. She squirms from the coldness.

I return my finger and rub the puckered hole for a second. She writhes and tries to encourage me to enter her. I do and she moans loudly. "Damien, fuck."

"So good." I encourage her as I pick up the pace and continue to press around the edges. When she feels stretched enough, I work to insert the metal plug.

"Are you ready?" I ask, even though I know the answer.

"Yes!"

I add more lube and slip my finger out and grab the toy, rubbing the tip over her hole. She rocks her hips back. And I dip it slightly inside. "Oh, that's tight."

"Tight but good?"

"Yes." She breathes.

I push more inside and she takes a deep breath and then I push the rest in. She groans and grips the bed sheets tightly. "You should see how beautiful it looks."

"Mmm." She rocks.

She's so fucking beautiful I can't hold back anymore. I need to fuck her. Fill her.

"Roll onto your back." I grunt.

She does and cute noises leave her mouth, and I know it's because the plug hits differently when she moves around.

I settle my hands next to her head. The sunlight beams on us through the window. She's beautiful all lit up.

My cock jerks, knowing it's so close to fucking her tight, wet cunt. "I'm going to fuck you now."

She nods frantically. "Okay."

I sink my hips and enter her tight hole.

The gem in her ass is making me crazy, and I have to control the urge not to fuck her hard.

I thrust, and when I hit all the way in, she cries out.

"I'm not going to last long. You feel too good and those fucking sounds are making me crazy."

She has the nerve to side-eye me and I cock a brow.

"Are you challenging me to fuck you hard? Because I wouldn't tempt me."

"Give it to me hard, sir." And the way she says sir is like she's playing me and she's so fucking hot.

"You are going to be the death of me," I say as I slam into her hard and only my name leaves her lips.

I pull back and thrust inside her again. The tightness is torture but the best fucking kind. I continue to thrust repeatedly. Picking up my pace, I feel her walls clamp down before she spills her next words.

"I'm going to come." She moans.

I thrust a little harder now. When I feel that she's stretched and on edge, I reach around and gently wiggle it in and out. Before removing it, she cries in pleasure as she violently shudders from an orgasm. Unable to hold back any longer, I come hard. Emptying myself inside her. I watch her flushed face gasping for air. I'm breathless too. That was the most intense fuck of my life. The best fuck of my entire life. Nothing and no one will compare. She's ruined me.

When I somewhat recover, I pull gently out and collapse beside her and hold her to me. When I find my breath again, I get up and carry her to the bathroom.

"What are you doing? I can walk."

"No, I'll carry you. We need to shower before our ride gets here," I answer as I turn on the shower. We stand under it for a lot longer than we should, but both of us are still coming down from the peaks of our orgasms.

We quietly shower, pack our bags, and get inside the taxi then onto the plane.

Both of us are quiet, deep in thought. I keep my hand in hers and watch as she's engrossed in a movie. I reflect on our weekend and it makes me realize something about her.

The fact is, truthfully, she scares me. I worry Marigold could choose herself too just like my ex-wife did because, why not?

My life is in a different stage to hers, but I have to remember she's not my ex and she has only shown me how much she wants me and a relationship.

She chose us.

Me and Samuel.

I need to choose her and face the consequences that will come my way from this decision. But she deserves all of me.

No more secrets. No more hiding.

CHAPTER 32

DAMIEN

SHE UNBUCKLES HER SEAT belt, but I reach out to stop her. I'm not ready for her to leave. My hand on hers has her brows pulling together.

"What are you doing?" she asks, threading her fingers in mine.

My gaze looks down at our joined hands. Admiring how small and perfect her hands fit in mine.

"I don't want to end our weekend yet." My voice cracks, giving away how sad I am to have this end.

Her exhale and soft expression make me think she was wishing this wasn't ending either.

But it is and there's nothing either of us can do.

Her lips part, but I speak first, wanting to turn this sad talk around.

"And I know a five-year-old who keeps asking for you to come over."

Her face brightens at the mention of Samuel. "We can't have him upset, can we?"

This weekend would have cost her a lot of important study time. She tried doing it on the plane rides and once at the cottage, but as a past student, I know it's not enough. I see her tired, puffy eyes and I would hate to think she'll be up all night studying tonight because of me. I can't be selfish. So as much as it pains me, I think even though I want her to come to my place now, I need to look after her.

I sigh heavily. "No. But I know you need to study. You didn't get a lot done the last two days."

She smirks. "We were busy. And I needed a break."

My mouth tips up at her insinuation. "We did. But I know this is a big year for you."

She nods, unable to disagree with me.

"I have an interview with Lincoln LLP firm," she announces, straightening up in her seat.

"Congratulations. Where is it?"

She hesitates, nibbling on her lip, and I'm not looking forward to what she'll say based on her body language.

"New York."

I swallow the disappointment I feel and think about how important this is for her. "Which division?"

"I chose criminal."

"How long will you be gone for?"

She swallows and glances down at our hands again before meeting my gaze. "Eight to ten weeks."

That feels like a kick in the gut. The thought of not having her around is unbearable. "How will I live not having you with me?" I blurt, moving my other hand to the back of her head to bring her face closer to mine.

"Lucky, we have phones," she breathes.

I groan and tip my head back. The woman who was made for me thinks I will be fine without her. I don't think she understands how much she means to me. "It's not the same. Now that I've had you, going online for that long won't be the same."

"I know but it won't be forever."

"What if they offer you a full-time job?" I ask in disbelief. She wouldn't be able to turn down a good offer. And I couldn't let her give up her life for me. I don't want to hold her back, even if it kills me.

She shakes her head. "I won't take it. I'll find a job here."

The way she says it makes me believe her. But it doesn't sit right. "Don't give up your dreams for me."

"I'll get a job here. I won't give up my dreams, but I won't give you up either." She reaches up and touches my cheek with her palm. Her thumb dusts along in a soft, reassuring way.

My heart pounds harder in my chest. "You make it hard to fight."

"It's why I'll make a good lawyer."

I chuckle before I turn serious. "You will. You'll be unstoppable."

She smiles bashfully at the compliment.

I move my face closer to hers to lay a kiss on the tip of her button nose, where it's flushed. "Will you come to my place after you unpack and study?"

She tugs her lip into her mouth as if contemplating something. "What if I promise to study for an hour before I come?"

I gaze into her bright eyes and she looks so happy. "How can I say no?"

"You can't."

I lay my forehead on hers. I'm not ready for her to leave the car, but I have to let her go. And the quicker she gets into the house, the quicker she'll be back in my arms.

"Go and I will see you soon," I whisper sadly.

We kiss one last time and she slips out and enters the house, but not before looking into the car as if she knows I'm watching her. After she's fully inside, I tell my driver to take me home.

As much as I'm disappointed to let her go, I'm excited to see Samuel. I've missed him. I can't wait to hug and kiss him.

And it always makes me wonder how Lucy just left and never missed him.

But just as I'm confused, it quickly changes to anger.

Samuel deserves a woman who wants him and loves him. And Marigold does.

I can't wait to get home and tell him she's coming over.

As soon as the driver parks, I'm out of the car striding to the door to look for my son.

There's clashing in the kitchen, so I can bet my mom is cooking or cleaning.

"Hey, Mom," I say, finding her putting dishes away.

"Son. How was your trip?"

"Good. Where's Samuel?"

"In his playroom. We just finished lunch. Did you want me to make you something?"

"No, I've eaten. Thanks for looking after him."

"I'll let you go and spend time with Samuel. He missed you."

I know she doesn't mean to say that to make me feel guilty. But it does. Will I ever be able to do something for myself without drowning in self-disgust?

"Thanks." I kiss her cheek and head toward the playroom.

I step into the doorway, and I can finally breathe.

"Hey!" I say, moving closer to him.

Samuel's head tips up and a huge smile erupts on his face.

"Dad!" he replies, dropping the Legos he was holding as he stands.

I squat and open my arms wide in time for him to jump into them.

I clutch him close and stand.

"I've missed you. Did you have a good time with Nana?"

"Yeah. Can I go play now?"

"Yes. I'll shower and then I have a surprise for you." I lower him down. But he doesn't walk away from me to sit back with his Legos.

"What surprise?"

I hand him a souvenir, it's a puzzle of Santa Barbara. "This is one. But there's also someone you've been asking to see."

Samuel's brows lift. "Mari!" he yells.

I can't help the grin that forms on my face. Yeah, I'm definitely not the only one smitten with her.

I shower and turn the TV on in the living room. I've put on a movie for Samuel and me.

Samuel said he didn't feel well when I got out of the shower. I checked his temperature, and he had a fever, so I gave him some Tylenol and told him to rest.

The door sounds and Samuel's little head tries to lift, but he struggles. I slip out from under him.

"Let me open the door for her and she can come here and watch the movie with us."

His head moves up and down slowly, but he doesn't speak. This isn't him.

I stride to the door. I open the door and find her in jeans and a sweater. Fucking adorable.

"What's wrong?"

I tried to muster up a grin for her but I feel pretty grim, so I guess I look like it. I hate it when Samuel's sick. I want to make it better for him.

"Samuel's sick. Fever and just not himself."

"Do you want me to go?"

"No," I reply quickly. "He wants you. You should've seen when I got home and told him you were coming over. I'm pretty sure he's more excited to see you than he was to see me."

She steps in and I grab her waist and yank her to me. I need a kiss from her. Even though I had so much of her mouth and body already, it's just never enough. I can't get my fill of her. All day and night with her is still not enough.

We separate and I take her hand and lead her to the living room where Samuel is resting.

He shifts on the sofa. "Mari."

"Hey, Sammy, your dad says you're not feeling well." She moves closer to him and squats beside the sofa.

His hand reaches out from under the blanket, and he wraps an arm around her neck.

My chest feels like it could burst. She puts an arm around him and rubs his upper back so softly.

"Do you want some back tickles?"

He nods.

She moves to sit beside his head, where she puts the pillow on her lap, and he lays his head down. Her purple nails going on his back.

I take a seat at Samuel's feet, momentarily rebuffed.

My mind is a jumbled mess of emotions and thoughts. I try so hard to focus on the car movie, but I zone out. Samuel sleeps and I expect him to wake up better, but just before the movie ends, he wakes up and vomits all over the rug.

Marigold gets up and I grab Samuel and take him to clean him up. But he wants to vomit again. Marigold asks where the bucket is and gets it.

He's sick again and then I go about cleaning him up and getting him fresh clothes.

This time, I take him to his bed. He snuggles in and falls asleep.

I go to clean the bucket, but she's already washed it.

When I move to deal with the living room, I find her on her hands and knees cleaning the carpet.

I stare at her for a moment before I join her. I've never had help. My mother, yes. A partner, no. And Marigold doesn't seem bothered by tonight. It's not sexy at all. Yet this is why she's so different. I don't have to tell her what to do. We're a team. I've not been a part of a fucking team in a long time. I shake my head because if I think about it, tears will form and I'm not crying about it. Even if they're happy tears.

After we clean up, I go to the kitchen to make her tea.

It's the least I can do.

Her hands circle my waist.

"Thanks for your help. You know I don't expect it."

"I know. But I want to. I want this."

I turn in her arms, and our faces are close. I'm lost in her eyes when footsteps sound and I'm too late when it dawns on me. Fuck. It's a Sunday afternoon. I got so caught up with Samuel, it slipped my mind. Here I am, standing in the middle of my kitchen, embracing Marigold with my hand on the top of her sexy ass. Her hands hold my head close to hers. I'm too late and I stare at my best friend Elijah's disappointed gaze.

CHAPTER 33

MARIGOLD

ELIJAH STRIDES TOWARD US. Damien drops his arms from me instantly. My brother doesn't miss it though, and he scowls harder. He flicks his narrowed gaze between our hands and our faces.

He knows.

Elijah reaches us head-on. He marches straight up into Damien's face. I can practically see steam coming from his ears. He grabs onto Damien's shoulder, and I gasp, thinking he's about to hit Damien. "What the fuck? I thought I made it clear I didn't want you with her."

"Elijah, stop," I interrupt with a desperate plea.

He drops his hands from Damien's shoulder. My brother's upset gaze is fixed on me now. "No. I'm mad at you, too. Damien was hurt by his ex and he needs time to heal." He squeezes the back of his neck. "And fuck, are you really ready to take on someone else's kid?"

I wince. His words slice my heart layer by layer.

But it not only hurts, it also angers me. Something I've never felt. And it lights a fire in my belly. "That's not your business. I'm happy. We're seeing each other."

"Like fuck you are," Elijah spits back, cutting me off from further talking.

I see red. My eyes narrow at him and there's so much tension inside of me that my words come out in a snarl. "I'm an intelligent woman who can make her own damn choices!"

Elijah snorts. "Seems to me you can't. Acting like a child. Going behind my back when I said focus on school and let him focus on healing."

I grind down hard on my teeth. Thinking about my next words carefully.

"You need to accept our decision. You have Jackie. And remember she's younger," I argue. I try to get him to see he's happy, so why can't he let us be? Stay out of my business. I know he loves me and it's fair to be shocked, but he's the one acting like a child.

He wipes roughly over his face and whisper-shouts, "I was there when Lucy left him. She ripped his and Samuel's fucking hearts out."

Elijah's eyes flick between mine and Damien's. "You two had a nice little vacation together, didn't you?"

"We did until now," I snap.

He ignores me, of course. "It's all a lie, you get that? Holidays are a fake sense of happiness. Reality is you're in college and he's a workaholic dad."

"I'm well aware, Eli," I sneer. He acts like I haven't given this much thought. I can't help the way I feel about Damien. My heart wants what it wants. And I want Damien.

"Fuck!" Elijah yells and his hands curl into fists.

"Eli," Damien warns.

Elijah's hard gaze whips back to Damien.

"We need to talk. Alone," Elijah demands coldly.

I've never heard him speak to a friend this way. Damien's eyes hold mine and they turn from cold and detached to fury before they flick to Elijah's. "Okay. But first, Elijah, don't fucking speak to your sister like that. Angry or not. She doesn't deserve it. She's done nothing wrong."

Elijah's jaw is twitching. He knows it's true, but he's upset I betrayed him. I didn't listen and give Damien space to heal. I won't get a sorry from him right now. He's enraged. He needs to calm down and realize that Damien and I are adults, and this is our choice. I get he cares for both of us. But fuck, let us work it out.

I run my hand through my hair. My magical weekend is now ruined. This is not the end. "I'm not going anywhere. This involves me and I'm not—"

"Listen to your brother." Damien's voice cuts through and silences me.

My mouth opens and I go to talk, but it feels like razor blades. I swallow the pain and use my firm voice. "You have five minutes and then I want to talk to Damien." I'm proud of myself at how controlled I sound, even though inside I'm shaking. I'm on the verge of crying. I concentrate on breathing in through my nose and out through my mouth as Damien glances away.

Neither of them answers. Elijah turns and grips Damien's arm and pulls him to the side.

I standalone in the kitchen. My body is shaking with a mix of hurt and anger.

I pull out my phone from my bag and text Clara. I ask if she's busy tonight because I might need to come over. She asks why, but I see movement and the boys are walking back, so I tuck my phone into my pocket. Elijah's face still looks angry as they stand in front of me. I turn my face to Damien, who looks at me with pity-filled eyes.

No...

I grab Damien's arm, ignoring the way his hot skin feels in my hand. The tingles won't help the turmoil I'm feeling. Only his words tell me he's still with me. We're still an *us*.

When we're out of Elijah's earshot, I look away from the asshole who's going to watch us with angry eyes.

I grip the necklace he gave me. As much as I love it and its meaning. If I'm his Goldie, he needs to choose me.

"What's going on?" I ask in a hushed voice.

He looks at me with sad eyes, but I don't like the way he's not touching me. With his hands in his pockets, he keeps avoiding my gaze. The body language is closed off and I'm scared.

Scared my world is falling apart right now.

"Your brother is right. I'm carrying trauma with me. I'll hold you back in life. There's no way for me to answer him with one hundred percent certainty whether I want to have kids or get married again. And as he reminded me, that's totally unfair to you." His voice is so quiet and detached. As if he's already decided.

"I feel like you're punishing me for your ex," I grit out.

My heart is breaking. He's making all these assumptions without talking to me. We never spoke about marriage and kids because we only just started seeing each other. And now he's already shutting me out.

"Your brother, he's important," he says. As if I don't know. He doesn't have many friends and my brother was there for him. I get it. I really fucking do, but Elijah will get over it. I won't. I'm sick of people hurting me and never speaking up. Not today. Today he's getting my honesty.

"And I'm not?" My voice is loud and shaking. The amount of adrenaline pumping through me is like a million shots of coffee. I'm so fucking angry.

"You know you are. I just need time to think...to heal...like Elijah said."

"Fuck my brother. If he can't get on board with our relationship, then that's his problem. But let's get real, Damien. Deep down you haven't completely let me in."

I'm sick of being the girl that gets hurt. I'm so fucking done with falling, only for the other to not fall too.

I want to be loved wholeheartedly in return. Hell, I deserve it.

He brings a hand up to the back of his neck, squeezing it. "I've given you more than I've ever given a woman before. I've known your brother for years and I'm struggling with...I'm fucking broken. No matter how much I want you."

"You're not. You just have to let go of the past and open your heart to love. For a future. Saying you want me and doing it are two different things."

He drops his head, and his hand returns to his pocket. Silence. That's all I get back.

No, I'm so fucking done.

"I choose me," I snap and storm off, ignoring my brother calling out my name in his stupid, authoritative voice.

I grab my phone and unlock it. Through blurry vision, I scroll to find Clara's name and call her. As soon as she picks up, I choke on a sob.

"I'm coming over," I cry.

"Of course. See you soon."

I hang up without another word, swipe the fat drops of tears that are rolling down my cheeks away and get in my car. Not once do I bother looking back to see if either of the guys has followed because a part of me knows they didn't, and I cry harder.

"What a dick!" Clara interjects. "And your brother is an asshole."

"Yep and yep," I say in a raspy voice. The sobbing has changed the sound of my voice.

I cried my heart out on the way to Clara's; I barely remember the drive except for how shaky my body was.

"I seriously can't believe he said nothing." She made us tea, but instead of sitting in her dining area, we're sitting in her room in case her roommates come home. I'm not in the mood to see anyone.

I sip my tea. Grateful for the warm liquid soothing my dry throat.

"And I warned him," she mumbles.

My brows pinch together. "You did what?"

"On your birthday, I told him to not hurt you."

I reach over and squeeze her hand. "Thanks for looking after me."

"Anytime. I'm sorry. I should have told him to break it off with you."

I shake my head. "No. Our weekend was so special I never want to forget it."

"Yeah?"

Memories of the weekend flood my mind. The chats, sex, and sweet moments. "He even made me tea. He looked up on Google how to make it and thought he screwed it up. It was cute," I say with a sigh, but it doesn't help my heavy heart when I think of how blissfully happy we were.

Clara crosses her arms. "It's cute, but I'm still angry."

My lip twitches, but even with her kindness, I can't smile.

Clara continues to stare at me.

I don't know what else to say. My soul feels shattered.

I blow on my tea and take a sip.

"I've never seen you look so sad," Clara whispers.

I try to put a smile on my face, but it's fake.

"I'll be okay," I say, as if to convince myself as well as her.

"I need to find a job. Because keeping myself busy will do the trick."

She takes a big sip of tea. "Distractions work well. Are you thinking about going back online?"

I shake my head. "No."

God no. I couldn't think of anything worse. All the good memories we shared are there and I'll end up a blubbering mess, rehashing them.

"Do you need help with looking?"

I sigh. "Not yet. I'll see what I can find in law, maybe a secretary? I don't really know. I can't think properly, but something fresh."

She nods. "New is good."

I leave Clara's house after we watch a trashy old movie, which I can't even remember the name of. As soon as I get home, I strip for a nice shower. The necklace he bought me shines under my bathroom light. I stare at myself wearing it in the mirror and fresh tears fill my eyes. I touch the metal and tears fall as I take off the necklace. And with trembling hands, I put it away in a drawer.

Out of sight, out of mind.

Just not out of my heart.

CHAPTER 34

DAMIEN

I WAKE UP IN a cold sweat. Sitting up in my bed, frantically looking around. I'm gasping for air. I rub my face when I realize I was dreaming.

I'm back to barely sleeping because every time I try to sleep, I have a fucking nightmare.

I feel like I'm drowning. I need her air like I need to get to the water's surface. This longing for Marigold is an out-of-body experience.

I can't blame her for wanting more than what I was giving her. What kind of man doesn't stand his ground and fight for her?

Me. I didn't.

I let her down. And every day it's been eating away at me.

I'm a big fucking coward. Who doesn't deserve her.

She never once made me feel unworthy, yet I made her feel that way. I know what that pain feels like. And it fucking sucks.

Elijah hasn't spoken to me since telling me to stay away from his sister. He left me standing in my kitchen.

It's been a few days since I saw her last, and I'm back at home with a now healthy Samuel and work.

Like, before...

Before she came into my life.

I've finished writing notes for a patient I discharged this morning. Leaving my office, I head to the theater changing rooms. I've got a case with Doctor Alex Taylor.

"Here's the man," Alex booms as he walks in and I'm putting my scrub top on.

"Hi," I reply.

Definitely not in a cheerful mood because now I have to confess what a shitshow my life is.

"And you come back quieter and grumpier than ever. What happened?" he asks, changing into his pair of navy scrubs.

"It just didn't work out," I mumble. He doesn't know who she is or any of the finer details.

"Bummer. But hey, plenty more fish in the sea," he says with a shrug and a cocky smile.

I shake my head in disbelief. Women weren't in my plan. However, Marigold was different and there'll be no one like her. I want to throw myself into work and forget about the heaviness in my chest.

"I'll see you at the sink," I say as I leave the room and find my way to the waiting patient. I introduce myself to the young woman with a benign tumor that Alex will remove. I will close it up, so she doesn't have a large ugly scar. It will take us the rest of the day.

At least here, I can make one person happy, even if it's not me.

After hours of surgery, Alex and I return to the changing rooms. I shower and dress in silence. I'm still struggling with the idea of going home to another restless night of sleep. I want to reach out to her, but I don't want to betray Elijah.

"You're really down about the girl, aren't you?"

My head whips around to see Alex staring at me from the seat where he's putting on his work shoes.

"Yeah, we only just got together," I confess. Not really understanding why I feel the sudden need to tell him, but it feels good to talk. My mom and Samuel aren't the right people to unload this information on, and Elijah is a major problem, which leaves me with a few work colleagues.

I sit forward in my seat, my hands clasped together, and talk. "I was actually dating Elijah's sister."

"The brunette? Young? In college?"

"Yep. That's her."

He whistles. "Nice."

"It was..."

He shuffles in his seat. "But?"

"Elijah told me not to go there."

"Listen, I wouldn't love it if any of my friends were with my sister, either."

"See," I say.

"But I'd get over it. Eventually. Because seeing her happy is more important."

I rub my hands over my face as I remember Elijah's words. "You don't know Elijah like I do."

"He seems easy going every time I've met him."

"Yeah, he usually is. Just not about this," I say with a sigh.

I get it, I do, but it's harder to accept when your heart gets involved. It makes it difficult to listen.

"Have you told him you love her?"

Staying silent, I blink slowly in his direction. I can't deny it. I've been falling in love with Marigold from the second we met online. We connected on a sexual and mental level.

"No."

"Sounds like she's worth fighting for. Tell him you love her."

"Would that seriously change his mind?"

I doubt it.

He shrugs and stands to lean forward, slapping my shoulder. "It's worth a shot. I need the less grumpy version of you back. It's way too quiet now."

A pathetic laugh leaves me.

And as I wave, it's also a silent thank you. He nods and leaves the room. I sit by myself, grabbing my phone, defeated. There's still no call or texts from either Marigold or Elijah. I wonder if I should message her. But what do I say? Nothing has changed.

I stand, shoving it away in my pocket and leave to confront Elijah.

I stand at my best and oldest friend's modern front door.

There's a small part of me that knows he'll probably want to punch me as soon as he sees who's standing on his front porch. But first, I need to explain how sorry I am. Then second, how deeply in love I am with Marigold.

I suck in a deep breath and bring my fist down on the door, banging hard on it.

The door opens and I twist back and come face to face with one of my only friends.

A tightness settles on his face as soon as he realizes it's me.

"What are you doing here?" he asks as his gaze travels around me, looking to see if I'm alone.

"To talk."

He snorts. "You should've done that ages ago."

"I know. I know, and I'm sorry. I just needed time to see if it wasn't a phase."

He scrunches up his face and I realize it's probably appearing if I only wanted casual sex with her.

"She might've not wanted anything serious," I explain.

"And you did?"

Oh, no. I'm going to have to be open and he's going to hate me, but it's the truth. If I want to mend our friendship, I need to be honest.

"I didn't think I was capable."

"Capable of what?" he spits as if I'm being ridiculous.

I'm messing up my words from the nerves.

"Of being in a committed relationship again."

He crosses his arms. "She's thirteen years younger. I'm still struggling with that."

I jut my chin up, not backing down. "I know. But I can't help it."

"You can't control your dick?" He sneers and I understand his frustration.

"I can and I did. I haven't been with anyone since my ex."

Elijah's silent for a beat before he replies. "You two are so opposite." He rubs the back of his neck." I don't get it."

"Oh, I know. I think that's why it works. She has this easy-going nature that calms me. For the first time in a very long time, I feel happy."

His features soften slightly. He knows my past and how dark I've been, so I'm sure he understands how big of a deal it is for me to confess my happiness.

"Jackie said she could see something between you two," he mutters to himself.

"I'm in love with her," I say boldly.

He stares at me with a bewildered expression before it finally sinks in.

"Hold up." He thrusts out a hand. "You're in love with my sister?"

My heart is racing as I finally say it out loud. Those words I haven't uttered to a soul, but now that I have, they feel good leaving my lips. Like the weight of the world just lifted off my shoulders.

"And she loves you for some reason. Does she know you love her?"

I stare wide-eyed and my heart is thumping wildly inside my chest. *She loves me?*

The feeling of knowing that information is overwhelming. My mind is spinning. I didn't fucking know she loved me.

I exhale heavily. I wish I could go back and tell her. "No."

"Hence why you look like shit."

I choke out a laugh. I've barely slept since she stormed out of my house.

"Have you spoken to her?" I ask.

"Nope, she won't answer me. She's being damn stubborn."

I smother a smirk. I'm proud of her. She's standing up for herself. Finding her worth and not wasting a second falling in love with someone who doesn't love her back. Only she doesn't know I do. I love her so fucking much.

"I hate that she's blocked me from her life when all I want is for her to be safe and happy," Elijah says.

"She'll forgive you. She probably wants a little time to think."

He seems to mull over those words. "Are you sure about this?"

"I've never been more sure about anything."

"If you break her heart, I won't forgive you." His eyes turn hard as he hits me with a piercing look. The warning. It warms my heart. I love how protective of her he is because it's how I feel.

"I promise you I won't."

"Now good luck figuring out how to get her to forgive you because I sure as shit have zero chance right now."

I wink. "I'll put in a good word for you."

CHAPTER 35

DAMIEN

THE NEXT DAY, I enter the school grounds to pick up Samuel after school. I don't even get five minutes before I'm mobbed by the moms.

I grit my teeth together as the flutter of eyelashes and shoulder touches begin. My body freezes at the unwanted attention. I know being a single dad is attractive to some, but there's only one woman on my mind.

"Who was that brown-haired woman picking up Samuel?" the bleach-blonde mom asks.

I rub my jaw that's beginning to ache from clenching too tightly.

"A friend."

Her red lips part into a wide smile, and she turns to her friends to say, "Told you." Before she faces me again. "I said she was too young to be your girlfriend."

I say nothing. My life isn't up for discussion, and if I was with Marigold, I don't care what they say. It's not up to them.

"Dad!" Samuel calls as he runs with his school bag that's still way too big for him.

Glad he's here and I can get away from the women.

I catch him in a hug. "Hey. How was your day?"

He pulls back and rolls his eyes like the thought exacerbates him. "I don't want to talk about it."

If I didn't think this kid was mine, those words are how I feel when I think about my day. The only time I've ever wanted to open up was with Marigold. Which gets me asking Samuel. "Did you tell Mari about your day?"

"You called her Mari!" he says, shocked, as I walk with him to the car.

"I did. Did you tell her about school?"

"Yes." He exhales again, not happy with my question. But inside I know why he would've opened up to her. She just draws it out of you, without feeling like you're rehashing, but more she wants to hear about it. That she cares about how your day was. Her kind heart is one thing I love about her.

We stop at the car, and I turn to hold him. I wrap my arms around him a little bit tighter. Missing her sucks.

"How about we go past the arcade on the way home?" I ask, not ready to get into the car.

"Yes!" He claps.

I take his bag off him, and he helps so fast I can't help but laugh at his enthusiasm.

We spend a few hours playing and laughing together. The arcade was the fun I needed to pull me out of my bad funk.

Watching Samuel wear a smile and play games was the highlight. I helped him with a few games to get him to win more tokens to get a big prize at the end.

As we step out of the Arcade, Samuel squeals. "Mari." He's waving frantically.

My heart beats harder in my chest from the anticipation of seeing her again. I've not laid eyes on her since...she left me standing in my kitchen with her brother.

"Hi, Sammy," her soft voice says back.

He hugs her, and it's unexpected and makes her stumble. I reach out and grab her. The electricity shoots up my arm from the touch of her warm, familiar skin. The way my body hums to hers is something else. I don't get time to figure it out. She shakes me off. And I let her go, even if my fingers tingle with disagreement.

Samuel lets go of her leg. "Are you coming to my house to play with Legos?" His hopeful face beams.

My stomach bottoms out with the situation we're in. It's my fault and Samuel doesn't know. The way he is with her is so unlike anything I've ever seen before. It's ripping my heart out. A part of me wants to beg for forgiveness, but the other part knows I have to sort myself out first. I need to think of her happiness over my own. She deserves to be loved unconditionally and lately, I've been selfish and asked her to hide. I should never have done that.

Her eyes hold mine and I don't miss the mix of sadness and anger swirling through them. She's not happy to see me.

"Hey," I give her a small grin.

"Hi," she says, but it's not her usual happy self. It's snappy, short, and angry.

She squats down and lays a hand on Samuel's shoulder.

I've decided I hate her being angry and upset. It's making me rattled. I usually feel a sense of calm, but right now, I'm getting panicky. I scratch the back of my neck and I look over her all-black activewear.

I try to concentrate on breathing and not how much of a fuck-up I am.

"Not tonight. I'm sorry I have work," she says with a genuine smile.

What work?

Horror dawns on me...no, she wouldn't be back online...would she?

"Soon?" Samuel asks.

"Yeah, I can do that." She straightens and her hand goes to her throat.

"Are you going back online?" I ask, even though I have no right. It falls out of my mouth like I need to know.

She stares at me for a good second, not saying a word. I see the wheels turning and I hate the waiting.

"No. Not that it's any of your business, but I'm an admin for a legal firm."

My shoulders drop as relief hits me.

"Congratulations. I'm happy for you."

She dips her chin, watching Samuel play with the toys he won at the arcade.

She swept her hair up into a ponytail and it shows off her exposed delicate neck and it reminds me. "Where's your necklace?"

"I put it away just like you did with our relationship," she mutters, without looking at me. Her focus is still on Samuel. Who's distracted playing with the toys.

"That's unfair..." I trail off.

"Is it?" Her head whips around to look me in the eye. She cuts me off angrily. The hurt talking now.

I look at her pinched face. It pains me deeply. I stand there with my mouth open until the words, "I'm sorry," slip out.

A tear sits on her lashes. But she blinks it away as if she can't let it fall. She doesn't want me to see her weak. I don't think that at all. I see her only as strong and beautiful.

"Mari." The sound of Samuel's voice shakes me.

She blinks, sniffing away the sad evidence, and puts on a smile for him.

"Yes, Sammy?"

"Would you have dinner with us too when you come next time?"

She clears her throat while mine is closing up from his words.

"Ah. Sure. That sounds nice. What would we eat?"

"Hmm, pizza!" He beams at her with a twinkle in his eye.

"My favorite. Well, I better get home now, but I'll see you soon, okay?"

"Kay," he says back and hugs her again. This time, she expects it, so she doesn't tumble backward.

"Bye," I say.

She waves and quickly looks away. I sigh. "Are you ready to go home and I'll cook us some pasta?"

"Yep. No sauce, just cheese."

"Just cheese," I repeat and grab his hand and walk back to the car in a daze. Seeing her again should have cemented that her leaving me was the right decision. That she's better off without me. But it didn't. In fact, it did the opposite.

❦

Later that night, I'm cooking dinner when Samuel walks in holding a piece of paper.

"What have you drawn, bud?" I ask.

"A picture for you," he replies.

I grab hold of the paper. Leaning in closer, I draw my brows together. "Who's that?"

The woman with long brown hair isn't my mother....

"Mari," he replies as if it's no big deal and completely natural.

I stare at the three of us. Samuel's holding each of our hands.

"I'm in the middle of Marigold and you," he says.

"I see. I love it. Look at our smiling faces."

"Yeah, let's put it on the fridge."

"Good idea," I say, acting like I'm happy and nothing is wrong.

Yet. Inside, I'm fucking sad. I miss her. And it's clear he misses her, too.

I put it on the fridge with magnets and step back, unable to stop looking at it. When Samuel runs away, I sigh and start making dinner.

I stare at the ceiling later that night, unable to sleep. I lie there thinking about everything that's happened between

Marigold and me. How she acted toward me today. The kindness evaporated and was replaced with hurt. I keep expecting her to come to fight for me. As if she's my ex-wife.

She's not.

In fact, she's done nothing but beg for me to risk everything for her. And yet I'm still asking her to fight for me. Who's fighting for her?

Fuck, who's fighting for us?

She has been fighting alone.

No more. I'm going to fight for her. Show her I'll give her all of me if she gives me another chance.

Will she?

I shake my head. Don't think. Like she always pointed out. I'm controlled and planned and fuck so unhappy.

I'm going to find her tomorrow and talk to her. No plan, just see what comes. And if I give her everything and she doesn't want me, I'll have to walk away. I won't like it, but I have to understand.

CHAPTER 36

MARIGOLD

IT'S THE THIRD MISSED call from Elijah in a row. I find it hard to ignore and not pick it up to know what he wants.

I'm not ready for his opinion. He doesn't want to listen.

I return to my class before I head to my new job for a couple of hours.

I've only been here a couple of days and the team seems nice. Knowing the terminology and being able to ask questions are helping my studies immensely. Later that night, I don't miss my brother's car in the drive.

Seriously?

What the hell could he want so badly?

I'm tired from college and work. The last thing I want to deal with tonight is Elijah. He got what he wanted, so I don't need to see his gloating face. He thinks he did the best thing for me, but he's trying to control me. I knew what I was getting into with Damien. If it was to fall apart, then that was for me to discover. Life lessons are from some of our greatest pains.

I storm up the drive and enter my parents house. I'm ready to go to war with him. The smell of a roast dinner fills my nose. My stomach grumbles, reminding me I haven't eaten in a while.

My eyes flick to see my parents talking to Elijah, who's sitting in his navy suit in one of my parents' dining chairs. He's eased back as if he hasn't been blowing up my phone all day.

"Hi, love, how was your day?" my mom says, but her face seems a little too happy.

Now my worry peaks. I'm not used to surprises or secrets, so I have this unsettling feeling sinking in my lower stomach.

I kiss my mom's cheek and look at my dad, who looks no different. I move over and kiss his cheek.

"It was good."

"Hi, sis." Elijah smirks.

His face annoys me, and I can't hold myself back a second longer. "What's going on? You've been persistent."

"And you never called me back," he replies, staring at me with a blank expression. He gives nothing away.

"I had college and then work."

He sits up in his chair. "And no time to reply to me?"

"I'm still angry at you."

"Please don't fight. He was only protecting you," Mom interrupts.

I get up and grab a bottle of water for each of us before sitting down and drinking some.

"You're my parents. I expect lectures from you." My eyes flick from my parents to Elijah. "You warning me that Damien's not right. Too old. Too grumpy...what else am I missing Elijah?"

He stares coldly back with a tick in his jaw.

"He loves you," Mom cuts in.

"Listen, I'm glad he asked. I've been concerned since your mother told me about you and Damien," my dad speaks.

I twist to meet my dad's eyes head-on. "Well, why didn't you speak to me?" I ask with a frown.

"I didn't want me, your mom, and Elijah all to say the same thing. I don't want to hurt you, or worse, push you away, so I figured one could speak for all of us."

"Oh," I mumble. My dad's right. How would I feel having them all gang up on me?

I wanted support and I guess they have, as well as being honest with me. They want me to go in with my eyes open.

"Now I've heard you and I'm sorry I upset you, Mari. Let me make it up to you," Elijah says.

"What do you mean? How?" I ask, skeptical.

"Let's catch up on Saturday, and I promise we won't talk about Damien."

Even hearing his name hurts. The pain in the center of my chest is turning into an ache.

"Only if you bring Jackie," I say, knowing she'll make this more bearable. I don't want to hang out with just Elijah yet. I'm still upset about how he's handled the situation at Damien's.

"Fine," he grumbles.

"Okay, I'm glad you two sorted everything out, but can I serve dinner now?" Mom says, slipping on her oven mitts.

"Yes, please, I'm starving." I sit up in my chair and finally a little bit of my appetite is back.

My mom comes over, lowering a plate, and kisses the top of my head. I turn my head, and she gives me a smile and I return a genuine back. The first bit of calmness returning. Let's hope it helps me sleep tonight.

Elijah texted me this morning and asked if I could meet him at the teahouse. I know what he's talking about because it's where I get my tea from.

And the thrill I'm going to a favorite place of mine makes me slip on my favorite blue jeans and a green top. I pop my mascara and gloss on and have my hair in a natural wave. The drive only takes me ten minutes. I look around for Elijah's sports car, but it's not here yet. I don't wait. I'm going to browse the tea. I'm curious to know what new flavors they've got in.

I step inside and smile at the store assistant who's serving someone else at the moment. But the lavender and mint hit me, and I move over to the pots.

I'm about to pour myself a cup when she comes over. "Good morning, Mari." She smiles, standing with her hands joined in front of her. "They're new flavors. I'll get you a cup. Let me sit you down where your booking is."

I glance at my phone to see where Elijah is, but no missed call or anything. Hmm, this is strange. He's never late.

I'll have a cup while I wait for him and Jackie.

She shows me out back where the tables are, and we go to the very back. My walk falters when I see the man with his heavy, lust-filled gaze running over me.

All emotions are hitting me at once. A mix of excitement down to fear. What's going on? Are Elijah and Jackie coming? Or is this a setup? But why?

I don't get to think any longer because Damien stands to his full height, and I suck in a sharp breath. His dark gray suit and a white shirt but no tie with his hair perfectly swept in gel are making my heart flutter and my lower body come alive.

A white shirt still sits at home buried deep in a drawer with fun memories of how sexy they can be.

No need to imagine what's under his suit because that memory is seared into my brain. His sculpted yet dark sprinkling of hair reminds me just how manly he is. I wish I could have it all again. Rewind to the time we were happy.

A brow quirks up high on his face, and I know he has caught me thinking about him in a filthy way.

"Marigold," he says in his low, deep voice. I'm not the only one affected by our reunion.

"Damien," I say, and it's breathier than I want it to be. I don't miss the lift in the corner of his mouth.

He walks around and I inhale his spicy pear scent. And it's so strong I don't smell lavender or mint anymore. I only smell him. It's heavenly. I threw out the body soap the moment I got home from Damien's house. I cried, stepping into the shower and seeing the bottle mocking me.

Not having it for a while and now having it so close reminds me how much I love it. I love him.

I sit down and drag the chair close to the table that's set up for lunch. He steps over and takes a seat opposite me. His gaze fixed on me with so much warmth.

Where's the sadness gone?

I don't want to get my hopes up.

The assistant brings me a cup of tea and I thank her and don't waste a second before I pick up the cup and drink it. The warm fluid hits my parched throat perfectly.

I lower it down.

His brows pull together. "You changed your nail polish."

I peek down at the green color matching my top.

"Yeah, I wasn't feeling the purple anymore." I shrug.

"I love the purple, it was you," he says in a sad tone.

I pick up the cup again. His gaze still holds mine.

He picks up his cup and sips it before he lowers it.

He winces.

I lower my cup.

"It's unusual," he mutters.

"You're drinking tea?"

"We're at a teahouse." He gives me a lopsided grin.

"I know, but you hate tea."

"But you love it."

I flick my hair off my shoulder. "You're drinking it for me," I whisper in disbelief.

"You're worth drinking dishwater for," he grumbles, clearly disliking the taste.

My heartbeat skips at his meaning, though. But I can't get too excited. He still hurt me.

"It's not that bad," I argue. Secretly, it's not my favorite either, but it's not that awful.

His eyes flick around as if to make sure the assistant isn't around. "Are you saying you like this?" He gestures to the cup.

"Not my favorite," I admit.

He waves and calls the assistant over.

"Can we get different tea and then get the cake of the day?"

"Sure. What tea did you want?" she asks.

He peers over at me. I understand he's looking at me for guidance.

"Can we get black tea and maybe some sweetener, sugar and honey?" I say.

I know she'll understand I'm getting him to try the tea with different sweeteners because he's bound to find one combination he likes.

She leaves and I sit staring at him, waiting for him to talk. Did he organize this...date?

"I spoke to Elijah," he starts.

Does he forget I was there? "I know. I was at your place too, remember?"

He shakes his head. "Not then. This week."

"Oh."

I try not to show any reaction, even though I'm on the edge of my seat waiting for him to spill what they spoke about.

"Elijah said nothing to you yesterday?"

I shake my head. "Only to meet him here."

"I got him to help me."

I blink rapidly, not understanding how Elijah switched so easily.

"Okay..." I say, still confused by everything. I'm waiting desperately for him to explain himself.

He grabs my hands and encases them with his. "I missed you."

I want to say *I miss you too*, but I need to stay quiet and let him speak.

"Seeing you but not being yours ruined me. I never wanted to try again. To be fair, I was bitter and angry about women. Then you, my Goldie. From that very first online meeting, I knew you were different."

I nod slowly, letting him know I'm listening. A wobble of my chin has him shuffling in his seat, edging closer to the table. His grip is tight on mine. His eyes reflect so much anguish that I have to bite the inside of my cheek to prevent myself from speaking.

"The scar running through my heart I thought was unfixable. But slowly, you threaded the needle and stitched me whole. I'll never let you go. I'll do whatever it takes to make you happy. Tell me what to do and I'll do it. Just please don't let this be the end. I'm not good at this, but I'll try."

A tear leaks from my eye, and it rolls down. He's my wounded man who's telling me I'm healing him. Words I've hoped to hear, but never thought he'd say. And now he's finally saying them, and I can't speak through my tight windpipe.

"I love you, Goldie. You're everything to me."

Words a man has never said back to me break me. A dam of tears breaks, and I pull my hand out of his grip to cover my face and cry hard into my palms.

A chair sounds on the floor and the touch of a hand on my back makes me cry harder.

"I'm so sorry. I don't mean to upset you. If you don't want me, I'll respect that. No matter how much that hurts me, I'll let you go. Your happiness is more important."

Is he kidding?

I rub under my eyes with my fingers and gaze at him lovingly through the blurry vision.

I sniff. My hands drop to clasp together on my thighs. "You idiot, of course I love you. I've been waiting forever to hear those words and hearing them from you means everything to me."

He gives me a deep exhale and then a lopsided grin.

"Well, nothing is stopping us now."

"Elijah?" I ask, double checking he's no longer going to be a barrier for us.

"Is onboard."

Which means no one is holding us back from being together now.

Those two words hang in the air between us. I try to wrap my head around the fact this is really happening.

"So, can we start again? This time with nothing holding us back? Will you be my girlfriend?" he asks with a longing look.

"Definitely." I choke on another tear as more fall, but this time, happy ones.

CHAPTER 37

MARIGOLD

"What happens now?" I ask Damien.

His hand holds mine across the table. He's barely touched his tea. I know I won't get him to convert to tea. But I'm happy he tried for me. His willingness to try was so sweet.

As long as I get it, that's all that matters.

"Let's go back to my place and see Samuel."

My smile widens at seeing Sammy. "I was hoping you would say that. But..."

My voice lowers, and I cast my eyes down at the table.

"But?"

I sigh and slowly bring my gaze to meet his gentle one. "I wanted to mention something."

"Hmm. Tell me. Anything." He runs his hand over his jaw before reaching out and clutching my hand.

My heart beats wildly inside my chest. I keep my eyes on Damien's. "Sammy told me he wishes you'd play with him.

He thinks you don't have time. I feel bad for breaking his trust and telling you, but I'm not sure you're aware."

He sits back slightly. His hand is still firmly on mine. "I wasn't aware. My life is highly structured and organized. But it's something I need to change."

The conflict on his face is hard to watch. It's like he's riddled with shame. There's no need. Just like he is with me, he needs to change his life for Sammy, too.

"Listen, just play some Legos with us. Then here and there, do it, just you two."

He nods. "And I might buy more Nintendo controllers so we can all play."

My lips tremble with the need to smile. "You liked playing Mario Kart with me that much?"

"I loved it. And now you're a part of my life. We will all hang out more," he says, the warmth of his smile echoed in his voice.

A fear knots inside my stomach. "Speaking of. Are we going to tell Sammy?"

Damien leans forward, and I sip the rest of my tea. "I'm going to just hang out and see how he seems. If it feels right, I'll tell him today, but if not, I'll give him another day or so, but not too long. I don't want to keep secrets."

My mind battles with a crazy mix of hope and fear. "Me either. I'm nervous."

"Why?" he asks, an eyebrow rising a fraction.

"Because I love Sammy and I hope he accepts us."

A sympathetic, curved smile settles on his face. "He loves you, I'm sure of it. I'd be shocked if he doesn't accept us, but if he doesn't, we can figure out our next step together."

My smile falters but then with his confidence I draw in a breath, more determined we can do this. Everything will be okay. "Alright, well, let's do this."

"No time like the present." He winks, removing his hand from mine and pushing out his chair. He strides over to me. I look up and without hesitation, I stand and take his outstretched hand and we leave the teahouse.

"Leave your car here. We can come back later and grab it. I'll drive us."

We get in his car for the quick trip to his house. I sit in silence, holding back the apprehension that sweeps through me.

Arriving at Damien's, I follow his lead from his car into the house, and he grabs my hand and walks us through the house.

I can hear the television on and noises in the kitchen. We enter the kitchen, and his mom is busy cooking.

"Mom. This is Marigold. Marigold, my mom."

I smile through the anxiety spurting through me.

"Hi. Can I help?" I ask, looking at the pots on the stove and the bowls on the counter. The mess in the kitchen makes me feel more settled. Maybe his mom is less organized and more organized chaos like me.

Her face brightens at the suggestion. "No, thanks, dear. I'm done now."

"Dad! Mari?" Samuel's voice calls from the living room's direction.

His tiny form comes running into the room and barrelling into his dad's legs for a hug.

"Hey, bud. You watching TV?" Damien responds, bending down to hug him.

Samuel lifts his head away from Damien and peels his body away from him. "Yeah."

Samuel walks over and hugs my leg. I melt on the spot. I didn't realize how much I needed that until now. Though I feel my heartbeat racing from his welcome arms, I keep my composure.

"Hey, Sammy. Do you wanna play something?" I ask, peering down at him.

He pulls back slightly, tipping his head back, wearing the cutest grin. "Like Legos or a game?"

He pulls back, tipping his head back with the biggest, cutest grin. "Yeah."

"Only if I can join in, too."

Samuel's head twists to look at his dad. "Yeah." He turns to me, his eyes brighter. "Right, Mari?"

My mouth curves with tenderness. "Of course. It will be way more fun with the three of us."

"I've always wanted a mom," he replies. His entire face spreads into a smile.

A spoon hits the pot in the kitchen, causing a loud bang. In the corner of my eye, I see his mom scrambling to pick up the spoon. She's clearly shocked, too.

"I always wanted a son," I say with a calm smile. Those words feel as natural as breathing. I never knew I needed him and Damien. But once I fell for them, I can't see my life without them.

Samuel peels off my leg and runs off to his playroom, yelling as he goes. "Come on, let's play."

I'm still shell-shocked, wrapping my head around the bomb Samuel just dropped.

I peer at Damien, finding him staring with luminous eyes widened in astonishment.

"I can't thank you for what you just said. It wouldn't be enough. But just know those words mean everything to not only Samuel, but to me. The fact you could love my son like your own..." He looks away, running his hand through his hair and down to the ground. Appearing to take a second. He looks back up. "I thought I loved you before, but it's immeasurable now."

He steps forward, grabbing the sides of my face, and presses his lips to mine in a slow, seductive kiss. It's full of so much passion it makes my knees buckle. I sink into him. When we pull apart, he whispers, "Meet me when you're ready."

He turns to go and play with Samuel, and I realize he needs a few moments with his son alone.

I watch his sexy figure leave the room and when I turn around, I find his mom staring on with tears leaking from her eyes.

She wipes them away. "These are happy." She sniffs.

I break into an open, friendly smile.

"I've not seen my son smile in a long time. Or seen him tell a woman how he feels. To see this change in him is every mom's dream. He deserves to be loved, and so does Samuel. Thank you, Marigold, for choosing them. Because they've chosen you and I know you'll be very happy together."

She wipes away more tears. I swallow hard and bite back my own.

"He's a good man and I'm lucky to have him and Sammy in my life," I say in a shaky whisper.

"Did you want a cup of tea? I noticed Damien's selection. I figured it was you." The corner of her mouth lifts. No more tears leave her eyes.

"Yes. I'd love one. No sugar or cream. Actually, we were just at a teahouse."

"How lovely," she says, moving around the kitchen to make us tea.

"I got Damien to try tea."

"You did?" She gasps.

I giggle at her shock. "I did."

"And?"

I shake my head. "Hates it. Sugar, honey, or sweetener. He still won't drink it."

She laughs and pours water into the cups. "You're definitely pushing him out of his comfort zone. I love it. Come sit and have some tea. Let's give the boys some time alone and we can catch up."

She lowers a cup in front of me. "Thanks. I think that would be good. Samuel needs time with his dad."

"He hasn't allowed himself to do anything other than work. He's been on autopilot for so long," she says.

I nod and blow on the tea before taking a sip, excited to spend some alone time with his mom. Until I hear my name being called out by Samuel.

"I'm coming," I call out. "Sorry. I better go in there and play."

She reaches out and rubs my arm. Her face is gentle and understanding. "Don't be sorry, go to your boys."

I smile at the words, *your boys.*

I walk into the room and find them both eagerly looking at me standing in the doorway. It feels like a dream. To have them both stare at me like I'm important to them. They do not know how much I need them. My life is now filled with so much love. Love that's reciprocated.

"What took you so long?" Damien winks.

They are playing a game of Trouble.

"I was letting you boys warm up." I step into the room, rubbing my palms together and walking to sit between them. "Now I'm going to win."

"Nuh-uh," Samuel replies. "I'm gonna win."

A light laugh leaves me at his competitiveness. He's definitely like Damien. But I'm also super-competitive too, so I know this game will be fun.

"Nope. I am," I say back, screwing up my nose at Samuel, who is trying to mimic me, and it's adorable.

"I'll beat the both of you," Damien states.

Samuel groans.

"Come on, let's start. Sammy, you go first," I say.

Samuel begins, and I watch with interest. But I can feel the heat of Damien's gaze on me. But it's his soft touch on my knee that has my head tilting up.

I love you, he mouths.

I love you too, I mouth back.

EPILOGUE

MARIGOLD

"YOU'RE AN EXCELLENT PAINTER, Sammy," I say, staring down at my nails. He's painting them, using his dad's favorite color on me. Purple. It's been our new thing. We hang out, play Legos, Trouble, or his favorite, Nintendo.

It's been so easy slipping into their life.

"I'm done," Samuel says, putting the brush back in the polish. And screwing the lid.

"Thank you. Now I need to wait for them to dry before I get dressed," I reply, blowing on the thick layer.

"Are you Daddy's mommy?"

"Do you mean girlfriend?"

I roll my lips as I wait for his answer.

My heart is in my throat at his direct questioning. Damien's not in the room, so I'm going to go with what I think is the right thing to do.

"Yeah."

My lip lifts at what he's trying to ask me.

"Would that be okay?"

He gets up and moves to his box of Legos.

"Yeah," he replies.

I think that's the end of the discussion when he carry's the box over. We both pull out blocks when he speaks again.

"Will you live with us?"

Seriously, where is Damien?

I don't want to answer these questions wrong.

"Would you like that?"

"Yeah."

"Maybe we can ask Da-Daddy."

"What are we asking?" his voice calls from the doorway.

My gaze flicks over to him. He stands effortlessly in gray sweats and a gray shirt.

His face is pinched lightly. Is he laughing at me? I still feel panicked and he's laughing.

"Samuel asked if I will live with you two."

My gaze doesn't leave Damien's. And I expect some fleeting change. But he doesn't even flinch.

"Yeah, I think that's a great idea," he replies smoothly.

"Today?" Samuel asks.

"Not today, bud. We have to celebrate Mari's graduation."

"Oh." He moans.

I turn to face Samuel. "I'll start moving stuff tomorrow. How does that sound?"

He builds his house out of Legos with his brows pulled together. "Good. Now will you play Legos?"

My lips part into an easy smile. Samuel is the sweet, easy-going kid I never knew I needed. The only sign that he's cranky is either in the mornings when he wakes up or when something doesn't go his way. Damien's expressions sit on his face. And on a five-year-old, it's hilarious.

Since we officially started dating, Damien works less. And refuses to be on call on any important dates—like birthdays.

I told him I have a job at a local firm starting soon, so I'll be busy and not to worry about me. But, of course, he won't.

My whole life finally feels settled. Even picking up Samuel from school, the whispers are slowly disappearing. The women, initially finding out I'm Damien's girlfriend, sent them into a tailspin. Now I'm becoming old news. But ultimately, I don't care what anyone thinks. I've fallen in love with the man, not his age, or the fact he's a single father. His heart is what matters, and he's treated me better than anyone ever has.

Samuel still hasn't heard from his mother. He has never asked, but I ask Damien. I still can't understand her reasons and wish I'd get to speak to her to ask why. But I'm sure I wouldn't like the answer, anyway.

The love Damien and I give Samuel is hopefully enough that he doesn't feel like he misses out on anything compared to his peers.

"How about you get ready, bud," Damien says.

"I'm almost done." He moans.

I sit, watching him finish up the last pieces before Samuel jumps off the chair and runs to the bathroom.

Damien comes closer to me. He lays a lazy kiss on my lips. And a sweep of his tongue along my bottom lip. A promise of what's coming later.

"I love that color," he says in a gravelly tone as he looks down at my nails.

I smirk. "I know."

"I'll get Samuel ready, and then will you be ready?"

I bite my lip, knowing he's trying not to push me, but the way he glances at his watch, I know he wants to leave on time. Some things haven't changed, but they aren't relationship breakers. They're his quirks. His acceptance of me into his life without reservation or worries about anyone else has been all that I needed, so I need to accept all of him.

For my graduation, we have dinner booked as a big family. Mine and Damien's family are all together in one room tonight. It's our first big catch up and I'm excited to have everyone together. No one has had any reservations about our relationship since we made it official. Samuel looks at us with so much love and happiness that it doesn't matter what the world thinks.

An hour later, we leave the house, and our driver drops us off at the Ivory Tower. We are a trio now. I'm holding both my boy's hands as we celebrate. It's not something I'm used to, but I also don't hate it. I worked hard to finish and the excitement both Damien and Samuel have shown me has made me want to throw this dinner party.

"I love your purple dress," Damien whispers in my ear, so Samuel can't hear. "I can see the outline of your nipples."

I touch my Goldie necklace and look down at my pale silk lavender dress with a smile before running my gaze over them.

"And my boys look so handsome in their matching suits." The sense of pride in my heart explodes. I've never been so full of reciprocated love. But these two boys have given me it in abundance.

"I love this suit. Do I get to keep it?" Samuel asks. I love the black suits with the lavender shirts. The matching family is my new favorite thing.

"Yeah, bud, it's all yours," Damien says back to him.

"Yesss!" Samuel says loudly, clearly excited by that information.

We step out of the elevator and onto the dark floors. Everyone is already sitting down at the long candle-lit table. I come over and say hello to every person. I notice a few friends are here too.

"Elijah. Jackie, how are you?" I say with a smile.

"Mari. Congratulations. We're so proud of you," Jackie says, handing over a bag.

My gaze slides to my brother, who looks at me, smiling. "Congratulations, sis." He stands and hugs me.

At first, I'm shocked, but then I hug him back.

I next say hello to my parents and then over to Damien's parents.

I finally sit down. Samuel between Damien and me.

We eat a mix of meat, chicken, and fish with an array of side dishes.

Before I know it, two hours have passed, and we need to get Samuel to bed.

As I'm getting ready to leave, Damien's hand slips over my lower back.

"Are you ready?"

I frown. "To go where?" I ask.

"I'm taking you away for the weekend."

I twist to face him. "Sa—"

"Will be fine with my mom. She's taking over from here. We need to celebrate you graduating properly." He wiggles his eyebrows and I know exactly what he's thinking.

"Where are we going?" I ask, totally ignoring the sexual innuendo.

"A surprise."

I groan. "Unfair, but I will not beg because I know you won't tell me."

"Listening to you begging is definitely persuasive."

I lift a brow, wondering if I should start begging.

He shakes his head. "But no, it won't get me to spill. I want to surprise you."

"Damn it!"

We say goodbye to everyone, leave the tower and the driver takes us to the airport.

We board the plane, and the pilot announces Santa Barbara. I side-eye Damien, who looks annoyed by the fact it's no longer a surprise.

I'm buzzing about going back to the same place. It holds special memories for me, and I totally relax there and get the one-on-one time I crave with Damien.

We arrive late, and the sun is already down. I expect to go to bed, but he finds the blanket and ushers me outside. I'm about to lie down on the blanket to watch the stars, but he speaks.

"Open your graduation present," he whispers.

I open the envelope to find a set of keys.

I frown, not understanding.

"Keys?"

They don't look like they are at his house. So what else could they be for?

"This place is ours."

I blink and look around. "You're serious."

He nods with a smug smirk. "I think you like to call my gifts excessive. So here is another one you deserve."

I shake my head. And before I can say anything else, he speaks again.

"I never want this moment to end."

"Mmm, me either." I smile.

"The stars shine just as bright as you. You can't help but smile as you stare at it. Goldie..." He shuffles to get comfortable before he drops to his left knee.

He removes a large solitaire ring in gold from his pocket and slips it on my finger.

"Oh my God," I splutter as the back of my eyes prick with tears.

"You are the woman of my dreams. I never want you to doubt my love for you. Wearing this ring would be a symbol of how far we've come and how serious I am about our future. I want a future with you until my very last breath."

"Damien," I choke as tears spill over my cheeks.

"Marigold, will you marry me?"

"Yes! Yes, of course," I sob, leaning forward to kiss him. His Goldie.

We kiss and I tear off his jacket. There's so many emotions pouring through me, but right now, I need him. All of him.

"I love you Goldie," he says between kissing me hard.

"I love you too," I rasp between another passionate kiss. "My excessive fiancé."

The End.

BONUS

MARIGOLD

I STARE AT MY reflection with tears filling my eyes.

I've always loved the idea of getting married and wearing a big poofy princess dress. And today is finally that day. With a sequined bodice and so much tulle, I feel like a real princess. I've always wanted a big wedding. And as I stare at the woman in front of me, I realize I'm living that dream right now. Damien is waiting at the end of the aisle for me.

With one last breath, I run my hands over the tulle bottom. I'm happy with how I look. My purple nails are on both my hands and feet. I haven't changed them again since he pointed out that the purple was his favorite.

I adjust the tiara in my hair, loving the way I swept my hair into a sleek bun. I wanted the total fairytale vibe and I have it. Everything has been a literal dream.

I can't wait to see Samuel waiting next to his dad. He didn't know who he wanted to spend the morning with.

A part of him wanted to see me look like a princess, but the other wanted to look after his dad.

I think he knew his dad needed him today. This step is huge for both of us. Something I dreamed about, but also something he never thought he'd do again, so I guess that would play havoc with him.

"Are you ready?" My dad comes into the room with Elijah.

"Hey, you're not supposed to be here." I shoo my brother away.

"I know but Damien insisted I come and give you something, sis." Elijah steps forward, holding out a bag for me to take.

My brows lift to my forehead, wondering what present he's bought me today. Damien is definitely a giver, and it's always the most meaningful gifts.

"I need a moment, Dad," I say.

"Of course. Take your time."

I take the present into my room and open it up. There're beautiful blue panties and a matching bra. He wants me to wear this while I say my vows?

Something blue...

I don't waste a single second before I slip off my other lingerie and pull these panties on. I'm not wearing a bra with my wedding dress because the top is like a corset.

I check myself in the mirror. My mouth curves into the widest grin. I'm ready to see my boys.

I walk out and my dad stands.

"Are you ready?"

"Yeah."

"Let's go get you married."

We walk out and climb into the car. The drive isn't long, and when I arrive, I don't feel nervous. The butterflies swarming my stomach are from excitement.

Those steps to Damien and Samuel can't come quick enough. Luckily, my dad keeps the pace and prevents me running to them.

The vow exchange to the first kiss is way too slow. I just wanted to hear *I now pronounce you husband and wife*.

"You may kiss your bride."

After a quick peck, we head to the reception. After food, dancing, speeches, and cake, it's time for our honeymoon. Inside the car, I kiss him like I did the first time on my way to the airport. In his lap with pure love and excitement.

"Wait," I say, needing to tell him something important.

He's breathing heavily as he stares at me with confusion.

"I'm off the pill," I confess nervously.

"Goldie," he says. "Are you saying you want a baby?"

I bite my lip and nod my head.

"Yeah, I'm ready if you are," I say.

I didn't expect him to be ready so soon, but I need to be honest with him.

"The thought of you carrying my baby inside of you is hot, and fuck, seeing you pregnant is going to be even hotter."

"Truthfully, I was worried you wouldn't want me sexually anymore if I was pregnant." I laugh as happy tears now spill from my eyes.

"No, Goldie. The opposite. It's a turn-on like nothing else."

I smile with pure happiness seeping out of me. "Well, Mr. Gray, you better get moving and fill me with so much cum I'll be sure to get pregnant."

He growls. "You got it Mrs. Gray."

Mrs. Gray.

ALSO BY

The Chicago Doctor's

Doctor Taylor

Doctor I DO

The Gentlemen Series

Accidental Neighbor

Bossy Mr. Ward

The Christmas Agreement

White Empire

Saffron and Secrets

Resisting Chase